Because of...Friday

*To: Pam
Enjoy! :)*

By

Diane Ganzer

Diane Ganzer
and
Sammy St. Croix

Avid Readers Publishing Group
Lakewood, California

Because of ... Friday

Avid Readers Publishing Group

http://www.avidreaderspg.com

ISBN-13: 978-1-935105-04-6

Printed in the United States

Other books by Diane Ganzer:

Patrick the Wayward Setter

A Christmas Miracle

Summer School Blues

And with Sammy St Croix:

Steel Destiny

Trail Boss: The Quest

Hope Survives

Llama Tails: Ricky's Adventure

Check out our website:
www.writeinyourearproductions.com

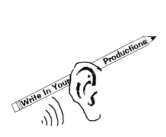

IV

"...Just do your thing and rejoice in your memories. We don't ponder in depression of the losses we endure, we rejoice in the knowledge that they ever were."

Sammy St. Croix 1/13/07

Chapter 1

Brett Pearson looked at the wall clock through the cell bars for the umpteenth time, waiting for his wife to come down and bail him out of jail. DUI. Despair assailed him as reviewed the events of the night. He just had to have the last drink! Well, why not? He was with friends and the mood was high. Now he was in a sour mood, dreading what Eva would say. This was the third DUI in two years, and he was caught driving after his license had been revoked. He was in deep trouble this time.

He ruminated on his past while he paced his cell. On his own since he was sixteen, he scraped his way to where he was now. He had held numerous jobs that barely paid his way, all the while dreaming of the "someday" when he would be well-known. He laughed that one off sardonically. Hadn't Eva always said he would be a nobody? She had worked for the same firm for over twenty years, grew up in a well to do family; she knew all about stability. He had only his mother; he didn't even know who his father was, the old man left when he was young. His uncle, also an alcoholic, kept Brett from time to time until he could survive on his own. Unfortunately, Brett's cocky attitude

1

oftentimes did him in; then it was another new job, a new location, until he got married. Eva said for him to do his job and keep his opinions to himself. His temper, however, wouldn't allow him to deal with other's inferiority. After completing classes in radio broadcasting, he secured a job at a well known radio station. The pay was good, but his ideas clashed with those of the strong on-air morning show host. Realizing that to stay was like beating his head against a wall, he quit, sure he would be missed.

He wasn't.

He stood still and looked at the clock again. Where was she? Or would she even care this time? He wished he could have a cigarette; he really needed one. Unfortunately, his last pack was in the car and that was towed away when he was arrested.

Eva put the phone down and hugged her arms together. Brett's one and only phone call sounded frantic. At this point she was beyond caring. Let him stew in jail for awhile! Then she sat down and reflected on their marriage. For too many years she had to pick up the pieces- she had to show him the way. He was very intelligent, but his arrogance was a fault, one she didn't want to have to deal with anymore. Picking up her purse and the keys, she slowly dragged her feet to her car and drove to the jail. It was two a.m.

"Pearson, you're free to go, your wife just posted your bail." The clanging of the keys in the lock drew his attention. Quickly, Brett got to his feet as her visage appeared behind the officer. Her lips were pursed together and she said nary a word as he collected his things, signed the paperwork and slowly fell into step behind her, his head pounding more from what he knew lay ahead than from the hangover that was sure to come. Instead, she drove home in silence, then after locking the front door behind them, stalked to the bedroom and reappeared in the living room with a blanket.

"I don't want you in my bedroom tonight, or any night

from now on. Do you realize how much your little party is going to cost us? You're not working! Where is the money coming from?" she shrieked, her voice ringing in his ears that were already buzzing from the booze.

Looking at her helplessly, he shrugged. "I'm sure some work will come in," he began lamely.

"I hardly think your emceeing a wedding reception every other Saturday will pay for what you did tonight. I should have just let you rot there!" With that, she slammed the door leading to the bedroom, causing Brett to jump. Watching it's silence, he sat at his desk, defeat evident in the slump of his shoulders. Reaching out, he turned on the monitor, then the computer and, while it warmed up, got a cigarette and took a long drag on it. Exhaling forcefully, he sat down once again and watched the screen as the Windows logo popped up, then his desktop picture glowed brightly in the dim light. Clicking on Internet Explorer, he surfed the web, looking for a music channel he could listen to when something caught his eye. It was an interactive radio channel and they were looking for DJ's. Interest made him fill out the application. It was voluntary, but he thought of the possibilities it would afford him: name recognition world wide. It would be the break he was looking for!

Someone else also was looking for worldwide recognition. Sandy Malone had written a manuscript that was picked up by a small publisher and the news about its release made it to the front page of the daily newspaper. She needed all the publicity she could get and seemed flattered with the attention as she spoke with local dailies and made small appearances, touting her novel, *"Winston the Wayward Spaniel."* By day she worked in a high school cafeteria and that very fact made her an anomaly. One newspaper dubbed her the "Deli Lady," a moniker which seemed to stick. Sandy knew of the hard work she had ahead of her to become better known and prayed for that chance to happen. She was a sweet woman, married since she was seventeen and had four children. Her celebrity seemed to embarrass them only slightly and, like her, they were pretty humble about their mother, the author. She carefully cut out her articles and put them in a file, thinking that even if she didn't make it "big," this was her fifteen minutes of fame and she was enjoying every minute of it.

Brett sat at his computer, putting together a morning show program for his new "job," as he called it. The radio station was interested in him due to his background in the industry and suggested he have a sound board ready and gave him two daily spots a week to begin. He selected music and added, subtracted, deleted and started over so many times until it became an obsession with him to get it just right. He did his own promos and finally, after two weeks of twenty hour days, was ready to present his show. Eva thought he was being foolish; his energy should have been put into something that would pay the bills. Indeed, his DUI was costing them over five thousand dollars, money which she did not have. The frustration mounted in her until they were either constantly shouting and nagging or living in complete silence. Each day she remembered her marriage vows: for better or worse. Brett gave her very few reasons to want to commit to them. Watching him agonize over his soundboard, she angrily grabbed her keys and left for work. He didn't even notice her departure.

Later that morning, he picked up the newspaper. Glancing through it quickly, his eye caught the story about the Deli Lady and he read with interest. Sandy had written a story for children about the adventures of a puppy who loved to get into mischief. Smiling to himself, he set the paper aside on his desk; he would get to it later. His program was going well. Already, he was now up to three shows a week and was always on the lookout for talent he could showcase on his program. Maybe an interview with this author would be a great interest story for his listeners, kind of a rags to riches sort of story. Looking at the clock over his desk, he

4

realized that in three hours he needed to meet with his probation officer. That would just be jolly, he thought with a sardonic snort. First, he needed to pee in a cup, give up some blood for a drug check, then sit and talk about all his "problems," ending with admonishments to stay clean. The blood tests to check for drugs as well as the urinalysis cost him each time they needed to do it.

They needed it every week. What a hassle! He may as well as molested a young boy, he thought ruefully. Sex offenders seemed to be running rampant nowadays and at least he would have enjoyed it. Sighing, he got up and made a sandwich.

Sandy was hard at work cleaning the steam table wells in the cafeteria when she was summoned to the telephone. "Oh, what now?" she thought. She hoped it wasn't the school nurse about one of her kids being sick, or worse, the principal! Taking the phone, she tried to ignore the two women who were sitting at their desks counting out the days collection of lunch money.

"Hello? This is Sandy," she began.

"Sandy? Brett Pearson here, from Listen to it Live!, an internet radio station I operate from my home. Do you have a minute?"

"Why, uh, yes I do." Sandy wondered if this was some sort of a prank, but he sounded sincere, so she listened.

"Sandy, I read your story in the paper and I was wondering if you would be interested in an interview with me, on air?"

Sandy mulled it over quickly. This guy really made her nervous and the last thing she wanted was for some weird person to be calling her at work. As if he could sense what was on her mind, he asked her if she had many people hassling her due to her celebrity status.

"Me? Yes, I have run into two people already! I am just a bit apprehensive because I have never heard of your station. What did you say it was again?"

"'Listen to it Live!' You can find it on the Internet. You are smart for asking. Don't worry," he chuckled, "this is completely legitimate! Are you free tomorrow?"

Sandy gulped. Tomorrow? She didn't even know who this person was and he was asking about tomorrow?

"I need to check out my calendar at home first, can I have your phone number to call you back?" She was going to check this out thoroughly, although deep inside, she had her reservations about the whole thing and hoped maybe he wouldn't want to have her after all. Brett gave her not only his number, but his address and said he looked forward to her call.

Sandy hung up the phone and smiled at the women, who had stopped counting long enough to listen.

"Everything OK?" one of them asked.

"Why, yes, somebody just wants me to do a radio interview for the internet, is all," Sandy didn't sound too convinced.

"Well, if I were you, I'd check him out with the police first, you never know how many weirdos are running around out there," the other cautioned. Sandy took it under advisement and left the office, one part of her excited about this new prospect, another apprehensive about the outcome.

Brett hung up and was impressed with how sweet she sounded. So pure, not stuck up like a lot of his guests were. He hoped she would return his call as he completed more promotional work for the station.

At home, Sandy typed the web site into the computer and waited to for it to connect. When the site popped up, she scrolled at the various links, then went to the part that said, "Meet the Team." Scrolling through, she found Brett's name and profile and read it and seemed impressed with what she saw. What a picture that accompanied it! He was quite handsome, with longer locks of brunette hair and a come hither look that melted her heart, which threw her for a loop because, by the sound of his voice on the phone, he sounded a lot older. She had pictured him to be maybe in his mid-fifties, yet the picture showed someone in his early twenties. Then she felt more comfortable with her decision as she picked up the phone and dialed his number that he had given her. No answer, so she left a message with her home number. Butterflies loomed in her stomach, but she quelled them away and put it into the back of her mind.

The next day at work, at almost the same time as before, once again she was summoned to the phone. Taking it, she heard Brett's voice.

"Well, are you up for an interview?" Brett pushed. He really needed some new topics for his program and held his breath as he waited for her response.

"Yes, I went to the web site last night and am impressed with what I saw, so I would very much like to do this."

"What days are convenient for you?" he asked

Looking at the calendar in front of her, she picked out Friday morning and gave him a time.

"Great!" he said, "We do a variety of things on that day anyway, so it will work out fine. Do you want me to give you directions to my house, or will you Mapquest it?"

"I'll Mapquest it," Sandy replied, hating the thought of traveling by herself to a place she had no idea of where it was.

"Good, I look forward to seeing you then," Brett was happy that he had one more slot filled and wrote it in his appointment book.

"Sandy, if I were you," one of the ladies interjected, obviously having listened in to the conversation, "I would take your oldest son with you. You don't know what you are getting yourself into."

"I'll take that into consideration," Sandy mused, feeling lighthearted that she had one more medium in which to publicize her book. Just think, the Internet! It was broadcast all over the world! The sales would go right through the roof, she was sure of it.

As the days crept closer to her interview, she rehearsed over and over in her mind what she would say and how she would say it. She didn't want to blow her one big chance by sounding like an idiot and so, kept going over and over in her mind what she would say. It progressed to the point where she was rehearsing at night before falling asleep as well as during the day while she made lunches for the kids. Her children were excited for her, and she asked her oldest son, Jake, if he would like to drive her there. Being seventeen, he welcomed any opportunity to drive and agreed. Everything was in place and ready for the big day. Sandy even went to the web site and listened in. She liked what she heard and saw and felt more relaxed than she had in awhile.

Eva was paying bills when she looked at the total left over in the checking account. There was little money left and a lot of bills to pay. Looking over at her husband as he scrolled his list of music up and down on the computer, she felt a surge of resentment well up in her. The burden fell to her, as it always did and she was exhausted from juggling all the creditors until the next payday.

"When are you going to find us a nice, paying job?" she demanded to know. Her shrill voice pierced the silence and he flinched, before stopping what he was doing, looking to her.

"You know I have been looking for a paying radio station, there just aren't a whole lot out there looking for my type of talent," he tried to assuage her. "Besides, I would have to drive and as you know, I no longer have a license to do so."

"You *were* at a paying station and decided to create conflict! What is wrong with you that you just can't get along for a change?"

"Get along?" Brett asked angrily. "I do get along! Is it my fault if others can't do things the proper way, instead of half ass all the time?"

"Your version of the story, not theirs, obviously. Honestly, I don't know how you expect me to…"

"Look, I do a lot around here so that you don't need to!" Brett interrupted her. "I cook, I clean, isn't that enough?"

Eva stared at him, fury etched on her brow, brown eyes

blazing. "Enough? We need money, Brett, to pay for your DUI and it doesn't grow on trees! You need a job! See that it happens! Wait! Where are you going?"

He had removed himself from his chair and was headed to the front door, a cigarette in his mouth. "You keep throwing that in my face. What do you want from me? People make mistakes..."

"Mistakes? Brett, that was your third one. The penalties just get higher each time you are caught. Don't you realize that?" Eva pleaded.

Brett just shook his head and walked out the door. Eva watched it slam behind him and put her head into her hands and cried.

Two hours later, Brett came back. He had walked at least four miles and was exhausted. He regretted that his license had been taken away; getting around was such a hassle, another reason why he couldn't find a good paying job. On his walk, he'd stopped into a liquor store and bought a six pack, now only three cans were left. The terms of his probation were that he not drink anymore. Screw it, who was going to dictate what he could and couldn't do? He did what he wanted, and his rebellious streak was why trouble usually found him.

Going into the house through he back door, he put the remaining three cans away in the refrigerator and went in search of Eva. She was lying down on the couch in the family room, eyes closed. He studied her visage for a moment, realizing she was just as beautiful now as the day he married her ten years ago. Going up to her, he kissed her eyes, then worked his way down to her warm mouth. She slowly responded at first, then with more fervor, until they were locked in the throes of passion. Even after all these years, with all the pain behind and beside them, he could still make her quiver. Afterwards, she cursed herself for letting her passions get the better of her as he went back to his computer. She got up, went to the bedroom, closed the door and cried. It wouldn't have mattered if the door was wide open. Brett wasn't paying any attention to anything except his music list.

9

The day of the interview arrived and Sandy was prepping not only what she would say, but how she looked as well. She wanted to make a good impression. Getting into the car with her son, Jake, they drove the route detailed on the map as she quietly gave him directions. They made it with five minutes to spare.

Brett was sitting at his computer, preparing for the days show. His music list was all in order, his promotions that he had prepared for others was intact. His stomach quaked a bit however, as he anticipated his guest list. Sometimes they just didn't show up, which left him with a hole he needed to scramble to fill. Looking up at the wall clock, he noticed it was five minutes before show time when the sound of the doorbell broke his reverie. Eva, who was preparing for work, went to answer it.

Sandy stood outside and surveyed the neighborhood while she waited for the door to be answered. Brett lived in a serene neighborhood filled with mature trees and sprawling ramblers. Envious, Sandy mused that someday, she could live in something like this, if only her book would make it big time. Just then the door opened. Sandy smiled at Eva, who ushered her and Jake in. Sandy admired the plush carpeting and large pieces of furniture as she was shown to Brett's den. Brett stood up with relief when he saw who it was as Sandy held out her hand. He admired her cute face and pleasantly plump body, her shoulder length blonde hair held in place by hair combs.

"Hello, I am Sandy Malone and this is my son, Jake. You must be Brett Pearson."

He shook her hand warmly, impressed with the way she presented herself. She was outgoing and pretty without any signs of arrogance that he found so distasteful in other guests. So many times it was all about them and yet, Sandy seemed totally unfazed by her celebrity. Brett showed her to her chair, offered Jake a place to sit and observe, then discussed how the program worked, showing her the controls and where she would need to project her voice.

"Keep it within these levels and you will do fine," he suggested. "Not too loud or too soft, we want everyone to hear what you want to say. Ready to go?"

Yes, I think so," Sandy tried to stop the butterflies from escaping her stomach and flying out of her mouth. She gripped the arms of the chair, waiting for her cue.

"I am sorry I can't offer you coffee yet, I just started a new batch, it will take a bit before it is ready."

"Oh, that's ok, I am fine," Sandy said.

This was a station that had an interactive chat line as well. People could type in messages and requests or just hang back and discuss whatever was on their minds. Brett signed in with his nickname and they began. He started off with a blonde joke, one of many which he was so fond to tell and Sandy laughed out loud at the punch line.

"What do you call a blonde with two brain cells?" Brett asked, looking at Sandy. She merely shrugged, smiling back at him.

"Pregnant!" She laughed then and watched the chat screen, but her angle only afforded her a side glance and she was also watching her voice level as the bars vibrated up and down according to her voice inflections as she discussed her book while Brett asked her questions.

At one point she mentioned that she used to work at a boarding kennel for dogs and he surprised her by saying he had also.

"No kidding, which one?" she asked, curious. He named it. "No way! Get out of here!" she was stunned.

"Why?" he asked.

"That was only a mile away from where I was. Small world!" she said, sounding impressed. One more thing they had in common was a love of animals.

All too soon, it was over. Sandy glanced at her watch and realized that fifty five minutes had already gone by. Brett switched on a song by Weird Al Yankovic, then he showed Sandy the favorable responses in the chat room. One gal named Callie even mentioned how impressed she was and where could she buy the book? Brett typed in the information as Sandy beamed. She had a positive feeling about this as she stood up, ready to leave. It was then that Brett remembered the promised coffee, which by now it was too late to offer.

"I am so sorry about the coffee. I guess the time just got away from us. Tell you what, how about a cold soda?" Sandy nodded and he went to the frig and offered her a Pepsi as well as one for Jake. Gratefully, she took it and then he walked her to the door, but only after checking to make sure he had enough time left on his music.

Sandy held out her hand once again. "I sure had a nice time today, thank you for inviting me over."

"My pleasure, I just hope all goes well with your book."

Sandy decided to go out on a limb and ask for a repeat performance. "I have my second book coming out in two months. Would you be interested in a repeat of today?" she asked, her heart thumping in her ears.

He mulled it over, then agreed. Why not? It would be one guest he knew would show up and he had had a good time too.

"All right, I look forward to it, then," Sandy flashed him a sincere smile, then turned to leave.

On the way home, she mulled over the interview as Jake drove. She was definitely on a higher sphere and nothing could bring her down for a long time.

Chapter 2

Brett was making dinner when Eva came home from work. She checked over the mail, then checked the inside of the large pot simmering on the stove.

"Hey, hun, how was your day?" Brett asked lightly, mixing the ingredients for a salad.

"Shitty, how about you?" She walked to the frig, grabbed a wine cooler and sat at the table and flexed her feet.

"It was nice." He walked over to the stove and checked the pot.

"How did your interview go this morning?"

Brett stirred the chili that was simmering, then looked at Eva. "It went well. Sandy Malone is a very nice lady."

"She is very pretty," Eva said, "for a children's book writer."

"Oh? Are they supposed to be ugly with a wart on their nose?" Brett teased.

Eva merely shrugged her shoulders, then went to put on something more comfortable. Brett went back to stirring his chili and thought again about his interview. Yes indeed, Sandy Malone was a fine looking lady.

Sandy sat down at her desk and selected a thank you card from her box of stationery. She found one with violets on the front and wrote:

"Dear Brett,

Thank you for having me on your show today. I certainly had a good time and hope it will help the sales of my book. You certainly have a wonderful program and I wish you all the best!

Sincerely,

Sandy"

She looked it over and, satisfied with what she said, she put it in the envelope and prepared it for the mail. She always thanked people who helped her in any way with publicity for her book, because one never knew how long their fifteen minutes of fame would actually last.

Summer was in full swing one morning as Brett was chatting a blue streak with another DJ via web chat when the chat room began to light up. The regulars were signing on and he glanced at it as he finished his conversation.

"And if you want to join us, just sign into chat, where we are all friends and loving every minute of this day! Let's see who is in there…I see Angel, Callie, stoker, "come again, softly" and …deli lady?" His voice held a question as he looked at the name while punching in a song. Could it be THE Deli lady that he had interviewed? Deli lady made her greetings and small talk, then Sandy was surprised when suddenly she saw a message for her on the screen. Who would know her identity?

The message read, "what are your plans for today, Sandy?" Taken a bit aback, she scanned the names on the chat screen, but didn't recognize anyone. Then it dawned on her that perhaps Brett was using a nickname in chat. It said next to the message, "Symba, Airwaves Warrior." Warrior, eh? What an ego! She typed in that she needed to go to the store for groceries, but that she just wanted to say hi. Next thing she knew, he introduced her on air and announced the title of her book and where to get it.

A warm feeling surged in her heart to know that he remembered. Sometimes a person is here today and gone tomorrow, but he still regarded her with respect. A smile slowly crossed her face as she continued to join in on chat, interjecting her opinion. Brett was surprised at the depth of her sense of humor, she had everyone in stitches as even he was "rofl," as it said on the screen. He also was amazed at how much knowledge she had, for a blonde! Usually blondes, in his opinion, were pretty shallow, but she knew her subjects, and as the days went on and she became a regular, he looked forward to having her on. He would chat with Callie, who it seemed, was always in chat, and Sandy got along with her very well. He knew that they had quite the rapport going, and others would join in with their camaraderie, but it didn't match Sandy's wit or the speed at which she could keep up the typing in time with his news, stories or jokes.

Several days later, she received a surprise phone call from Brett just before dinner. Eagerly she picked up the phone when she saw his name on her caller ID.

"Sandy! How are you?" he asked with genuine concern. He held her thank you card in his hand, touched by the gesture. No one had ever thanked him before after they did a show appearance. This gal had class. An idea had been floating in his head for awhile and he wanted to run it by her.

"I am fine, how are you?"

"I am doing great! Say, I had an idea that I thought I could run by you," he began.

"Sure, what is it?" Sandy asked, flattered that he would even think to call her.

"Your book, I was thinking of how great it could be in an audio CD format."

"Oh, well, there's an idea that I hadn't thought of before, but it sounds great," Sandy mulled the idea over. "I don't know, though, if my publisher could do it..."

"Well, I was thinking, if you would be interested, I could do the voiceover and put it on a CD for you, then you could have copies made and sell them to whoever you think might be interested. What do you say?"

"Well, I..." Sandy was wondering what he wanted out of this idea.

"Sandy, I would do it for free, just because I want to," he hesitated, as if reading her mind. "You have a great story with lots of potential."

"You know, Brett, I do need to check with my publisher about the copyright laws concerning infringement and all. Can I get back to you on this?"

"Sure," he said easily. "Call me when you know something. Who do you suppose would be interested in it?"

Sandy thought it over. In her excitement, marketing went right over her head. She hated the whole idea of marketing, because she wanted to concentrate her time on writing as opposed to selling. "Well, how about day care centers, schools, even nursing homes or the family car? Just pop it in a CD player and there would be a great story to listen to while one is driving."

"Good ideas. Well, I'll tell you what, you think it over and contact your publisher, and we'll talk again. Like I said, there is nothing in it for me, but I would like to help you out."

Sandy was flattered. "Thank you again. I will talk to you soon. Take care and thanks for calling!" Hanging up, she immediately composed an e-mail to her publisher asking the very question Brett needed information on. Hitting send, she resumed making dinner, her mind buzzing with new ideas.

As time went on, Rick, the station manager of "Listen to it Live!" noticed that listeners were beginning to complain at how raunchy Brett's morning show was becoming. He and Brett had never really seen things eye to eye and now he noticed that each morning were promos that were a bit over the top and even in chat, Sandy could lead a group in a slightly off color joke that would instantly hook Brett into something even more suggestive. Sandy took the bait and ran with it until everyone who could tolerate it were getting carried away. The day came when the manager called Brett to say he needed to tone down his show.

"What do you mean, tone it down? The listeners are enjoying it and no one has said anything to me before about it. Who the hell is complaining?" Brett was incensed.

"Pearson, you have been riding a fine line for quite some time now. I run a G rated station and am offended by your promos.

Stop your raunchy program right now, or I will pull the plug on it. Believe it when I say that. This is a family program and I don't need the complaints!"

"You know damn well that I have the highest ratings of any of these DJ's here and without me, you would have nothing!" Brett replied adamantly.

"Remember what I said. Tone it down and clean it up, or I pull it off and you are history!" Rick hung up.

Brett was furious. Thinking for a minute, he typed in on the screen, "there will be a change in format folks, sorry." Suddenly the music changed from the classic rock Sandy loved to bubblegum hits such as the theme from the Partridge Family TV show and the Mickey Mouse song. Sandy was confused and the others in chat didn't really catch on to it yet, so she typed in her concerns.

"What is going on?"

"Brett got a call from the manager. He needed to tone down his show because people are complaining," Callie typed in.

Tone it down? It was wonderful and Sandy said so. In fact, the more she typed, the more furious she became until she was throwing barbs in the direction of the station manager. Suddenly in mid-sentence, he caught her in a private message and told her to tone down her response in the chat room or he would black her out of it. She typed back how unfair he was and he couldn't censor what everybody enjoyed listening to.

"If they don't like it, they don't have to listen," Sandy reasoned. "There are music stations in this market that play even worse and are very highly rated!"

"Deli lady, remember what I said, you need to be respectful in the chat room or I will pull you out. I want a respectable show!"

Sandy was angrier than she had been. She'd stood up for Brett, mainly because she felt she owed it to him. He had given her the break she needed with her book, she wanted to repay him.

17

Besides that fact, she really felt a connection with him and liked him as a person. Suddenly her private message screen lit up.

"Deli lady, the person you were talking to is Rick, the station manager. He is trying to tell you what you want to listen to. Leave the chat room and perhaps the others will follow. Let it dry up."

"Brett, what is happening?" Sandy typed back.

"I have never played anything blatant, only suggestive. He doesn't like anything I am doing. Just leave and let the chat room dry up." He typed in the words with more anger than he had felt in a long time.

Reluctantly, she signed off, her mood soured for the day. Then it hit on her to write an e-mail to this Rick and really tell him what she thought!

Her writing skills came in handy as she politely but firmly explained that if people were offended, they didn't need to listen and that Brett wasn't doing anything wrong. He was a superior DJ and without him, then she would not listen to the program and felt sure others agreed with her. She challenged him to contact her so that they could discuss it further. Hitting the send button, she thought it would be a matter of time before she heard from him.

He never did reply to her message.

She also sent a message to Brett, telling him how sorry she was about the program and that, despite her best efforts, she felt as though she had failed him. She hit send on that one, more upset than she had been in a long time.

After the worse show in his history was over, Brett promptly pulled the CD and tossed it into the garbage. That was absolutely ridiculous! He checked his e-mails, even as he did so his heart warmed to the thought of deli lady and her courage. While most everyone else stood back and let what was happening take place, she actually had the courage to stand up for him.

Nobody had ever done that for him before! Usually it was he who was left holding the bag. He had been arrested and in trouble more times than he cared to admit since he was sixteen just because people had these sick ideas of letting him take the fall. It had come to the point where he just didn't give a damn anymore and he was tired of fighting. Yet here was someone who was well-known and put her own writing career on the line to step in for him. His admiration of her rose quite a bit.

Just as he thought that, he noticed a note from her in his inbox. Clicking on it, he read the message and his heart swelled with both pride and sadness. Quickly he typed in a reply.

"Sandy, thank you for what you did today. I will quit before I let him fire me. I will find a station that appreciates what I do. I will never forget what you did for me. Brett."

Sandy read that message later and inwardly wished him the best, sad over the loss of a great DJ. She typed out a message in reply.

"Brett, let me know which station so that I can listen in. I will be your #1 fan! Good luck to you and take care. Sandy." Hitting send, she thought about the waste of great talent this station was losing. It was too bad that his tenure had to end as it did.

The following night, out of boredom, Sandy clicked on to the internet radio station, mainly to see what the response was to Brett's leaving. Imagine her surprise when, as she scrolled down the chat list, she saw his nickname there! Symba Airwaves Warrior. Timidly, she made her greetings, and being subtle, asked him how he was. He typed in that he was fine. She then broached the subject that had been on her mind all day:

"Are ya staying, then, Symba?"

"Yes, I'm staying," was his reply.

Her heart warmed as she left it at that. The rest of the evening ended in a blur; he was staying.

Eva, who had been told by Brett of his troubles with Rick, had hoped inwardly that this situation would be what would push Brett to quit the station. She felt that his talents would be better spent at a paying station, and yet he was putting in so much time, not only filling in for other DJ's who couldn't fill their spot, but was also doing promos for just about all the other DJ's. She would have been happy if he would have quit.

Brett had been becoming more and more unhappy with Rick's attitude concerning his work, and subtly voiced his displeasure through his shows. There were times when Sandy would gently remind him through the chat room that his comment or little cameo that he had just played were over the top, but as time went on, he became more aggressive about it. She had a bad feeling about the whole matter and knew deep inside, that it would just be a matter of time before he was fired.

One morning in late July, Brett was tinkering after his program with his late model Chevy van that was his pride and joy. Music thrummed from within the garage on his state of the art speakers, giving the neighbors a blast of Led Zeppelin. As he pulled out the dipstick to check the oil, thoughts were running through his head and he methodically checked off each one, trying to decide which would be the better idea. Then the thought occurred to him; invite deli lady back on for an encore interview, except keep it as a surprise. She was well known in chat and always when she was there, the show became livelier with her infectious sense of humor. Wiping his hands on a towel, he went to the computer and clicked on to his e-mail list. He typed in:

"wanna do a surprise appearance?"

Hitting send, he waited for her response. This was going to be sweet revenge for everything that Rick had put him through.

Sandy came home from the grocery store and, after putting away the few things she had bought, checked her e-mails. Seeing one from Symba, she eagerly clicked on it and read his message. Desire surged through her that she could not explain. A surprise appearance? It would mean being with Brett again, something she wanted to do. He had a hold on her that, over time, grew into a longing she wanted to see fulfilled. She typed her message:

"Sure! when, where, why and with you?" She hit send and went about her chores, her heart practically floating through her chest.

Later that day, Brett went back to his e-mails. Seeing Sandy's reply made his mouth water. Now, he knew he that was not being fair to her. Literally, he would be using Sandy to get his revenge against Rick, but the ends justified the means. It would be cleverly designed so that Sandy herself would not know what was happening, yet others would catch on to his meaning. He typed in that he wanted her to come by that Friday at eight o'clock and sent the message. Then he went to his vast library of dirty jokes and stories and selected various bits that he would use on the program. Chuckling to himself, he thought of how Rick wouldn't know what had hit him.

On Friday, Sandy prepared for her appearance. This time she would be going alone; she wrote in her appointment book, "radio interview 8 a.m." For reasons she couldn't understand, she didn't even tell the kids where she was going other than "out." Then as she prepared to leave, she glanced at herself once again in the mirror, satisfied with her looks, for good measure, spritzed perfume on her neck, then in a naughty gesture, also spritzed some below her belt. She didn't know why, but she hoped that the show would end in a romantic way.

All the way there, she rehearsed what she would say. She brought along the second copy of her book just in case he wanted her to read snippets of it on air. The day was warm and sunny as she pulled into the driveway of his house. This time, Brett answered the door himself, thanked her for coming over and apologized for not having shaved. He said this was a surprise for his wife as well, for she didn't know what he had planned. Sandy just smiled, a feeling of something she couldn't quite put her finger on growing in her stomach. She was a pretty good judge of situations and right now, she felt something was amiss. Brett offered her coffee this time and as she accepted the steaming cup, she thanked him and got comfortable in her chair next to his. Lifting the mug to her lips, she admired the rich aroma and sipped. He could sure make a pot of coffee! It had a flavor of hazelnut and something else she couldn't quite name. Sipping again, she brought out the sequel to her first novel.

"I brought my book along, I thought we could maybe share a bit from this sequel..." she began.

Brett looked at it and explained that he would plug it, but there was something else he had in mind. Sandy shrugged and set it down next to her. She gripped the coffee mug in her hands, delighting in the fragrance. It was delicious and she felt spoiled by his attention.

Once again, they needed to share the same microphone as he explained how the controls worked. She knew the routine this time; yet when he introduced her after telling yet another blonde joke, her greeting was way off the wall.

"Speaking of blondes, ahem! I happen to have a blonde sitting right here next to me. Would you care to say something... deli lady?"

"Hello, world, down under, up over and everywhere in between!"

He laughed a bit, and inwardly hoped she could relax and enjoy this. He certainly was! He made introductions and told everyone that deli lady was making a surprise appearance.

"You remember her, the writer of *"Winston, the Wayward Spaniel."* Well, now she has a sequel, *"The Miracle of Christmas."* Available now at any book seller."

"Hello, everyone, it sure is nice to be back here," Sandy said warmly.

Brett held out the paper and said that although he usually did the horoscopes on Fridays, because Sandy was here, he would give her the satisfaction of doing so. The listeners in the chat room immediately flooded the line with their astrological signs so that they could hear their horoscopes and as Brett read off each sign from the chat screen, Sandy detailed what their day would be like. Brett was impressed with the steady way she read, adding her own brand of humor to each person, for instance, telling someone who had only two stars to stay home that day!

Then he had his endless lists of blonde jokes, lists of top ten this and top twenty that. Between songs, he asked Sandy if she wanted to read from a particular list. Sandy agreed.

"Top twenty things guys wish they could hear from women," Sandy began. Because she was reading this cold, she had no idea what she was reading. "Number one, I'll swallow it, every drop!" Sandy stopped and looked at Brett, who was laughing hysterically. Being a good sport, she continued. After the eighteenth one, she stopped and related a story that she had experienced with her husband.

Brett listened, then asked her to finish. Number twenty was a repeat of number one, which by this time, Sandy read with relish.

Brett was switching gears and played what sounded like a woman in the throes of ecstasy. "Rick," he thought, "eat your heart out." Then he tuned into a selection of songs, and, looking at Sandy asked her if she wanted a drink.

"Strawberry margarita? Please?" he begged with a smile.

Sandy didn't know anyone who drank in the middle of the day, but he obviously knew what she liked, mainly because twice in the chat room, she had said that a strawberry margarita was her favorite drink. She agreed, knowing that now, they were playing with fire.

Jumping up, he whipped out the ingredients and pulled out the blender and had it ready in under one minute. Impressed, Sandy took her drink as he poured one for himself. Raising his glass, he offered a toast. She raised her glass and as they touched glasses, she took a sip. It went down smooth. He took a couple of swallows, then went back to his computer, Sandy following.

The buzz began inside Sandy's head before long because she was not accustomed to drinking. Soon their banter on the radio became more casual; at one point, Sandy asked Brett on air for a lap dance. He looked a bit uncomfortable, then merely asked her to bring him dollars. To himself, he thought how this was going better than anything he had expected. "Rick, you bastard, eat your friggin' heart out. The woman is like putty in my hands!" Then he stunned Sandy by telling her a sad story from his youth, of how he bid adieu to all that was familiar to him after someone robbed him of everything he owned and destroying what they didn't take, going so far as to stab his cat to the wall!

Sandy listened in shock and awe, then gave him a shoulder rub; she felt so bad for him. It sounded as though he had had a hard life, and she was the type who wanted to erase the pain and make it better, no matter the cost.

All too soon, the show was over. Brett pulled his headset off and leaned back, looking thoroughly exhausted.

"It takes so much effort to do this," he said, rubbing his hand through his long mane of blonde hair. Sandy just looked at him and smiled, secretly wishing it were her hand through that mane. Then, taking a pen, she autographed the latest copy of her book and handed it to him. He read the inside, "to Brett, thanks for everything. Love, Sandy."

"Thank you again for having me here, I really had a good time." Sandy offered him a smile and he thought once again of attractive she was.

"How much time do you have before you need to go?" he asked.

She looked at her watch. "At least one more hour," she replied.

"Good! How about we get a refill and then I'll show you around." Going to the kitchen, he refilled their glasses and, once again, raised his glass in a toast. No probation officer was going to tell him he couldn't drink. Actually, he could hold his liquor quite well.

This time, Sandy raised hers and replied, "cheers, honey!" and downed her margarita in a smooth gulp. It went down so well; she never had one as wonderful as this.

Brett took her on a tour of his house, obviously proud of all the improvements he and Eva had made to it. He introduced her to his cats, who were lounging in various rooms. Sandy stopped and petted each one, her love of animals evident in her handling of them. He admired a person who loved cats. He then took her outside and showed her the garden, reveling in tales of how each plant was special in it's own way. He loved tomatoes and had several varieties growing there. Sandy listened, fascinated by his knowledge and asked questions, too. Her head had a mild buzz and she reeled a bit from the liquor coursing through her veins. Finally, she looked at her watch and announced it was time to go.

"Really? Do you have to leave so soon?" Brett asked, realizing that he didn't wish to see her go.

"Yes," Sandy smiled at him, disappointed that nothing more had really happened. She was hoping for...what? Ravishment? The man was married, damn it, and so was she! Still, the romantic part of her wondered how much farther it might have went. He had a charisma that oozed sex appeal. Yet, she had to go. Her kids were waiting for her.

"Can I have a hug?" Brett asked, stepping forward with his arms extended.

"Well, certainly!" Sandy was delighted as he grabbed her up in a big hug. She impulsively turned and kissed the side of his head just before she released him. Brett was surprised at that response, yet it warmed his heart also. Then he felt a twinge of regret that he brought her here to exact his anger towards Rick. Something inside of him, a feeling he couldn't name, nagged at him and he felt a sense of frustration. He watched her as she stepped into her car and drove away.

Chapter 3

As he put away his material from his show, Brett felt a mixture of satisfaction as well as loss. He wanted revenge and yet, now that his installment of the show was complete, he felt as though he wanted to punch something. Going into the garage, he had an idea of adjusting the stereo on the van, but thought better of it and wandered aimlessly through the yard, stopping occasionally to pet one of his many cats.

Sandy had left an impression on him he didn't see coming. Her sweet demeanor threw him for a loop. She had a natural energy that impressed him, as well as the other listeners in chat. Going to his instant messaging, he noticed another DJ had left a message.

"Hey, Brett, your guest…deli lady? She was great today! What an infectious laugh!"

"I am glad you liked the show," Brett typed back. Then he noticed another listener, one who was paying him particular attention lately, was online.

Her nickname was "come softly again," and she was a looker as well as a tease. Over time, she became more intimate with Brett online, going so far once as to ask for his help in setting up a porn web site for her. She was an exotic dancer by trade and sent Brett some pretty explicit e-mails of her in the nude. Brett drooled over the pictures and kept them in a folder on the computer. Today she wanted him to direct her to a sexually explicit web site, but she was having problems connecting to it.

"Sure, hun," Brett typed. "I'll help ya."

"Muah, sweetie. When was the last time somebody made a man outta you?"

"Been awhile, darling," was his reply.

"Here, feast your eyes on this and have a blast, rocket man!" Suddenly, up on the screen was another picture of her in a very revealing position. Brett fondled himself until release came, then, after typing in a hearty thank you, he went to clean up. What would he do without his cyber groupies, he wondered. After considering it for awhile, he came to the conclusion that if she asked him to, he would have left Eva in a heartbeat for her. Never mind the fact that other than her sexy pictures and his constant desire for sex, they had nothing in common. Feeling empty despite his recent orgasm, he again got up from the computer and made himself a sandwich. How low could he sink, he wondered, before he crashed and burned?

That night, after the dinner dishes were washed, Eva sat down at the computer to look up some information on a credit card that she wanted to apply for. Brett was napping on the couch, so she was quiet as she typed in the information needed to apply. Then, as she waited for the information to download, she noticed a folder in the toolbar that Brett had left open. Curiosity got the best of her when she saw one that was quite full from someone or something titled, "come softly again." Opening it, she was stunned to find picture after picture of a woman in various poses, the graphics so detailing that she gasped in shock. Where did this come from? Was it possible that her husband was into porn?

"Brett, wake up, wake up! Do you hear me?" Eva stood over him and shook him awake. Groggy, he wiped his eyes and wondered what was wrong. "Tell me about these pictures! Who is this?"

"What the...why the hell are you trespassing on my computer? Those files are private!" Brett protested.

"Private? Yes and also boobs and butt and everything else I wouldn't expect to find you hoarding on the computer! Who is she, Brett?"

His mind furtively thought for a minute, then he decided he would just come clean. No point in trying to hide it.

"It's from a cyber groupie. I have been helping her to set up a web site for her... business..." he began contritely.

"Business? What is she, a hooker?" Eva's eyes blazed and her face flushed from the effort of trying to remain calm, but realized also this was the last straw. To her, he may as well as just had an affair with the slut.

"She is an exotic dancer."

"And you met her on air?'

Brett just nodded, remorse evident in his whole being.

"This is it, the last straw! I am giving you an ultimatum. Me or the show. You can't have us both! Either or, Brett..."

"What?" Brett asked, shocked. "That show is my life! How can you say that?"

"Your life? What about me? Where do I fit in? All those times I have bailed your damn ass out of jail, other times I waited so patiently for you to finish your time in it! Yet, you tell me this is your life? You have got some serious thinking to do! Either or, Brett. I will not share you with that goddamned program anymore! Or the sluts, whores and beggars that go with it! You devote all of your time to it and I sit here like a bitch who has nothing better to do than to wait for you to finish. You have no money and I'm tired of supporting the two of us and your laziness. Get a real, paying job or get out of my life. Is that clear? I will expect an answer from you tomorrow!" With that, Eva grabbed her purse and stormed out of the house.

Brett cringed when the door slammed, the reverberation echoing though his mind. Slowly he went to the computer and, closing the file window on the pictures, he sat down with his head in his hands as he stared morosely at the screen. How did he get himself into these things? What could he do?

Eva drove around and finally ended up in a parking lot of a nearby strip mall. Pulling in a private spot away from observing eyes, she gripped the steering wheel so tight her fingers turned white. Was she prepared to follow though with her threat? But then again, it seemed lately that the only thing that prodded

Brett into action was a threat or the refusal to buy him a new toy. Stereos, DVD players, it seemed a high ticket item usually kept him in line for awhile. But then the novelty wore off, the credit bills came rushing in, and Eva felt as though the whole world was crashing in on her. The whole agony of her marriage to Brett made her feel older than her years. What was she going to do, she wondered. She was in no hurry to return home. That very fact alone scared her.

Brett finished his resignation notice for radio management. He perused it to make sure it said what he wanted it to. Short, sweet and to the point. Clicking on enter, he watched it go up on the screen of the radio's web site.

"It has been a sweet ride, but I need to leave Listen to it Live due to financial difficulties. Good luck to all of you in the future. Brett Pearson." Then he realized that he needed to find someone to cover a spot that he had promised he would fill for someone else. So, going back to the screen, he typed in that information as well. Pushing away from the computer, he knew that he craved a drink. Something hard that would make him drunk fast. Going to the refrigerator, all he could find was a can of beer. No good, he wanted something more, damn it! Depressed, he pondered his future and realized he had many days strung out ahead of him, one after the other, with nothing to look forward to. No prepping for a show, no promo work, nothing. He might as well as be dead.

Depression was nothing new to Brett. It seemed that whenever life dealt him a blow, he just wanted to curl up and die. When he admitted it to himself, he realized that it was Eva who was his anchor, she brought him back to reality. But just how many times would she do that before she gave up? That was why he gave up his program. When he admitted it to himself, he knew he was doing the right thing.

Sandy spent two whole days trying to set up instant messaging on her computer, per Brett's suggestion the last time she saw him. He said it was a great way to keep in touch, and after the fourth time, was finally able to sign on. Imagine her surprise at seeing his e-mail address on the screen, her first contact! She added it to her contact list, then tried to send a message. His contact card showed that he was offline right now. Disappointed, she shut down her computer for the night and, after giving her husband a kiss, went to bed.

Harry was beginning to wonder what was up with his wife. Sandy was listening to that interactive radio show each day, Monday through Friday, for the whole four hours Brett was on. Luckily it was summer and she wasn't working until the afternoons at a part time day care position, but what would she do in the autumn? Also, she had set up instant messaging. When Harry asked her what it was for, she acted secretive as she shielded the screen from his prying eyes. The antenna went up in his mind; was she having an affair? She was sure acting secretive lately. Also, her interest in sex was waning and the few times he inadvertently listened in, she would turn down the volume on the racier parts of Brett's show, as if she was hiding something from him. He would wait and watch.

The next day, Sandy was up early as usual and signed in to her instant messaging first, before she connected to the internet. Right away, a blinking light alerted her to a message from Brett! Clicking on, she read: "There won't be a radio show today, or any day for that matter."

Shocked, she wrote, "why?"

"Eva gave me an ultimatum-her or the show."

Sandy sat in stunned silence, although she assumed this day would arrive, it seemed too soon now that it was here.

"I am depressed." Brett wrote.

"Hang in there, hun." Sandy wrote back. "What happened?" As if she could feel his anxiety, she waited for his next words, so wanting to help him, yet knew that this was the beginning of a long descent into hell for him.

Suddenly a graphic picture showed up on his contact card. "When your husband asks you who that is, tell him it is me." It was a man with his pants down, mooning the world with his male organ showing.

Oh, boy, he really was depressed. Sandy panicked. If her kids saw that, she would be embarrassed. Gently, she wrote in and asked if he could change his picture so as to not offend her kids. A new picture blended in, one of a pair of dogs.

"What will you do?" Sandy asked

"Find a station that pays." Brett typed in. "Eva wants me to make money. Big money." He thought over the events of last night, when Eva came in from her drive. Her face was white, her pupils large as she looked at him, defeat evident in her very soul. She went to the bedroom, closing the door without a backwards glance. He would let her know about his decision today. It still didn't make it easier for him. Already he wondered what the others in the chat room were up to.

"Please go to chat and tell them that I won't be there," he typed to Sandy.

"I will. You take care and hang in there! I am thinking about you. Hugs!"

As Sandy signed off, she went to chat where only two other people were there. She explained that Brett had quit. As shocked as she was, they asked why. Sandy replied it was because he needed to find a paying job. Nobody had anything to say after that. There was no need to. The Warrior had left the building.

The days after that were a discombobulated blur. For Sandy, it had become a quick addiction to listen to Brett's show. Now she had nothing to do for four hours each morning except all the things a wife and mother should do.

Sandy moped. Then she realized that she could IM Brett each morning, just to touch base with what was happening in his life. It would have been so easy to just up and walk away. It would have been over and she could have just gone on with her life. She had only known him for three months, but time had a way of slowing down sometimes.

She found that she cared that much about him, and when

31

someone is drowning, she never threw out an anchor.

The first week, all he talked about was the loss of his show. Sandy allowed him to grieve, typing in words of encouragement. Brett found out that, without the show, he was able to concentrate on things that had passed his attention before. But the huge hole that had been his show was a void he found insurmountable. He would type in quips so full of pain and pessimism, Sandy wished he would reach bottom, just so that he could climb back up.

The lawn was mowed regularly, a long overdue land-scaping project was finished, he was able to clean the gutters and trim the trees and paint the den, all things he kept putting off because he had to prep for the show, do promos for the show, do the show, get ready for the next show. When he really thought about it, it was a catharsis to put the pain of the past into his work around the house and get things accomplished. Eva noticed the slow but steady results and inwardly was happy that perhaps her decision, as drastic as it was, brought about results. One evening, Brett came in all flushed and sweaty from laying patio blocks. Eva had just come home from work and was perusing the day's mail left on the kitchen counter. Brett grabbed her in a bear hug, resulting in a squeal from her.

"Brett, you're all sweaty and smelly. You need a bath!"

"I know," he purred in her ear. "Want to come with me?" He kissed the back of her neck and nuzzled her ear, which she eagerly returned with slow but steady interest. Taking her hand, they soon forgot all about dinner as the sun went down and the full moon came up over the eastern horizon.

Sandy felt that maybe what Brett needed was a shoulder to cry on. It was on a beautiful sunny morning that she took a deep breath and invited herself over for brunch to his house during their chat session. Rather presumptuous of her, but what else could she do? She offered to bring something or they could go out, she asked. He couldn't drive, so it was either this or nothing. Unbeknownst to her, he did drive, carefully taking back roads to get to the store for bread, cigarettes and liquor. He just never admitted it.

He typed in, "when?"

"How about Tuesday of next week? I start back to school on Thursday, it will be a nice send off."

"OK, do you like eggs or muffins? I will cook for you," he wrote.

"Anything is fine. I look forward to it," Sandy sent it with relish. This time, she vowed, something had to happen. Unfortunately, she wanted to take advantage of a man in pain to get it.

Chapter 4

The day before her brunch, Sandy sat at the computer, working on the edit for her third book. Book sales were going strong for the first one and she was working on promoting the second one. It was frustrating trying to get book signings at book stores, because they wanted to showcase big name authors, not small ones, although Sandy thought bitterly that if she didn't get a break, she would be no author at all. Suddenly, Brett's IM came up on screen.

She clicked on it and asked, "what's up?"

"I am gullible and forgiving," he wrote.

Sandy looked at that and wondered what was up now. So she asked, "gullible about what?"

"I have made too many stupid decisions that have wrecked what I thought were friendships. If you want to leave too, I will understand."

"What is going on? Talk with me," Sandy pleaded.

"I am a nobody,"

"Brett, that isn't true, you're very special to me. I will not leave you. Why would I do that?"

"Because I have fucked up everything that is good in my life."

"Brett, you don't need to cut yourself down. Look at the strides you're making! I can see a difference in you. Don't back down now!"

"I am making a demo for a new radio station. Hopefully someone will want to hire me."

"Of course they will," Sandy wrote. "You have a talent that is so remarkable, why would nobody want to hire you?"

"Gonna use clips from my shows and put it together. Then I will look into who is hiring out there. I believe I can take a station and turn it around."

"You already have one fan and she is right here. Hang in there, I know things will get better. Be positive."

"Sandy, that groupie, "come softly again" lied to me. She made me think I was her #1, then when she realized I have nothing, she left me."

"She didn't have a whole lot going for her anyway. Stick with people who love you, people like me," Sandy was being forward, she knew, but she didn't care.

"Why haven't you left before now? I am a washed up DJ..." he began, but Sandy cut him off.

"Now listen to me, you have a pretty home and a pretty wife. I am here for you, don't go on like this!" It hurt Sandy to admit that about Eva, but some rational part of her needed to confirm that he was, indeed married, as was she.

"Your husband and my wife, they don't have a clue. We should have met a long time ago," Brett typed in.

Sandy sat stunned as she read that. So he recognized that too. "Yes, we have so much in common, we should have met sixteen years ago. I am driven and so are you. We would have been so good, but that is a moot point right now. We have to go on."

"You are a good friend. Thank you. I need to go make some dinner now. I will see you tomorrow."

"Yes, we'll talk tomorrow. Good night, Brett." Sandy signed off. Then her mind went into overdrive. She looked at her husband slouched in the recliner. Married almost seventeen years, she felt the ravages of time on her marriage. Too often, she had to pick up the pieces for him, and what she admired in Brett was that he spoiled his wife terribly. He cooked for her, made her lunches, and always it was, "Eva this..." or "Eva that." He held her in high esteem. Turning back to the computer, she shut it down and pondered on how life handed out unfair sentences.

Sandy told Brett that she would be there at 8:45 a.m. Turning into his street, she was shocked to see Eva's car still in the driveway. Heart beating fast, she assumed that maybe she was late for work, so Sandy went down the street and parked discreetly, waiting about five minutes for her to leave. Then a feeling overtook her that perhaps Eva was supposed to be there, so she turned back and parked by his driveway. Getting out of the car, she grabbed a flyer for her next book signing, and took it with her as an excuse perhaps for Brett seeing her. The last thing she needed was conflict between husband and wife. Knocking timidly on the door, she was greeted with a male voice asking, "who's there?" from inside the house.

"A pervert," was the first thing that popped out of her mouth, which she instantly regretted.

"Come on in!" Brett called.

Stepping inside, she was assailed by a variety of smells from his small kitchen. Brett had onions chopped fine on the counter, bacon sizzling away and eggs cooking in a skillet. He had just applied cheese to the eggs and turned to say hello to Sandy. She smiled at him, then remembering her manners, she looked at Eva and made her greetings.

"Hello, it is good to see you again. You must be so spoiled to have Brett make breakfast for you." Taking in Eva's attire, she assumed that Eva was off work this day. Was there a mix up on Brett's part? He never mentioned that she would be home.

"Oh, yes, any time he wants to, the kitchen is all his!" Eva teased. She washed her hands, then excused herself to go catch up on the daily paper.

Brett handed Sandy a mug of coffee, which she gripped with a nervous squeeze, then he went back to his omelet. "Take some grapes there," he offered. Picking up one plump little grape, Sandy popped it in her mouth. Then remembering the flyer, took a magnet off his refrigerator and stuck it on.

"This about my next book signing in two weeks. If you can, it would be nice to see you there," she offered.

36

He glanced at it, then admitted that Eva had became angry with him for not going to the last one. Sandy merely raised her eyebrow, but said nothing, sipping her coffee, she fell into a relaxed silence. He asked her if she wanted cottage cheese and went to get the container from the frig.

"Any nibbles yet on your demo yet?" Sandy asked.

At that, Brett dropped the cottage cheese, as Sandy grabbed it and returned it to his hands. He looked at her and realized again how beautiful she was. "No, not yet, but I am still looking."

"Good. I know something will turn up," Sandy said with a smile. Then, feeling nervous, she stood in the division between kitchen and dining room so that she could converse with both Eva and Brett. They made small talk about the latest hurricane down south and the vagaries of people who stay in a hurricane's path. Brett kept busy with the breakfast, and wished he had told Sandy that Eva would be home. He could sense the tension, but knew that Sandy was a real people person and could make anyone feel at ease.

"Come and sit down, breakfast is served," he called out. "How many pieces of bacon would you like?" he asked Sandy.

"Oh, I will have two please."

"Only two? I worked so hard on this! How about you, hon?" he asked Eva.

"I'll take three please," Eva said.

Brett heaped on the eggs, bacon, cottage cheese and put two pieces of English muffins on her plate and handed it to her. Sandy was stunned. Eva was very petite and not even Sandy could eat all that he had just handed to his wife. She received her plate, then Brett sat down with his.

Starting first with her cottage cheese, Sandy remembered her manners and addressed her questions to both Eva and Brett. She noticed that Brett seemed nervous, so she directed more questions to Eva.

"Are you on vacation this week?" Sandy asked.

"Yes, I do it every year at this time. Then we can catch up

on going places and doing things before Labor Day." The talk then turned to music trivia as well as wedding days. Sandy remarked that she was married on May first-May day! She told of how it was a time of flowers in baskets and springtime. Her husband, Harry, had other thoughts, namely the Communist parade in Red Square every year. Eva laughed at that one.

"If I remember right, it was cold when we got married," Brett said between bites.

Eva looked at him strangely. "Cold? Where did you come up with that? It wasn't cold."

Sandy looked from one to the other, waiting for what would happen next.

"I thought it was cold. Well, when did we get married? Wasn't it in November?" he asked, chewing on a strip of bacon.

Disgusted, Eva shook her head and refused to tell him. That cast a pall on the rest of the meal. Brett finished quickly, keeping his thoughts to himself.

When the plates were empty, Brett went to put the excess food away and clean up the kitchen, then sat at his computer in the den to work on his demo some more. He felt like a real bastard for ignoring Sandy, but he was not comfortable having her here with his wife. Why didn't he tell Sandy that Eva would be home and let her decide if she wanted to come over? Because he wanted to see her again, he enjoyed her presence. Yet he was so afraid that he would say something wrong or let something slip, such as his stupidity in not knowing his own wedding date. Sandy, being a real lady, kept the conversation flowing.

After a bit, however, she stood up and, washing out her coffee mug and plate, went in search of Brett.

"Well, this is where you are hiding out. I wondered where you were," Sandy said lightly, rubbing his shoulder easily. She'd hoped that motion would let him know that she could sense his unease and maybe he would loosen up.

"How about if we go outside and look at the garden," he suggested, getting up from his chair. Sandy followed him to the back door and they stepped outside. Brett started talking a blue streak about tomatoes, when Sandy gently cut him off.

"Brett, talk to me," she began.

"About what?" he asked as he picked up a stray crabapple, tossing it out into the street.

"What's going on?"

"What? Everything is fine."

Sandy was hoping he could talk but felt that maybe Eva's presence was making him nervous, so she got the ball rolling. "How is it going with you and everything?"

"Well, my PO will be here in forty five minutes. I have that to look forward to each week. I have to pay to pee in a cup every week and then I pour my guts out to a counselor as if I am a criminal or something." Brett kept busy, pulling small weeds and tossing more stray apples. Sandy followed him like a puppy as he worked, knowing that this was probably how he dealt with it.

"How does he expect you to have a job if you have appointments almost every day and you can't drive?" Sandy asked philosophically.

"My point exactly," Brett answered sardonically. "You know," he said, stopping for a minute. "I should have been a sex offender. They are walking the streets everywhere and I get treated like this."

Sandy rubbed his arm, then impulsively hugged him. They were by the side of the garage now where Eva wouldn't see them if she were to come outside. Sandy wished she could wipe the exhaustion from his brow and let him know that she was there for him. Maybe the hug would suffice. Sandy was careful, she didn't want to upset Eva, so she pulled away right away, disappointed that today, too, there would be no planned ravishment. What was wrong with her? He was obviously committed to his marriage, he had so much to show for those years. On the other hand, Sandy, even after twice as many years had little in the way of extras because to raise four kids takes a lot out of a bank account. She glanced at her watch and felt that now would be a good time to make her departure. Even though it had only been ninety minutes, if his PO was coming over, she imagined that he wanted to get ready.

"Well, kiddo, thanks for a great breakfast. You are an excellent cook and I wish I could have served you instead. It was my idea to do that."

Brett smiled at her. "I love to cook and I know that what I serve is better than anything you will get around here. I didn't want to go anywhere anyway."

"Hang in there and know that I'm thinking about you," Sandy smiled back, patting his arm once again, then went in the house to say goodbye to Eva. She was reading her paper again as Sandy walked over to shake her hand.

"It was so nice seeing you again. I had a delightful morning, but now I really need to go." Eva said as she got up and walked her to the door.

"It was nice to meet you and to have this chance to get to know you better," Sandy said. "Your husband spoils you rotten, you are so lucky to have him!" Eva merely smiled, thinking how nice this lady was. Turning back to Brett, she wished him a good day, then walked to her car.

As she drove home, her mind flitted from subject to subject. How lucky she was to have met Brett, yet how ironic that the one person she felt a strong bond with, was also married. His wife obviously ran the marriage, while Brett did exactly what he was supposed to. How was that supposed to be a happy union? Then she thought of the circumstances he dealt with: he had no money, no job, no job prospects at this point, couldn't drive and all obligations toward Eva, who had bailed him out and stood by him for so many years. No wonder he was depressed, he owed it to her. He had no where else to go. Sandy really felt for him. He needed a friend.

Chapter 5

School started again for Sandy and her kids. Back into the routines they all were familiar with, while, at work, coworkers grilled Sandy on her book signings and asked about the big royalty check. Sandy merely smiled and replied that obviously it hadn't come yet, or she wouldn't be here! She filled them in on the not one, but two radio interviews she did for her books, keeping out a lot of the details. Some things were better left unsaid.

The next several weeks fell into an easy routine. Brett and Sandy would instant message each other almost every morning early before Sandy went to work. She would do activities with the kids, chores, shopping, working on the edit for her latest book as well as book signings, all the while keeping Brett in her thoughts. Then came the day he broached the subject that completely took her by surprise.

"I have a deal for you," he typed.

"Oh? What?" Sandy asked out of curiosity.

"Be my co-host on the radio." He waited for her response with baited breath. She had such an easy, happy way about her, he really wanted to do this.

"Are you sure?" she asked.

"You have such a great sense of humor. The energy you gave off on the last show we did was wonderful. I want us to be a team."

Sandy was flattered that he would even think about this. "Sure! I don't want to sound desperate, but I would love too!"

"Desperate doesn't make for a good job. Love of what you do, that is the ticket to success. You love life and I want us to be together. I am wifenapping you!"

"Kidnapping me, from everything I know?" Sandy teased.

"Yeppers," was his response. "We need to get you a proper microphone and you will need to practice."

"How?"

"That is the problem. Your work schedule doesn't give us much leeway." He really meant hers and Eva's. He didn't want to do this while she was around. He learned his lesson last time. He wanted this to be fun for both of them.

"Screw my friggin' schedule," she wrote. "When do we start?"

Laughing at her response, he typed in, "How about next Friday morning? Eight o'clock?"

"I will be there," she typed in, her stomach in knots at this prospect. She would get to see him again!

Asking her boss for that day off from work, she mentally ticked off the days.

This time she didn't write the appointment anywhere except inside her heart.

This time, she vowed, the day would end in the result she had dreamed of.

Friday morning, she instant messaged him, just to let him know she would be there in two hours, whether he liked it or not. Soon the talk became more suggestive until finally they both agreed they needed a cold shower. He signed off with a "ttfn" and Sandy closed down the computer, breathing hard. Where would this lead? she wondered. More important, was she ready for this?

As Sandy drove the freeway to Brett's house, it was sunny and warm for late September. The sky was a glorious blue. Pulling up alongside his house, she noticed that Eva's car was gone. "Score one for Sandy," she thought. Walking up the sidewalk, she noticed the many little things he had done to beautify the place. Always it was something that kept him busy. Ringing the doorbell, she saw him run- yes, run! to answer it. Smiling, she stepped in and followed him to the kitchen, after first removing her shoes.

"Here's a cup of coffee for ya," he said handing her a steaming mug.

"M-m-m-m, it is delicious. What kind is it?" she asked.

"Some kind of hazelnut that Eva gets. Sometimes she gets these different flavors like coconut or raspberry..." seeing her wrinkle her nose, he hastily assured her that it was very good. Smiling, she sipped some more.

"I haven't shaved yet today, come on up with me and keep me company," he suggested. Following him upstairs, she watched, fascinated by this personal act of hygiene. Harry never liked it when she watched him shave. She made up for this by telling Brett funny stories of Harry's idioinsyncrasies.

"You wouldn't believe it, but he has fourteen white shirts, all for work. He gets mad if the two that he likes aren't cleaned and ready to go each day. Two! I asked him why he has fourteen shirts if twelve of them are useless. His reply? 'I like knowing I have shirts if I need them!' What a guy!" Sandy smiled at the recollection as she drank her coffee. Hearing a blue jay outside the open window, she bent down for a closer look. Brett looked over her head to see what she was interested in. Pointing the bird out to him, he admitted he had never paid any attention to that one, usually it was the cardinals that he liked to observe. Finishing up with a splash of cold water and a toweling, he applied after shave, then hanging up his towel and straightening out the sink area, he asked her to follow him downstairs. Sandy realized that his propensity for order obviously stemmed from all of the disorder in his life. It was probably nice to know that there were some things he had control over.

"Come on, let's go outside," he said, slipping his shoes on.

Sandy went to retrieve her shoes from the entryway and slipped them on by the back door. Brett appreciated her thoughtfulness when she explained that she did that at home, too. With four kids all running in and out, she needed to keep a sense of order, she explained. Brett took her to his garden and explained about his tomatoes and what he would do different next year. Then he showed her his fire pit as it burned some logs that he had stacked against his garage. Sandy loved the smell of burning wood and watched as he stoked and banked the logs and embers, turning away from it occasionally and regaling her with stories about friends he knew and his own camping experiences. He was more animated than Sandy had seen in a long time.

Soon talk turned to his old radio station. Brett was still mourning his leaving it as Sandy listened sympathetically.

"But look at all of the things you have accomplished since you left," she said.

Quietly, he agreed with her. He admitted that he felt pushed around and unappreciated by Rick. If only he had been told how good he was!

"Brett, you have a talent that is beyond belief. Don't keep beating yourself up over what no longer is! You are destined for greater things. You were doing it for free anyway. You're worth more than that. Go find your world, then fly with it!" Sandy looked starry eyed as she said this; sipping on her coffee, she felt she could do anything.

"But I want a station of my own. You know, at my treatment class the other night, I had to present my life story. It was the hardest thing for me to have to admit. At the end, most everyone clapped. But there was one woman who said I was arrogant. After everyone made their comments, I explained that the arrogance she sees, is really my confidence which I need to protrude on air. That didn't satisfy her, though."

"Brett, the last few weeks on the show, I could feel a frustration within you and you were not happy."

"How so?" he asked, wondering how much she knew.

"It was in your responses, the way you were becoming more withdrawn. You didn't like the way Rick controlled you and it showed. Then you started taking it out on yourself by drinking more."

That much Brett knew; in fact, he was amazed at how intuitive she was. He continued to listen.

"It's a survival thing, I guess. Growing up in a home that wasn't too happy, I could always sense when my mom was angry, so I learned to stay out of her way. So I can just feel it when things are not right."

Brett nodded, surprised at her depth of feeling.

Sandy. She felt his pain and gave him encouragement when it was needed. Brett was so happy she was here.

"Say, it is too nice out, let's go for a ride." Impulsively, he took her to his car and opened the door.

"But what about the demo?" Sandy asked.

"You know, I have been thinking about that. I don't have a station yet and you might forget everything I have taught you. Let's put it on hold for now."

Sandy had been looking forward to it, but the prospect of going someplace with Brett seemed appealing, too. The thought that he shouldn't be driving flew right out of her head.

They took all the back roads and ended up at a strip mall. Deftly backing his car in, Sandy turned and noticed that they were at a liquor store. Raising her eyebrow, she didn't say anything, but inwardly, wondered what he was up to. He jumped out of the car and asked, "strawberry margarita for you?" Nodding, she agreed, and, while she waited for him to return, hoped he was doing something he could handle.

About ten minutes passed before he came out with a brown paper sack and a twenty four pack of beer. He put the sack into her hands and the beer beside her on the floor. Then they drove to a gas station, where he bought three packs of cigarettes. On the way there, he explained about the many neighbors who had come and gone in his neighborhood, the smooth condition of the newly paved road and teased her about every little thing before he rubbed her shoulder when she pretended to take it personally. They pulled back in to his driveway and entered the kitchen, where he put the beer away and gave her the sack that held strawberry daiquiri and a bottle of Jose Cuervo. She set the bottles on the counter, then folded the bag and put it in the cupboard where he had stored other ones of various sizes.

"Here you go, make it!" he announced, pulling out the blender. Sandy had no idea how to make a margarita, and meekly said so.

"What is so difficult about it?" he asked, then got out a tray of ice, put it in the blender along with the strawberry daiquiri and a splash of Jose Cuervo. Mixing it together, Sandy watched a bit as it churned furiously around, then turned it off. Selecting a large eight ounce glass from the cupboard, she poured it full, then set the blender back on it's base. Following Brett outside, they watched the logs burn as Brett, downing his can of beer, talked about his hopes, dreams and desires.

The topics ranged from his latest camping expedition to what happened just before he and Eva got married. Sandy hung over the deck railing as she listened, careful to stay out of the way of the smoke as it occasionally drifted her way. Spotting several crows flying overhead, she watched their antics.

"What do you call a group of crows?" Brett asked her, following her gaze.

"A murder," Sandy replied looking him square in the eye.

Brett looked at her in amazement. "Not many people know that," he said, clearly impressed. "If I was working at the bar where I did my gig, you would have a won a prize for that!" Sandy just beamed. The smell of wood smoke intensified, making Sandy feel euphoric combined with the sensations of the drink. Brett joined her on the deck and they talked some more, comparing notes about music, Brett stopping occasionally to get another beer.

"Hey, you want to listen to a CD I just put together?" he asked, sounding like an excited schoolboy.

Sandy smiled and, taking another gulp of margarita, she followed him in the house. On the way to the basement, he topped off her glass with the remainder of the drink, grabbed yet another can of beer and went to his vast collection of CD's.

Sandy was stunned. There must have been over one thousand CD's stored in cases in the basement. The stereo speakers were each the size of a small person as he explained to her about his CD player.

"I bought it right before I had to go to jail. Then it didn't work, so here I was, trying to return it eight months later and the customer service rep wondered what had taken me so long!" Brett turned back to his music and picked out a song.

Sandy was thirsty and downed the rest of her drink in several large gulps and the buzz began in her ears and rapidly progressed to her extremities. Looking at her watch, she noticed she hadn't eaten in over six hours. This was not good. She felt woozy as the strains of a Pat Benatar hit churned through the speakers so loud her insides quivered. Brett watched Sandy's reaction and asked her a few questions, but she had difficulty getting the words out. He popped open another beer and, when the song finished, explained how when he had a music and lights show, it was cool because the lights would flash and pulsate on everyone in the room. He became very animated as he explained in detail how he performed each show.

"I have another one that I think you will like," he said and put in another CD. The room once again boomed to life as Brett turned the lights off over the pool table off. The strains of YES singing "Hearts" filled the room. The combination of music and darkness plus the hypnotic beat of the song put Sandy into a trance. Brett stood on the opposite side of the pool table and watched Sandy through half lidded eyes. She began to sway a bit with the sound, her mind captured by the feelings the images evoked.

"She's so beautiful, she looks like she probably did when she was sixteen," Brett thought. It was at that moment when he fell in love with her. After what seemed an eternity, the song was finished. The only sound in the quiet basement was of Brett crying as he took the CD out of the boombox.

"This song does this to me every time," he said as he fumbled with the CD case. Sandy went around the pool table, grabbing him in a hug. Putting down the case, he held onto her tightly as she turned and kissed the side of his face and hugged him some more. Her heart beating next to his was the only sound heard, the only sound she wanted to hear.

The rest of the afternoon passed in slow motion.

Chapter 6

Brett smelled so good and it felt so right to be here holding him like this. He then pulled away a bit and, looking at Sandy, took her face in his hands and kissed her mouth, slowly at first, then with more urgency. She repeated the motions, holding nothing back. He pulled the hair combs out of her hair in one swift motion, then pulled her shirt and bra off effortlessly. She reached for his shirt and did the same and kissed him again with a fervor that she never used with her own husband. She got lost in his beautiful blue-gray eyes as he caressed her hair and she his, reveling in it's length and softness. She wanted him with every fiber of her being, holding nothing back. Inside, she knew she would burn in hell forever. Another part of her didn't care.

"If I never have this again," she thought, "let me enjoy it now while I can!"

"Let's go someplace more comfortable..." Brett suggested, pulling away.

"Lead away," Sandy replied, taking his hand. Brett couldn't believe his ears. This gentle writer wanted him? He took her upstairs to the guest room and, with no inhibitions, she shucked off her jeans as he, laying a blanket down on the floor, led her to it and she lay down, totally unashamed of what he was seeing. She couldn't believe how exposed she was, yet felt nothing but how natural and good this was. He kissed her face and mouth, taking his time to thoroughly arouse her. Slowly he explored her breasts, then went lower, lower until he found that special spot of her and began to give it special attention. She writhed and moaned until she was almost at the breaking point. He kept at his ministrations until she cried out in ecstasy. He congratulated himself on giving her this wonderful gift as he slowly made his way back to her mouth and kissed her again.

Sandy reached down and, gripping him, pulled him inside of her and maneuvered to make him fit. He was so much bigger than she had expected, such a difference from her husband! He filled up every place that had lain dormant for years as she moved in a rhythm as old as time. He skillfully moved her, twisting, writhing, legs draped over him, then off to her side, as Sandy began to moan again, gripping the blanket and feeling as though her whole world was coming to an end.

Brett felt himself rise and ebb as he listened to her moans. He wanted release so bad, yet it just wasn't happening. Pulling Sandy to the side, he rolled her over and entered her from the back. She raised her back up higher as he moved in and out, so exquisitely slow that she wanted to scream out. Instead, she offered up her backside and felt him fumble, then he entered another orifice entirely. Sandy's eyes opened wide at the intrusion, yet because she trusted him so implicitly, she allowed him to do even this. It shocked her because she never liked it when she tried this with her husband, yet with Brett, it felt so good and right. She moaned some more and wanted his release so much, yet when it didn't happen, she wondered if maybe she was doing something wrong.

She'd only had one other man in her life, her husband. With him, sex was all "wham bam, thank you ma'am!" No talking, only perfunctory motions that would have Sandy so frustrated that afterwards, because she never came, would go into the bathroom and masturbate to end the need. This was totally new to Sandy that she could want someone so much and actually enjoy it. Then her fears of ignorance began to cause her to doubt. What if he thought she was some dumb hick? Sandy only knew what she experienced and although she had read her share of romance novels, nothing prepared her for this. Brett seemed pretty worldly and she wanted it to be good for him. She put the thought out of her head as suddenly, he flipped her up and over him so fast, she went sailing and landed next to him, laughing at the surprise. Turning to him, she crawled on top of him and put him where she knew he belonged.

"Why didn't we meet sixteen years ago?" she asked him as she gave his mouth special attention. "I could have kept you out of trouble and you would have spoiled me rotten!"

He only looked at her with sadness as he returned her kiss. He felt the same way.

"Leave your wife, I need you," Sandy begged. "We have so much in common, it isn't right that now that I found you, I can't have you…"

Taking her head in his hands, he replied, "Sandy, I am married to Eva. I have to be where I am. You will need to figure this out for yourself."

Disappointment coursed through Sandy as she kissed him, but verbally kept up her wish.

"OK," Brett laughed. "If she ever throws me out, you can have me, how is that?"

Sandy kissed him again and moved in a rhythm which he kept pace with. Crooning, he said to her, "go for it, let it happen… and when it does, it's all good." Her release came once again as she realized she had more with him than in all of her years with Harry. "If you want me to come, you're going to have suck it out of me," he told her softly.

"Do you want it low and slow, like the way you make your bacon, or fast and furious, the way I make mine?" she asked seductively. Gleefully, she kissed her way down his flat stomach to the promise of all that was good. Taking him in her mouth, she gently laved and sucked, all the while marveling at how she couldn't even take it all in. Brett became frustrated that he wasn't responding fast enough. Was it all the beer he had consumed? He didn't want to disappoint Sandy, she was trying so hard. Getting up, he went down to her and sitting astride, began a slow motion that increased with time. Sandy tried to keep up, but the buzz in her head was making her so dizzy and the lack of water and the effort all caused her to finally say she could no longer finish.

"You win, you are too much for me to handle! I can't do it any more!"

"What?" Brett asked, incredulous.

"I said," Sandy repeated, exhaustion evident in every word, "that I can't do it anymore. I need air and water!" Disappointed, Brett got up and walked away. Sandy watched him and felt a keening sense of horror at what she had just done.

Brett picked up his clothes and got dressed, commenting under his breath how "the man didn't blow." Then went in search of everything he took off of Sandy, being sure he had everything. He didn't need Eva finding it. Eva. What was he going to do? He had never betrayed his marriage vows and now, look at this. Looking up, he saw Sandy standing there and he handed her the shirt and hair combs. She had a shocked look about her.

"What?!" he asked desperately.

"I…I.." Putting her hand over her mouth, Sandy couldn't finish, depression evident in her every movement. She went and dressed in the bathroom, fixing her hair, then found Brett in the kitchen, washing out the glass and blender. She stood next to him and looked out the window.

"We crossed the line, didn't we?" she asked. "We went from friend to this."

"Yes we did." Brett answered quietly. Taking her hands in his own, he hugged her, then looked into her eyes. "When you make love to your husband, you will have this to look back on and remember how it was so good…"

Sandy kissed him and looked into his eyes once again. "I didn't use you," she said and kissed him. "And you didn't use me," she kissed him again. He shook his head, that no, they didn't use the other. "And I got to play hooky from work…" she said. He smiling at her, kissed her again. Then, sure she was feeling better, he released her and went to the den. He sat at the computer and checked his messages, talking about a new radio station that maybe he might want to sign with, but like the previous one, they didn't pay their DJ's.

Sandy was amazed that he could just pick up so quickly and go on. Women like to be held and cuddled after making love, but men? It's right back to whatever they had going before.

He answered an e-mail, talking all the while to Sandy, then listened to a phone message from someone interested in doing some work around Brett's house. Sandy looked at the clock and realized that if she was going to beat the traffic home, she had better leave now. Standing, she said as much to Brett.

"When will you come back?" Brett asked her.

I have a day in mid-October off if you are interested," Sandy replied.

Brett looked at his appointment book, then set it down and agreed, saying how they needed to get to the important stuff first while they had time. Sandy just laughed and headed out to the kitchen, Brett following.

"You might want to use mouthwash, to get rid of the tequila smell," Brett advised.

"Oh, is it noticeable?" Sandy asked, putting her hand to her mouth.

"I can't smell it because I have been drinking," Brett said. "Come on, let's get mouthwash." Going upstairs, he handed her the bottle of mouthwash, which she placed to her lips and, taking a swig, swished it around, then swallowed it. Brett laughed, "the girl will swallow anything!"

Smiling at him, she went downstairs and stood by the backdoor. "You take care and I will see you soon," she said.

Brett picked up the bottle of tequila off of the counter and, hoisting it in her direction, told her to keep laughing, because he loved the sound of it. Going outside, she turned back just in time to see him take a long swig from the bottle and an eerie feeling welled up inside of her.

The drive home was alternately sad and happy. Sandy feared what her husband would say. Harry would take one look at her and just know. She rehearsed what she would do and say;

her reaction was critical to keeping this day a secret.

Because it was Friday.

As she pulled into her driveway, she noticed that Harry was home already. "Shit!" she thought. "I don't want to have to see him now." Walking into the house, she saw him and said hello brightly and went straight to the kitchen to begin dinner. She wanted to hide her face which she just knew was flushed from her day. Like the song, about eyes having a mist from the smoke of a distant fire.

"How are things?" Harry asked her.

"Fine, just fine!" Sandy said, feeling guilt coursing though her veins. Harry gave her a funny look, then went to read his paper. Sandy exhaled her breath in a long gasp, unaware that she had been holding her breath. It was going to be a long night.

After Sandy had left, Brett putzed in the garage. A maelstrom of emotions coursing through his mind, the bottle of tequila nearby, dreading when Eva would be home. So many things were flooding his mind and he needed the tequila to take the edge off of his thoughts.

Sandy was so good and her heart so pure, why had he allowed things to get out of hand? It was one thing to lust with her over the computer, it was another entirely to act on it. The fact that he wasn't able to have an orgasm also hurt his pride. Damn it, why didn't it happen? It seemed to occur more often and he wondered if the booze was responsible for it. She had looked so disappointed and he wished he could have given her all of him. He was the world's only male nymphomaniac, he thought, needing sex twenty three hours a day. Here was his chance and he blew it. Taking another swig, he hid the bottle behind the stereo in the garage and went in to begin dinner, hoping his actions would not betray his emotions.

Chapter 7

If Sandy thought the next few days would be a breeze, she was sadly mistaken. This wasn't a happily ever after fairy tale; this was real life and she was caught up in a whirlwind of thoughts and emotions.

She spent Saturday feeling very euphoric as she shopped for groceries, then washed and waxed her car. Thinking of each moment, each caress from the day before only made her insides quiver as she put all of her energy into the motions of waxing. Smearing on the paste, she made sure she did the undersides of the fender as well as inside the doorjambs. Brett would be so proud of her thoroughness, she thought.

Going inside the house, she typed an e-mail to him:

"Thanks for the sweet memories. Can you send me a copy of that song "Hearts?" It is so haunting, I can't get it out of my mind. I have no more words left in me, only feelings! Nothing wrong with that! S." She sent it, then prepared dinner. Her kids wondered why mom was so happy as she sang her way through preparations.

Later, when she was checking her e-mails, Brett instant messaged her.

"We made salsa today. Big job, but Eva helped. I am sending you a copy of Hearts, accept when it comes through. If it is too big, I'll have to make you a CD."

"Got it!" Sandy wrote when it came in. She downloaded it to her files, then thanked him and signed off. Immediately, she played it and felt all the memories come flooding back. Tears welled up within her, tears which she couldn't shed. His message, "we made salsa today." We, meaning he and Eva and not he and

Sandy. It would be things such as this that she needed to deal with. Life went on for Brett and she wasn't with him to enjoy it.

That evening, she put all of those lustful energies into a sexual encounter with Harry. She climbed on top of him and rocked him to soaring heights. When she kissed him, she imagined it was Brett. She compared the two bodies, warm and soft versus hard and angular. She noticed different styles in lovemaking and determined that from now on, she was taking what was hers, no more masturbating afterwards!

When it was over, he caressed her arm and asked why she was amorous all of a sudden. Luckily it was dark, because Sandy's face flushed as she lied, "because I love you and you are so good to me." Rolling to her side of the bed, she felt as though she had betrayed Brett. Harry immediately fell into a peaceful slumber as Sandy listened to him snore softly.

That night, she tossed and turned, unable to sleep. The guilt began to encumber her as she wondered what Brett had done that day other than to make salsa. Was he thinking about her as nonstop she did him? Sandy wished she could be a fly on the wall to know.

Brett had spent Saturday making salsa from a recipe handed down through Eva's family. This was a yearly tradition and a good way to use the crop of tomatoes they had in their garden. They made enough to give away at least forty jars full of it. With Eva at his side, they chopped tomatoes and peppers, measured and poured ingredients of varying types and finally had it to simmering on the stove. Eva noticed he was quiet and wondered what he had been up to now. Hoping it was something she wouldn't have to bail him out of, she washed the utensils they had used thus far. Still, something was nagging at her, something she couldn't quite name. Slamming down the dish rag, she went to find him on the computer. Looking up radio stations as usual, he didn't hear her enter the room.

"Brett, what's going on?" she asked, with a touch of anger in her voice.

He jumped in his seat, not expecting her display of emotion and looked at her, guilt in his eyes. "Wrong? Why do you think something is wrong?" he asked trying to sound innocent. Oh, God, did it show? Did she know?

"Brett, I am not stupid, I know when you are up to something. You have been too quiet today and I want to know why!"

Getting up, he rubbed her arm and, kissing her head, told her he was fine. Then, for good measure, he hugged her, rubbing her back. At first she stiffened up, but as he continued his ministrations, she softened and began to respond. He went from her lips to her eyes and down to her neck, stroking her breast until she felt herself melt inside. Why couldn't it always be this way? Grabbing his belt and giving his pants a good downward yank, she dragged him to the couch and allowed him to slide her pants down and her shirt off. Giving each breast his own personal attention, he moved on top of her and began a slow steady rhythm until, he couldn't control himself and sped up the tempo until she called out his name. Where Sandy was soft and round, Eva was lithe and supple from working out. He appreciated the differences in each as he maneuvered into a more comfortable spot. Releasing his energy inside of her, he cursed the fact that just yesterday he couldn't do this with Sandy. Getting up, he went to the bathroom, leaving Eva to wonder what had just happened here.

The next day, Sunday, Sandy took the kids to church and listened halfheartedly to the sermon. Remorse hung heavy within her as she wished she knew what was expected to happen between her and Brett. He seemed so right, they were so alike and yet, she realized that men who cheat on their wives also cheat and lie to their girlfriends. Sadness welled up within her as a tear slowly made its way down her cheek. She wiped it away. Why did she think she was special? He wasn't exactly jumping up to leave Eva and what would she do if he did? He was a felon, he wouldn't be able to drive a car, hold a job, he would need someone to get him to probation meetings and treatment classes. Sandy had no money for a house and landlords did not rent to felons, legitimate landlords, anyway. He had no money and owed Eva a huge debt just for her being there all these years. He would be absolutely bored with Sandy and in the end, would resent her with every fiber of his being. Sandy couldn't do that to him, she realized. Oh God! Why did life have to be so complicated? The raw emotions coursed through her, threatening to tear her in two.

After Mass, she waited till everyone had left before approaching the altar. Sending her kids to the car, she told them to wait, that she would be out in a bit. Going to the candles, she lit two, one for her and one for Brett. Getting down on her knees, she began to pray:

"Oh, God, I am so sorry for ruining not only my life, but his and Eva's and Harry's. When one commits adultery, the ripples extend beyond just he and I. Lord, please, show me the way! The pain is too much for me and I am so confused, I don't know what to do. I want to let him go, but the pull is so strong. I want him as a friend, as we once were! Is it possible that we can return to that? Please, show me the way!" By now tears were pouring down her face and she made no effort to wipe them away. She stared up into the eyes of the Sacred Heart of Jesus, desperately wishing for his intervention.

Driving home, she felt even more empty.

It was hard to concentrate as she went about her chores. She washed and waxed Harry's car while he napped, ideas swirling around inside of her. Frustration built until her heart was hammering away inside of her chest; she feared it would fly out if given a chance. Entering the house, Sandy threw the rags she used for waxing into the laundry and, going to the computer, sat down and composed an e-mail to Brett.

"My soul has been turned inside out and I cry often. I wonder why fate has decreed that the perfect person, who is like me in everyway, who is so unselfish and can make me laugh, is involved with his own commitments; I wonder of the fairness of it all.

"I have no regrets, other than why this didn't happen sooner. We could have been spared so much misery and would have actually enjoyed our years instead of cringing at them!

"So now, we go our own ways, we say we are the absolute best friends, but what does that mean? I hold you in my heart and refuse to let go; you say you want me for your co-host, yet I wonder, if that big radio contract comes along just for you, would you accept it and walk away from me? I certainly wouldn't hold it over your head if you did.

"So many things running through my head, I can't sleep at night, you consume every dream I do have, every waking thought has you in it, what have you done to me? Where do I go from here? You said I need to figure it out for myself, yet that is something I have been doing all my life. Just for once, I want someone else to do it for me, please take the burden off of me so that I can breathe free. Is that asking too much?

"I think of my kids…they would be devastated and who would care for them? I sometimes just want to walk away from it all, yet Harry wouldn't know how to handle it long term. Never mind what he has done to me in the past, this would be the most heinous thing I could have ever done to him and I would never live it down. Never mind also that I have every reason to do this because he has been no support to me whatsoever since we married.

"I want to live, I want to love, I want to dream before I die. I don't know when that will happen, no one does, but before I go, I want memories to look back on and a friend to be happy with. Without hiding, without covering my tracks, without excuses, without regrets. Where does my absolute best friend stand on this? Because if it means as much to you as it does to me, then these thoughts must be running through your head, too. This is not some simple urge, like going to the bathroom. This is thoughts and feelings all rolled up into one. I do not have delusions that everything will be all right, but someone who can laugh with you cry with you and hug you isn't asking too much. I can't stand to lose you and I refuse to, I will do whatever it takes so that we can remain what we are…best friends.

"Do I dare to send this? Or will it turn you off so much that you will X me out of your life forever. You are an addictive drug I cannot do without. I need to know…what happens next? Love and best wishes…S".

Sandy hesitated over the send button for so long, her finger ached from the indecision to go for it. Finally, heart beating within her ears so loud she thought they would burst, she pressed send.

Brett spent Sunday in a haze of confusion and uncertainty. Emptiness welled up within him and he wondered if it was possible that he actually cared about Sandy. His marriage was not the happiest, but he was comfortable. It would be impossible for him to take up another commitment. It wouldn't be fair to Sandy if he tried to do what she wanted. He was no good for her, he had no job and wouldn't until a radio prospect entered the picture. He also wasn't supposed to drive and wouldn't be able to for another three years. Going to the garage, he found the tequila bottle and sat on the bumper of the van, taking a large swig. Why was life so complicated, he wondered morosely. Putting the bottle by the recycle bin, he went inside to check his e-mails.

There was one from Sandy, which he pulled up and read. His heart broke as he reread it several times. She certainly had a way with words. It was her gift of writing that turned him on to her in the first place. She was so pure, so sweet, how could he corrupt her by his presence? Yes, he thought of her also, but knew he could not leave Eva, she had seen him through some pretty rough times. Sure, it was tough and while Sandy had totally given herself to him, Eva always seemed to hold back, performing only in a perfunctory manner. Her passion could not hold a candle to Sandy's, Brett realized. He missed her and wanted her. He hit delete, not bothering to answer it and left the desk.

Eva went about her tasks and noticed that Brett was

too quiet again today. Her radar was up as she assessed his movements and realized that he was depressed about something. She wondered if it was about the fact that he was having a hard time finding a job on an internet station. Jobs were hard to come by in this market, most internet stations wanted DJ's, but most were volunteer jobs. They couldn't pay their bills on good intentions. Maybe that was it. Going to him, she asked if he was OK. He just looked at her and nodded, then went to find a project he could lose himself in. She followed him.

"Brett, I was thinking, how about if we go camping again, one last time? I can take the third week of October off. What do you say, huh?"

He remembered what Sandy had said about having that week off from school. He closed his eyes and felt trapped. Still, what could he say to his wife, except, "sounds good, hun. Just tell me where you want to go." He turned back to his project leaving Eva feeling bereft.

The next morning, Sandy signed in to her instant message account. Brett popped up and she cheerfully said hi. Talk soon turned to generic things and Sandy thought for sure that he would be gushing over what had happened, in his usual suggestive way. Instead, he kept the talk polite until she could stand it no more and asked him about Friday.

"Sandy, I belong to Eva…I have to be where I am."

Sandy looked at his words and the lump in her throat threatened to choke her. Nodding, she typed in that yes, she realized it, just as she was where she had to be.

"We have sown our oats," he wrote.

"No more oat sowing then?" Sandy wrote.

"We shouldn't." he replied.

Sandy felt a let down worse than anything she had ever felt, yet she knew this was the right thing to do, it just had to be!

"We are adults, at least you are anyway. We need to go on," Brett wrote, feeling miserable. "Friends still?"

"Yes," Sandy wrote.

He then gave her another blow by announcing that he and Eva were going camping.

"When?" Sandy asked.

"The third week of October," he typed.

That was when they had set their schedules to meet. She felt like a real shithead at that point. Well, of course. Life goes on and he said he was committed to Eva. Why should it be any different? What was he supposed to say to her, "sorry honey, but my lover and I plan to have exquisite, all-day sex that day?" Highly unlikely.

"Where to?" she asked, hoping to keep it light. It was useless to even remind him at that point of their plans. He wanted to be adult about it. Why bother?

"Not sure yet, it's up to Eva."

The rest of her day passed in a blur, as did Brett's. It was relatively quiet, however, until Eva went to throw out a bag of garbage and found the bottle of tequila. Snatching it up, she stalked into the house.

"Goddamn it, Brett! What the fuck do you think you are doing!"

He entered the kitchen and, seeing the bottle on the counter, felt his insides drop to his feet.

"What the hell is this and why is it here?"

Brett didn't say anything except that he didn't know.

"You don't know? What kind of response is that? Damn it, you just love to do this to me, don't you? Drink and get into more trouble. They'll put you away for ten years to life, you asshole! Does nothing pass though that brain of yours, or is it so full of booze that you don't care?" Going to the sink, she poured it out and tossed the bottle in the trash. Then she ran to their bedroom and slammed the door so loud that a cat jumped off the couch and hid under it. Brett was depressed and just wanted to die. Eva was so mad she wanted to see the deed done and, if prodded, would have done it.

Each moment, every second that night seemed an eternity.

Finally, not able to sleep, Sandy went to the computer at two a.m. and was surprised to see Brett online. She typed in, "Ya there?"

"Eva found the tequila."

"And?" Sandy held her breath.

"She poured it out with questions."

"What did you say?"

"I don't know."

"You don't know? That is what you said?"

"No."

"Then what did you say?'

"I don't know."

Sandy felt frustrated when she read next, "wanna die now, except being a felon...no weapons."

"Brett, what is going on? I need to know, did you just use me for your own release?"

"If you recall, release didn't happen."

Sandy was stunned when she read that. She typed in, "I know and I am sorry for that. What can I do?"

There was no answer. She waited a half an hour before she realized he would not be back.

That day she was exhausted. She had no sleep in over 48 hours and every muscle was fatigued to the breaking point. That night, she checked her computer, but Brett was offline and would be so for quite some time. He kept busy with various projects around the house needing his attention. He stopped when he found himself looking at Sandy's book that she had given him and realized that his promise to make her an audio CD never became reality. She had only mentioned it once, but it was just one more thing he needed to do on his list.

Meanwhile, Sandy fretted and regretted the time they spent together. In her anger, she typed him an e-mail that said in part how yes, she drank and responded, but so did he and if he wasn't supposed to drink, then he should accept responsibility for his actions. She mentioned that she respected his commitment to his wife and understood it. If this news hurt him to read it, it hurt her to write it. Hitting send, she alternately fumed and fretted and knew she was going out of her head.

Brett read her e-mail and, feeling sorry for himself, didn't know how to make it right. Eva had taken to keeping the bedroom door locked at night and only acknowledged him with grunts and stares the rest of the time. He felt like a real heel and just wanted things to be back to normal. He kept the secret of his tryst with Sandy, but by holding Sandy at arm's length, he knew he was alienating her also.

It came to a crescendo on Wednesday morning. At five thirty she saw an e-mail that Brett had left for her and eagerly read it .Looking at the time it was sent, she noticed it was at 9:17 p.m. Tuesday evening. Sandy smiled to herself when she realized she had shut her computer down only ten minutes earlier. If she had waited, she would have seen him sign on.

"I am OK. I should have sent that tequila home with you. I'll yap with ya in the morning. Bye." However, when she went to instant messaging, his line was closed. She felt that maybe he had lied to her and just made up an excuse. Glad that he really didn't hurt himself, she went to work, feeling like a wrung out dishrag.

While she was at work, her mind was on the pain within her stomach that an antacid didn't relieve. It gradually grew worse until she found herself gripping the counter to stand upright. A coworker noticed her paleness and advised her to sit down. Without warning, she passed out cold and even after efforts to revive her, she remained semi-conscious until the ambulance came. She no longer cared anymore. As her coworkers fretted over her, she vaguely heard their voices, but didn't respond. She was too exhausted to even try.

While Sandy lay on the gurney in the hospital for the test results, heart monitor wires attached to her, she had plenty of time to think about all she had done in just the last five days. Hell, just since June, which was only four months ago. Why did she even have to meet Brett? She wished she had never heard of him or his show or met with him. Because of Friday, she had hurt so many people without their even knowing it: Brett, Eva, Harry, her kids. The lies she told, the secrets she kept. Oh, what a tangled web we weave when first we practice to deceive! How, she wondered, did some people just have cavalier affairs, leaving destruction in their wake? All she had was one encounter, just one, and her world would never be the same.

Sandy needed a phone. She wanted to call Brett one last time and let him know where she was, if he even cared, she thought miserably. She knew he had a treatment class that evening at this very hospital, if they admitted her, she perhaps might be graced with a visit from him. Or was it asking too much?

Just then, a nurse walked in, holding a phone. "Phone call for you," she said. Sandy took the phone and spoke with the school nurse where she worked, who had been with her while the ambulance was enroute to the school. She asked Sandy how she was and Sandy mentioned all the tests they had performed, but that she didn't know the results yet. The nurse bid her well and hung up. The inspiration hit...call Brett. She dialed his number, but only heard his answering machine click in. She left a message, telling him where she was, then hung up. She wondered if he was really there, or out.

Brett spent the morning with his probation officer, who was telling him how soon he would be done with his bi-weekly meetings with her and then they would meet monthly. Inwardly he celebrated, one more thing soon to be done with. He wanted to have a drink, just to be spiteful, then he realized that was a stupid idea.

Eva was waiting for him in the car and drove him home. She needed to go back to work, so he fixed himself a sandwich and noticed the light on the answering machine was blinking. Checking the caller ID, he noticed it was the hospital. No big deal, maybe the meeting for tonight was changed. Listening, he was horrified to hear Sandy's raspy voice.

"Brett, I am in the hospital. I collapsed at work and they don't know what is wrong. I just wanted you to know so that you wouldn't panic if you didn't see me on the computer for awhile. I am hooked to a heart monitor. I'll let you know if I hear anything. I am thinking about you and miss you…" her voice trailed away, then the line severed. He stood in shock. What had happened? Running his hands through his hair, he felt helpless and angry all at once. One of his cyber groupies, "come softly again" tried something like this. She had one of her friends contact him to say that she was in a bad accident and dying in the hospital. When he tried to verify it two days later, he found that she had been lying. That was why he had cut off all ties to all of them. But Sandy would never pull a stunt like that, he knew. Besides, the number was from the hospital. He sat holding his sandwich, appetite gone, fear over the unknown replacing his hunger for food.

Eva sat staring at her computer monitor for what seemed to be forever. Her mind was on her marriage and future with Brett. He was high maintenance, that was for sure. She remembered when they met, it was at a bar where he worked as the entertainment DJ. She like his style and his way with people, though his come on line was derogatory at best. He, in turn, admired her zest for living. They soon moved into a town home and married after that. They saved money for a house, he working many odd jobs. All was well until three years ago when he got his first DUI. Then everything went downhill. Drugs were found in his possession; although he never used them, he did sell them. That was the first major crack in their marriage. Then just a year ago, he was pulled over while driving and found to be on probation with no license. Of course, that meant more jail time and this time, Eva couldn't afford the bail, so he spent the time incarcerated. When he got out, he tried to resume life as usual, but more cracks were forged in their union. How many times can a wall be repaired before it totally crumbles, she asked herself? She tried so hard with him, going into debt to keep up with his desire for technology, trying to support his desire to break into radio again. She couldn't go on much longer. Not even the prospect of camping excited him now. What was she going to do?

As it turned out, the tests pointed to the fact that Sandy had an illness that was incurable. Called lupus, it affects the internal organs, insidiously tearing them down until an organ failed or death set in. The doctor gave her some medication for the pain in her stomach, but told her that she would have only ten good years left before she would be debilitated, or worse, then prepared the discharge papers so that she could go home. Sandy cried at this. Ten years! What about her books? She wanted to leave a legacy behind and now, what would become of her? Harry had arrived from work earlier and was there to take her home. This was why she had been tired and fatigued lately, actually for quite some time. The drive in her was what kept her from noticing it until it was too late.

After Harry made sure Sandy was settled in at home, she picked up the phone and called Brett back. She reached his answering machine again, merely saying that she was home and for him to call if he had time. Sadly, she hung up and pondered the future.

Her books, which had been doing well, now reached a stagnant level in sales at the online booksellers. Sandy was frustrated that she couldn't do any more. Book stores were reluctant to have her come in for signings because she wasn't well known, and yet how would she be, if nobody gave her a chance? It had been her goal to leave a legacy behind, one that would be remembered. Harry had been of little help or support. Indeed, he felt that she was a good writer, but would never be a great author. Sandy now felt a sense of urgency that matched her frustration. Limited time and so much to do. She wanted to prove him wrong, that she had the potential for more, so much more. Where to begin?

As Harry drove back to work to finish out his day, he

ruminated on Sandy and her illness. She had always been the one to care for him and all the household needs. How could she expect him to pick up the slack if she was sick? The kids could help out, but he would have to do the balance of the work. He was not prepared to handle this, he thought as he turned back into the parking lot.

As it turned out, Brett did hear her message and went to the computer to IM her. She was online and he asked her how she was doing.

"What did the doctor say?" he was worried.

"I missed you!" Sandy typed back, referring to the days without hearing from him. He thought she meant when she tried to call him.

"I was at the probation officer's office today. I would have come and visited you tonight in the hospital after my treatment class, but it would have been after visiting hours were over."

Sandy beamed when she read that. "The doctor did a lot of tests today, but won't know the results until Friday when I go back in for a checkup. I'll let you know the results."

"I need to go and get something to eat and leave for my class. Keep in touch," he wrote, then signed off. Sandy's heart felt lighter than it had for some time.

Until Friday. After returning from the doctor feeling bereft from finding out the test results, Sandy noticed right away her instant message light blinking on the computer. Answering it with news about her visit from the doctor, she was stunned to read Brett verbally recounting how a former DJ at Listen to it Live was bashing his reputation on air. Sandy knew of it when she was listening in one evening and alerted Brett to it. She didn't realize, however that he had dwelled on it all morning and was spitting nails by lunchtime.

"I want it stopped, she is ruining my good name! I will not put up with it!" Brett pounded out the words on his keyboard.

"Brett! What is wrong? Are you mad at me?" Sandy felt a genuine fear. Not now, when she and Brett were communicating again. Perhaps she shouldn't have said anything, but still, she would have wanted to know if it were happening to her also.

"No, her! You contact her and tell her to knock it off or I will sue her for slander and defamation of character! I helped her and this is the thanks that I get? Grow with me or get the hell out of my way!"

"I am learning from you and I agree, nobody should stab you in the back. Why, you have nothing but helpful, to me and to everyone."

"That is why I want you to handle it. Tell her what I said."

"OK, I will," Sandy felt morose. Although she had liked the gal who had done this to Brett, lately she felt uncomfortable because this woman wanted to drag everyone down to her depths of despair.

"Hang on, I need to mellow out here...breathe, breathe!" Brett wrote. Sandy waited patiently. "Ok, I have my cigarette, now tell me what the doctor said."

Sandy wrote about what the diagnosis was and what it would mean for her. "Heart, kidneys, lungs, liver are all affected. The doctor said I may have ten good years before I am too debilitated to do anything." She felt so bad that she was literally giving Brett what amounted to a death sentence for her. He read her words in horror, then decided he needed to get tough with her.

"Here's the deal...you are tough...I am tougher. I am also healthier, or so I think. So let's cut the crap and you be awesome with me!" He sat back and waited for her response. He didn't care what her health was like, if there was some way he could be with her through this ordeal, that was all that mattered.

As Sandy read his message, her heart swelled. She had been so afraid that he would just ignore her or worse, cancel her from his life altogether. Yet here he was, telling her to stick with him!

"You wouldn't be the first co-host to drop dead on me. I

can handle whatever comes up."

"Oh, Brett, do you mean it?" Sandy asked. Then a thought occurred to her. "How many co-hosts have you done in?" she asked nervously.

"Figure of speech. Just take care of yourself!" Then he signed off. Sandy sat back and reread his message. Harry didn't take the news of her illness well at all, going so far as to whine about how he would have to care for her, should the need arise. Yet Brett was her pillar of strength, telling her to be awesome with him. Those words would ring in her ears the rest of the day. Remembering what Brett had said about the DJ, she set about composing an e-mail and gently but firmly explained that Brett didn't appreciate what she has said on air and that she needed to keep her thoughts to herself. Hitting send, she gave thanks to God for bringing Brett back to her. True, not in the way she wanted, but for now, this was good enough.

Brett completed his required treatment classes and stayed busy with things around the house that needed doing. Still, there was an unfulfilled need within him, a desire to aspire to greatness. He knew had what it took to take a floundering radio station and turn it around. He spent hours honing a demo CD and pitched it to various stations, only to be told he would start at the bottom and have to work up, or worse, that he wasn't good enough. Slowly, depression overtook him as he hit the bottle to drown his fears.

Sandy worked feverishly on her books and stories, submitting them to publishers as well as magazines, hoping someone would latch onto it and propel her into …what? Fame? Fortune? She realized that if she could just come out ahead, she would be satisfied. She loved to write for children, but was finding it hard to break into that niche. Book signings also were hard to come by. Everyone wanted their turn at stardom and book stores were careful in who they promoted. Frustration began to set in and Sandy's marriage took the hit.

Harry noticed the changes in Sandy and didn't like what he saw. She was at the computer night and day, literally shutting him out. He took to reading her journal hoping to find some clue as to her aberrant behavior. An entry caught his eye and he was stunned. He needed to read it twice, three times. Disgusted, he threw the journal back where it was and fled the bedroom. Anger coursed through him as he readied himself for work. Sandy had written about how her heart was breaking, it had only happened once and she didn't want to hurt his wife, so she thought it was best if they remained friends only. She used cryptic words, which frustrated him even more. Who was she referring to? And what had only happened once? Was she having an affair? She sure had been blocking him out of her life lately and he realized then that he no longer wanted her to be a writer, but would she want to be his wife anymore?

Sandy was waiting up for him when he walked through the door at ten p.m. An anger worse than anything he had ever known coursed through him.

"Good evening, honey, how are you?" she said brightly, not catching on to his body language.

"Get the fuck out of my sight!" He snarled at her.

"What? What is wrong? Honey, what's the matter?" Sandy's insides roiled at the unknown.

"I said to get the hell out of here! Go upstairs or something! I don't want to talk to you!"

"Honey, talk to me! You can't just leave me wondering what is wrong. We have married for so many years…"

"Those years have meant nothing to me! Now get out!" With that, he went outside to have a cigarette. Instinctively, Sandy knew something was up and she had a suspicion that he knew, somehow, about what she and Brett did. Going to the computer, she quickly composed and e-mail.

"He knows what we have done. This is the beginning of the end of my marriage. Sandy"
Signing off and closing down the computer, she slowly dragged her feet upstairs.

Tossing and turning in bed for the next two and a half

hours, Sandy could not take the suspense any more. Tiptoeing downstairs, she saw Harry sleeping in the chair and quietly touched his arm. His eyes flew open and he growled out his response. "Get the hell away from me!"

"Honey, let's talk," Sandy began.

"There's nothing to talk about! Now get away!" Once again, Sandy dragged leaden feet upstairs and curled up on the bed, forlorn. After several more sleepless hours, she went back downstairs, Harry, seeing her, decided to just go upstairs to bed to escape her. She turned on the computer and instant messaged Brett. He had read her e-mail and wondered what was up. He decided the best course of action was to play it cool. The last thing he needed was for Sandy to go off the deep end and for Eva to find out about it.

"He knows," Sandy typed.

"Knows what?" Brett asked.

"What we did. He is on the warpath."

"We have done nothing," Brett typed in, feeling as though he was betraying what he and Sandy shared. It was too beautiful and he would never forget it. But he needed to keep Sandy focused also. Through words, he kept her reassured, until by the end of their conversation, she was stronger as she typed in how after so many years of doing things for him, it was her turn and she could handle whatever came up. Truly she could. She was strong, she didn't need to feel as though she had to be married to Harry. What had he provided in the way of comfort to her marriage? It was a comfortable relationship, but also fraught with his insecurities which her writing only brought to the surface. She decided she would act on his anger.

Later that day, she began her search for a new place to live. Looking around her house, she realized she didn't need any of it. She could start over and would be better off for it. Calling various apartments, she left little notes about her search on the desk, oblivious about who might see them. She was beyond caring-she was into self preservation.

When Harry returned home from work, he saw her notes and his stomach quivered. His irrational tantrum was bringing him to a point the wasn't prepared to reach. Sandy? Leaving? What else would these numbers and addresses mean? He didn't know how to broach the subject, but felt it was in his best interest to not put it off.

Brett wondered how things were with Sandy. As he performed the work in his yard, his mind went to her again and again. She was a beautiful person, one he would have been glad to covet for his own. Her vitality was infectious and her laugh resounded in his heart. Not a day went by that he didn't think about her. Her passion overwhelmed him as he realized that Eva didn't hold a candle to her. But, he owed Eva a lot. It was she who stayed with him, bailing him out time after time. If not for their house, he would still be in jail, for she took out a second mortgage to pay his debts. Yet the debt he owed her didn't keep him satisfied at night. When they had sex, and as far as Brett saw it, that was all it was, he saw Sandy's face before him. Eva seemed only perfunctory about the whole act, whereas Sandy consumed him heart and soul. He was torn apart and didn't know how to heal from it.

Harry put on his coat and announced that he was going for a ride. Sandy asked him if he wanted company and he slowly agreed. As she retrieved her coat, the kids asked where they were going. They had felt the tension in the house between mother and father and wondered when it would end. She merely stated they would be back soon, as she was curious about where they were going. He rarely took her anywhere.

As he drove, the silence in the car was so thick, a knife could cut it. Finally, Harry pulled over to the side of the road, then looked at Sandy.

"Are you happy with me?"

Sandy began to cry. Her heart was with Brett, there was no point in fighting it any longer. "No," she answered miserably.

"Why not?" Harry wanted to know.

"Because, I haven't been happy for quite some time. I have tried, but I am not satisfied."

"Why haven't you said any thing before?" he demanded.

"Because…" and Sandy cried harder. "I thought I could do this! I really did. But I can't and I don't know how to fix it. I think it would be better if I left, or if you left." She wiped her eyes with the backs of her hands, the tears flowing constantly.

Harry felt as though she had punched him in the gut. His wife of so many years…not happy? He thought he had done everything right…well, there was that little affair of his a few years ago, but she had forgiven him for that, hadn't she? He turned to look at her.

"Is there somebody else?"

The image of Brett assailed her. Yes, there was. But, she was afraid that if she admitted it, his temper would flair and she was afraid of the recriminations. She would leave him and be done with it, that was it. Instead she answered truthfully.

"I wear my heart on my sleeve, you know that. I have had many crushes over the years."

"Is it Brett?" he asked, as if reading her mind.

Sandy looked at him. "Brett and I are very good friends…"

"Have you had an affair with him?"

Sandy was glad of the darkness in the car. Her face blushed as she lied, "no, we have not had an affair." Her stomach heaved at the response. It was beautiful, but it also had cost her a lot. She remembered the turmoil, not sleeping for several straight days, not wanting to lose Brett altogether.

Harry put the car back in gear as they drove home.

"What are we going to tell the kids?" Sandy inquired. "When are we going to tell them?"

"Why are you so anxious to do this?" Harry asked.

"I think they should know that one of us is leaving…" she began.

"Why should one of us leave?"

74

"Because, I am not happy. I don't think I can be happy with you! I want a divorce!" Sandy cried out.

"You do what you want," Harry retorted bitterly. "You always do anyway!" With that, he pulled back into their parking spot, shutting off the engine and exiting the car. Sandy felt numb. "You getting out?" he asked.

She exited the car slowly and followed behind him. When they entered the house, she watched him for cues, to see what he was going to do. He merely hung up his coat and sat in his chair. Frustrated, she went to the bedroom and closed the door.

Chapter 8

As time went on, Harry and Sandy were at odds with each other. They circled each other like lions in a cage, each spitting out the ominous words the other wasn't ready to hear.

"I am leaving!"

"Good, get the hell out!"

"Pack your things and go!"

Yet neither did anything about it. Sandy asked herself why she would have to be the one to leave, she wanted to be with her kids. It would be easier if he left. Harry felt it would be better if she left.

When all was said and done, neither left.

Sandy still communicated with Brett each day. She missed him terribly and wondered when she would be seeing him again. He kept busy getting ready for Halloween, his favorite time of the year. He asked her if she and her kids would like to participate in a live Halloween show which he put on each year for the families in the neighborhood. Eagerly she agreed.

She decided to be a virgin bride. Finding a costume at a store, she altered it to look very ethereal. Her middle son, Joe, was going with, the other kids all had plans. As the days counted down, she felt such anticipation. She was going to see him again! That was when he surprised her with his idea. He had taken her first book and set it to audio CD. Chapter by chapter he painstakingly narrated, until the finished product was ready to be packaged. It was only days before Halloween when he told Sandy of his project. She was stunned, so stunned when she saw what he wrote on instant message.

"For all of your hard work, it would only be right that you and I become partners. Everything I make, I will split with you 50%." Sandy typed in, gratitude welling up inside her.

Now it was Brett who was stunned. It was only his intent to help her out, he had not expected monetary gain from this. Yet as the days went by, they found themselves designing a CD case cover and packaging the CD's took up a lot of his time.

"Where will you be marketing these?" he asked her one day.

She typed in, " Oh, I don't know...day cares, schools, pet stores, wherever we can fit it in."

Halloween came, the weather, though chilly, was calm and bright. Eva wasn't too keen on the idea of Sandy's being a part of the celebration, but seeing at how happy Brett was feeling about it, decided to just watch and see. Sandy comported herself as a lady, playing the part of the virgin bride well. She decided to play act a bit as well, hoisting her skirt just enough to run throughout the display that Brett had rigged up, carrying on like a damsel in distress each time she saw some children headed her way. Brett's heart warmed when he saw how much fun she was having and wished it could go on forever. The fun stopped all too soon as the trick or treaters dwindled to a few, then nothing. Brett looked at his display and sighed. He didn't want to have to pull of this down, it took all day just to set it up. Yet, to leave it would mean it would certainly be stolen.

Suddenly a voice said next to him, "come on, I'm not leaving until I help you get all of this in. What do you want me to do first?" Sandy was right there, costume and all, picking things up and bringing them in, one by one. Her feet were freezing and her hands numb, but she continued helping him until every last thing was in and the cords and lights all put away. Eva was in the house, complaining all the while about how cold she was as she frowned at where Sandy and Brett were setting things down.

"I'll put this stuff away tomorrow," he explained. "I just want to get it in tonight."

When they were done, Sandy was surprised to see a pot of chili simmering on the stove. Eva handed her a cup of hot apple cider and then went to answer the phone. While she carried on a conversation, Brett ran out for cigarettes. Sandy felt a bit miffed and realized that such behavior was rude. She sat discreetly on the stairwell leading to the bedrooms as she waited for either Brett to return or for Eva to get off of the phone.

Finally when he came back, Sandy went to the kitchen, taking it upon herself to stir the chili. He got bowls and spoons out and began to dish it up. She took a bowl for herself as well as Joe, and they ate in companionable silence. She savored the warmth of the chili as well as the flavors and textures. When she was finished, she made her goodbyes to Eva and Brett as she collected her son and they drove home.

"Did you have fun?" she asked him. He yawned sleepily and said he did. Sandy mused on the events of the night and realized that she had fun also.

When they got home, Harry had just returned from work. He was not happy about where she had been that night and showed his disapproval by not speaking to her. She didn't mind, she was in too good a mood as she went upstairs to get ready for bed.

The following week, Brett instant messaged her that the CD was now completed. She was anxious to hear it as she drove back to his house, the day dreary and cold. Two visits in a week, great! she thought. As she sat at his desk and listened to the completed product, tears formed in her eyes. This was beautiful, her dream once again coming true. When it was finished, she cried as quietly Brett handed her a tissue. Getting up, she gave him a quick hug, wishing it were longer.

"Thank you," she said. "It is beautiful."

"Hey, it was a tag team effort," he said, patting her arm. Smiling at him, they discussed the ways they were going to finish designing and promoting the product. Sandy realized she would need to come over yet again to help with the stuffing of the cases and picking up various items needed for the endeavor. Eva kept a low profile, wondering just how much influence Sandy and Brett would have with each other. She intended to keep watch, all her instincts were alive. She did not trust Sandy even one little bit.

In mid November, Sandy went to Brett's to pick up some completed CD's. He had known that she was coming over, yet when she arrived, Eva came to the door and said that he was sleeping. Sleeping? Odd. Sandy explained that she needed his signature on some forms that she filled out so that they could consign the CD's to various stores.

"Just a minute, then, I'll go see if I can wake him up," Eva said, feeling extremely put upon.

"Brett? Brett? Wake up, Sandy needs you to sign something," Eva said.

Brett slowly looked around him, then at Eva. He was going through his own personal hell. Last night he had flashbacks and memories from his past that he would rather not have dealt with. He stayed up late, drinking as he put his thoughts into an e-mail for Sandy. It was his life story that was so filled with pain that he felt she would be so shocked to read, she'd have nothing more to do with him. Now here she was, didn't she take a hint? Going into his den, he saw her smile as he slid into his chair. She explained why she was there, giving him items to sign. When he completed the task, she looked at him like a cat that had caught the canary.

"I have something for you," she said, holding out a small gift bag. "It is from a little boy who had heard our CD and wanted to do something for you in return. Before you open it, keep in mind that he is autistic, but since you have come along, he is progressing very well! He has been listening to your CD every night and his father is impressed by what has happened."

Brett opened the package, removing from it a small ceramic cup. The words on it said, "every man's life touches so many other lives." He looked at it, stunned as he read the sweet note that came with it. Tears came to his eyes. He looked at Eva, then at Sandy. Nobody had done this before, it was so unexpected.

Sandy beamed as she watched him. Eva made a quick comment about how he cried over every little thing as Brett went into the kitchen to pour himself a cup of coffee into the mug. Sandy followed him, watching as he wiped his eyes. She gave him a quick hug, hoping to make him feel better. Unbeknownst to her, Eva witnessed it, her heart growing cold. Why, the little bitch, so that was what was up! Shocked, she sat at the desk and began to pay the bills. Fuming, she pressed hard on the checkbook, quelling her anger as Brett and Sandy laughed and talked out in the kitchen. When Brett directed a question at Eva, she ignored him completely. Immediately, Brett knew, she was jealous. Looking to Sandy, she knew right away what was up. Tearing a piece of paper from the grocery list, he wrote, "jealousy sucks."

"Well, I suppose I had better go," she said as she went to the den to grab her coat. Seeing Eva, she made her polite goodbyes.

"It was nice seeing you," Sandy replied.

Without looking up, Eva merely said goodbye, continuing her work. Sandy went to the kitchen where Brett was. He didn't want to see her go and stalled her by talking about an idea he had for a story about a vegetable salad in the making.

"Seeing as how you are the deli lady, you can pull this one off," he said with eagerness in his eyes. Sandy took the bait and ran with it, their conversation lasting another half hour. Finally she whispered that it really was time for her to go.

"I'll walk you to your car," Brett said. Once there, he hugged her, knowing that he was out of line of Eva's vision. He didn't want to let Sandy go, she felt so good and right in his arms.

"I put a jar of salsa in your bag, enjoy it," he said shyly.

Sandy's eyebrow went up. Salsa? "Oh, Brett, thank you, I can't wait to have some." She knew how he prided himself on it, made from the tomatoes of his garden. Getting into her car, she headed back home, getting caught up in a traffic detour, which rendered a quick twenty minute trip into a two hour ordeal.

She got home just one hour before she and Harry were due at a football banquet. Sitting down, she went to check her e-mails and was stunned to see what was waiting for her. A long letter from Brett, it was the story he had shared at treatment that had been so painful for him to write, that he had vowed that no one, not even Sandy would see it.

As she read it, she cried at all that he had to overcome in his life. The tears fell hot and bitter as she read his closing statement:

"Sandy, I could go on and on, but no one would really give a shit anyway. No one knows this, not even Eva. Only you. I love you and trust you that much. You are the one friend I have never had. I would appreciate it if you could stash this where no one will accidentally find it. I need one week of silence from you, I need to know that I still matter. Don't argue with me about this! I will hate to not have you for one week, but I have to have that barrier.
Brett"

No wonder he didn't want to see her earlier, he thought she already knew and he felt…what? Ashamed? Or that maybe she would drop him like a virus?

Quickly she composed her own e-mail back to him, even as Harry was complaining from upstairs that she needed to get ready for the banquet:

"Brett,

I have read this and I want you to know that this changes NOTHING between us. I still love you and consider you my friend. Do you understand? This changes nothing. I will be here every morning. If you like, you may come in and say hi, I will not force myself upon you.
Love, Sandy"

That night at the banquet, so many thoughts and emotions

flooded through Sandy, the tears welling up inside of her. How could one person go through so much hell? Poor Brett! It was so much like her own life story, which she had written into work of fiction for an agent who now was helping her to find a publisher.

The next morning, Sandy turned on her computer, signed in and was working on another novel when the instant message light blinked. Her heart warmed when she saw who it was.

"Hi," Brett said.

"How are you?" Sandy asked back.

"I am doing fine."

"I am here if you need anything. I read your story. I will not leave you," Sandy typed.

Brett's heart skipped a beat. He had found something he rarely had in his life: someone to provide unconditional love. What a treasure that was.

Chapter 9

Thanksgiving came and went, as Sandy was assailed by the anniversary she always thought of and set on the back burner. It was when she was sixteen years old that she had attempted suicide, and every Thanksgiving only served to remind her of that. She typed a note to Brett, telling him of her own pain from childhood. She was blunt and honest, feeling that if he could be open about his life, then so could she.

"You had mentioned bringing reading with you on Thanksgiving, so I felt it was time to tell you more of *"Hope Survives."* Except that this is not in the book, this will never be in the book, this will never be talked about on talk shows and it will never see the light of print. But, to help you understand it more, you need to know the whole story.

"My mom never wanted to be pregnant. She did everything she could to terminate the pregnancy on her own. My dad found out and was upset, so that ended her quest for the time being. It didn't stop her from trying after I was born, however. When I was 3 months old, after several colicky months, she and my dad were at wits' end. They had a nasty argument over who would care for the baby next, so my dad decided he would take matters in his own hands and shook me violently, throwing me in my crib afterwards. I stopped breathing. Luckily I survived with few ill effects other than needing surgery to remove the buildup of clots from my head, which resulted in blindness in my left eye. I also have scars on my head as a result. Most babies die from this. I should have been so lucky. Instead, I was subjected to years of torment about how I was unwanted and unplanned for. I was told repeatedly how I would never amount to anything more than being an imbecile, a parasite, a moron and other names.

"When I was about three, I remember my dad fondling me. I felt extremely uncomfortable, mostly because my mother had such a prudish way about her, that I would have bathed with clothes on if she could have made me. As I got older, it continued more and more. I was ashamed because I knew that if my mom knew, there would be hell to pay. I oftentimes think she suspected, however, because she always called me "daddy's little princess." She deeply resented the way my dad would "spoil me" with small gifts of money and such. I felt embarrassed and just wanted to die.

"As I got older, the molesting continued. I was constantly told by dad about how I was prettier than my mom and how he would be jealous when I finally married. I still hadn't told a soul, but was mortified beyond belief. It seemed that no one could help me...my mother increased her abuse of me, hitting and beating me every chance she got. She would come after me with knives and other things, hurling objects at me from very close range, then telling me when they made impact how glad she was because she wanted me to die or at least to suffer as she suffered. I felt so helpless and all I wanted to do was to curl up in someone's arms and cry and be comforted. The only comfort---not! was my dad, who always felt "bad" that my mom was hurting me, but couldn't stop it.

"My older brother was a delinquent since he was 10. He was put into foster care at 11. He would come over on weekends to visit and some summers also. When I was 12 and he 14, he took an obscene interest in me and threatened me at knife point, raping me and saying that if I told, he would say it was all my idea. I never told anyone, even though it went on for most of the summer of my 12th year. When he left after the summer, I never saw him again, much to my relief, yet here was dad, more now than ever- because now I was developing. The sexual abuse never stopped and I never told a soul. I was too afraid of the consequences.

"When I was 16, I attempted suicide. I couldn't drag myself out of bed or face the day anymore. I was like a druggie who had hit bottom. It was on Thanksgiving day 1979. I wanted so much to die, I didn't care about life, for it had been sucked out of me. After 3 hours and nothing much happened, I panicked and called my dad, who took me to the hospital. I had taken a bottle... about 50 pills, of Tylenol. The doctor said I should have died and didn't know why I didn't. I only knew that I had fucked up and was to continue in this hell of my own making, it seemed.

"When Harry and I were to be married, I couldn't take the guilt anymore and only told him of what my brother had done, but minimized the severity by saying it happened a couple of times. I was so afraid of losing him and he was my ticket out of my mother's hell.

"Harry was shocked and said for me to tell my mom. Well, that was a big joke. Suddenly she started calling me a slut and a whore and didn't believe me, saying how I must have done something to encourage him because brothers don't do that to their sisters. Then she told others what a slut I was too, because I had initiated incest with my brother. I was mortified. Good thing I didn't admit to what my dad did, although he was shocked because he wasn't the only one, I guess. I was glad to just get the hell out of there.

"However, it didn't stop there. Knowing what he did about my "past", Harry loved to rub it in my face about what happened, saying that if I really wanted to, I could have got out. I tried telling my counselor in high school about what happened with the physical abuse my mom dished out and she didn't believe me, so why would it have been different?

"Three months after we married, a drug dealer from up the street came by looking for Harry. He used to supply him with drugs several years before and sometimes would stop by to see if Harry had changed his mind about a purchase. After the Maplewood incident in 1978, when he was arrested for DWI

85

and Drug use, he quit all that, but this guy persisted. I said Harry wasn't home. He then came on to me. I was ripe…only 17 and he was 25. He felt I should have caved in to his charms, I just didn't want him around, period. When I rejected him, he said he would tell Harry that we did do it and that I lead him on. I didn't believe he would be so callous. He followed through on his threat.

"When Harry got home later, he was spitting bullets. He demanded to know what I had been doing that day. I said nothing, except to care for the kennel. He then said I lied and that Rick, this drug dealer, had said we "fucked". I hotly denied it. Harry said that if my brother did it with me, then obviously I was coming on to people and what a slut and a whore I was. He then proceeded to anally rape me, screaming afterwards there was more to where that came from. I was so mortified that this knight in shining armor was tarnished after all. What an idiot I was, to be so desperate as to sell my soul to him, just to escape my mother.

"For years afterwards, he always believed that if anyone even looked at me cross sided, I was having an affair. He never trusted me after that. I wanted again to just die, how could I have been so wrong about someone? This was coupled with physical abuse from his outbursts, which were frequent. After 8 years, I sought counseling, which resulted in the cessation of the physical abuse, but not the emotional from him. I am happy to say that after more counseling, I stood up for myself and realized that I am a human and will not tolerate that crap. He finally backed down a bit, but it has never been the stuff of romance novels.

"I have always tried to live up to my image of what I think people should live with…compassion and sympathy. Not nagging, not yelling, not screaming, name calling or hitting. I hope I have raised my kids to be an example of what I never had. I want to leave a legacy for others to follow and be inspired by.

"To this day, if I even see my folks in public, I freak out and run the other way. I can't stand the hypocrisy that they subjected me too.

"The nightmares are still frequent and if I am under a lot of stress, the tears come, too. Yet, you are the only one who now knows this. I can't tell others...I no longer want to be judged by my past, but rather my future.

"So, this is who I am. If it is a turn off for you, I will understand. I was always so afraid of losing people that I loved by confessing. I didn't want them to think I'm a menace to society or some weird person with psychotic tendencies. Nothing is further from the truth.

"As the anniversary of my Thanksgiving attempt at suicide approaches, I give thanks...because I have seen now why I am still here. I have much to do.

"Will you still be part of it with me?"

Brett read it while the turkey cooked in the oven. Good grief, she had withstood so much and yet, look at her now. He had known some of what she had experienced, but hadn't counted on this. Yet she was so normal, polite, sweet... He typed in his own message to her:

"Another Thanksgiving has arrived and this year we both have a new friend to call our own. It never ceases to amaze me what adults can do to the innocent, the vulnerable, the defenseless. It also amazes me that you're not messed up in the head or at least a severe alcoholic. Which just proves what the experts say about alcoholism being hereditary. I had my share of problems as I grew up, too. I didn't have to be an alcoholic, but here I am. There really doesn't seem like there's anything I can do about it, and for the record, if I can keep from ruining my life any further, I don't mind. Just circumstances I have to live with. You are a very durable person, Sandy. I respect you and your honesty as well as your drive to be who you always wanted to be. Unfortunately, it was far too long in the coming. But, you can now flush all the bullshit and move ahead with me as your friend, confidante' & partner in crime. Happy Thanksgiving!"

Activity geared up for the big holiday. Christmas. Brett

worked with Sandy, preparing the next CD for her second book, the continuing adventures of a spaniel named Winston. She had wanted to go on a book tour and take it with her to spur sales. Time wasn't on their side as they worked feverishly to complete it.

Sandy had noticed how tired and lethargic she was becoming, but attributed it to her heavy work schedule. Also, her monthly cycle was not really a cycle so much as she was gushing blood, going through as many as three or four tampons in an hour. Alarmed, she called her doctor. He scheduled a biopsy. When the results came in, he turned to her, folder in hand.

"Sandy, I have some bad news. Everything is pointing to cancer."

Stunned, she felt as though the world just stopped, yet she was flung through space. Clinging to the chair, she needed to get a grip, but she couldn't breathe.

"Cancer?"

"Yes. I am scheduling you for an appointment at the hospital. You will need more tests done to see the extent of this as well as the route will we use for treatment." Handing her a referral, he stood up, shook her hand and left.

Cancer.

For several days, she ruminated on it. She needed to meet with Brett to pick up the completed CD's, so on that Saturday morning, she instant messaged him the time.

"Can it be a bit later? I need to go to AA," he asked.

"Sure, I can come by later. I just need to stop by the hospital for some tests first. The doctor saw something that set up flags."

"As in, the military flag?" Brett joked.

"Brett, I may have cancer." She waited, her breath held for his response.

He sat stunned, then typed in, "hush!"

She went on to explain what was happening.

"Good luck, hun," he said. "I'll see you in a bit."

All throughout his session at AA, he could only think of her. He hoped for the best as he went straight back home with Eva, Sandy arriving shortly after. By then, he was making brunch and invited her to stay. As he cooked the bacon, she stood by him, telling him what she knew.

It was cancer, they would need to set up treatment times. They had given her pamphlets with titles such as, *"Coping with Cancer,"* and, *"How to cope when you are dying."* She was scared. Brett tried to keep it light, yet his heart pounded. His life was just becoming good again, which he attributed to Sandy. Why this, why now? he wondered. Handing her a plate heaping with food, he told her to eat, to keep up her strength, she would need it in the coming days. Gratefully, she accepted it.

In the weeks yet ahead of her, she had to look forward to radiation treatments, dealing with her children, work, Harry and her writing, all not necessarily in that order. She was glad for Brett, he kept her sane when her world was becoming insane. He was her strength, inwardly she fumed that Harry couldn't be the same. Instead, he was becoming surly and rude, contemptuous of her relationship with Brett. One night, they had a shouting match, leaving Sandy in tears.

"Don't make me choose between you, because I will choose him!" she sat in a chair, crying.

"Why?" Harry asked.

"Because, I love him," Sandy replied, tears coursing down her face. She hoped this information would be the momentum to propel him out the door. He got up, then knelt down by her.

"I will not leave you," he told her. "Is this because of my affair several years ago? Is this why you are doing this? You haven't forgiven me, have you?"

Sandy thought it over, then shook her head. "No," she weakly agreed.

He stood up, running his hand through his curly hair, now graying with the passing of time. She once had thought him so handsome. That was before he constantly took and took from her, eventually assuming she would handle all responsibilities. Sandy finally realized that her writing and her children were more important than being Harry's slave. As she looked at him now, she felt empty.

"What do you want me to do?" Harry asked, defeat written all over him.

"I want to be able to finish my work with Brett. When you see the little blinky light on the computer screen, don't get all carried away. He and I are very good friends, you don't need to get so jealous," Sandy explained.

"I won't," Harry didn't know if he could live up to that, but would try. His wife was dying. The least he could do was to be here for her. How would it look if he moved out or worse, sent her out? Image was all important to him.

"Are you sure?" Sandy asked. "I don't believe you,"

"I'll just stay upstairs. Then you can do whatever you want on the computer and I won't interfere." Harry responded.

Sandy just nodded, her heart feeling lighter than it had in awhile.

Harry's promise only held up for a short while. Then, a week later, he became rude once again as he crossed her path to get a drink from the refrigerator. The light was blinking as Sandy was editing another manuscript that was due at a publisher in a few days. Muttering under his breath, he strode back upstairs, stomping his feet in protest. So much for promises, Sandy thought. Stopping her typing for a bit, she wondered why, in the limited time she may have left, couldn't he fill her life with happy memories instead of making her sad and miserable. Putting her head into her hands, she cried.

She had exactly one hour before she needed to be at the dentist and needed to drop off supplies for Brett, so stopped over at his house. She just walked in the kitchen; hearing her, he met her. She was stunned to see his face was puffy, eyes red. His voice was shaky. He had been crying. Walking up to him, he hugged her hard, then took her into his office.

"I sent you an e-mail," he said, pulling it up. "Now that you are here, we need to talk."

She read it, pain washing through her. He said for her to give her daughter his phone number, to call him in case one morning she would no longer be at the computer. Holding onto him, they both cried, unashamed of the tears that flowed. She nuzzled his face and kissed him, sorrow slicing through her like a knife. This was hardest on those who survived. They had the opportunity to watch someone they loved slowly slip away. It wasn't fair! Getting up, she got a tissue, crying even more.

"Sit down, sit down," Brett advised her. She shook her head no. Getting up, he hugged her to him, feeling her body next to his. She was becoming thin, he could feel her ribs as he stroked her sides. Taking her head into his hands, he gazed lovingly into her eyes.

"I love you," he said. "You have made my life so wonderful. But you have only been here such a short time. Why did you come into my life, only to have to leave?" His eyes misted over again as he stroked her hair.

"I don't know. I'll fight this as hard as I can," Sandy whispered. Reaching up, she kissed his mouth once, twice, three times. He pulled her to him and held her tight, wishing he could just take her now, make love to her, as if by doing that, he could eradicate all the demons that were held between them. Then he slowly stepped back. He made that mistake once. Eva, if she found out, would be livid. She was not a forgiving person. He feared for his future. No money, no job due to his felony record from all his DUI's, no license, he was basically a nobody. Sandy told him often enough that despite those troubles, he was a somebody and used his work through radio as an example.

"You have touched so many lives, you just don't know it yet. There is a spot in heaven for you!" She patiently reminded him.

He was an agnostic, yet lately he found himself praying to a God he refused to admit he needed in his life. Looking at her now, he pushed her away.

"I have something to tell you, but it makes me uncomfortable to say it," he began. He pulled out a cigarette and, taking a deep drag, sat down.

Sandy looked scared, standing forlorn. What was it? She wondered. Going over to him, she sat next to him, putting her hand on his arm. Did he want her to leave his life? Could he not stand the thought of dealing with her after all?

"What is it?" she asked quietly.

"I can't say it, it sounds horrible..." he began.

"Say it!" she loudly responded, then quieter, "please, just say it. Or else I will always wonder, what if?" her voice ended in a whisper.

Looking at her, his eyes filled with pain, he made his announcement.

"I want to do your eulogy. Except that I can't, because if I were to get up there, all I will do for ten minutes is cry, then sit down. I will not have done you justice. So I've decided I will make a CD which can be played there. Sandy, I'm not going to your funeral."

She gasped.

"Hun, I can't! All I'll do is cry..."he pleaded with her.

Sandy cried once again.

"Nobody will care if I am there or not. I'm nobody to them. I was somebody to you. You won't be there. Why should I go? God, I feel like such a bastard now!" Brett exclaimed hotly. Getting up, he grabbed a can of beer, pulling the tab and drinking half of it's contents in one gulp. For all of his show about AA and meeting with his probation officer, he still allowed himself to drink. He was an alcoholic and he knew it. He tried and failed, just like with most things in his life.

Just like with Sandy.

He met her, now she was dying. She may not have another Christmas in her, she told him. He wanted to do right by her and now this! He couldn't even show up at her funeral. "Brett

Pearson, major fuck up, nice to meet you!" he thought bitterly.

Rubbing her back, he felt so awful for the pain she was dealing with. Sitting back down next to her, she put her head on his shoulder and surprised him with her words.

"Brett, you must do what you are comfortable with. I'll be watching you from wherever I am. If you don't want to go, I'll understand."

Looking earnestly into her eyes, he was amazed all over again at her kindness, her openness. The rush he felt was greater than any orgasm he had ever experienced, and he had experienced many over the years with many women. Yet this woman stood far and above all those other whores. She was a true lady. Giving her another kiss, he held her. Together, they dealt with the pain as only true friends can. Looking at her watch, she realized she needed to go. She would be late as it was. Turning to him once again, she bid him goodbye, giving him one last kiss. Then she was gone.

His heart lay broken and spent. He got another can of beer-then another; the rest of the afternoon becoming a blur as he sat at his computer, the alcohol having an effect on his memories. He sent Sandy several e-mails, each one becoming more unintelligible than the last. In one, he asked her to write a story that they could use on their current CD project about people triumphing over tragedy. In another, as the ragged memories came crashing through, he told her how, when he was young, he had been raped by several of his father's friends.

When Sandy got home from the dentist, she read the e-mails and immediately composed a letter to him, detailing their relationship into a story of heartbreak for their project:

"They met, as all people do, quite by accident. After the initial meeting, which was during a radio show, he was impressed by the way she carried herself, the memory etched into his mind. A few days later, he called her up, just to check on how she was doing. The conversation lasted well beyond a few minutes, as she regaled him with talk of this and that.

She became a good friend, and memories began to be made.

"She became his ally on the radio program he hosted, telling funny jokes through the chat line and keeping everyone upbeat with her quick wit. As the friendship grew, she included him in her latest writing projects, which escalated from just a one time happening into a full scale endeavor that took up most of his waking hours. He realized then that they clicked together in a way that many friendships do not. He looked forward to her mornings with him through the chat line, her witty e-mails, her silly jokes.

"His world came crashing down when she was diagnosed with cancer. Not this gal who kept up his spirits! He wasn't ready for this. It couldn't be! As she tried valiantly to fight off the invading illness, her body becoming thin, yet her demeanor stayed positive. The doctor, however, became the bearer of bad news.

"You will not make it through the next Christmas."

"That was when he realized that every moment that they had together needed to become firmly etched into his mind. Every conversation, every nuance of her voice, became for him a treasure which he savored.

"The day dawned cold and dark when the call came. She had passed away during the night, the fight was over, the pain was finally gone. It was then he took out a letter which she had written and made him promise that he would not open until now. Slowly he opened it, pulling it out of the envelope.

"If you are reading this, it means that I am no longer here by you. I tried so hard to beat this, but it seems the angels have won. As I write this, it is raining out. There are two crows zipping between the pine trees. I miss our moments together and wish time could have just stopped and never start again. You have given me so many memories. Who knew way back when, what a treasure you are? You have been my soul and inspiration. Without you, I would be nothing. With you, so many doors opened to places I have never dreamed of entering. You gave me strength, you gave me hope. You brightened my day and gave me reasons to live. Now, you must go on! Please, don't let our work- which was more JOY than work- be in vain. Take my name, my writings, my inspiration and let them loose! They are what I left behind for others. Now, what I have for you is this: I love you! you know, I have always loved you. You had that rare magic that made me want to aspire for more, you are that rare gift of a person who comes along only once in a lifetime. You have been my soul mate, my dearest friend, my twin. Why I lived so long without you is a mystery to me, but our time together has been so precious. I treasured each moment and had it stored within my heart. You were my strength when I couldn't go on-my rock in troubled times. Be strong and know I am watching over you. I have a spot right here next to me...I am waiting for you. You have done everything right, not only for me, but for everyone you came into contact with. Your legacy is the love you spread through the sound of your music, your voice, your actions, but most of all, your love.

I love you...Your P.I.A."

"He slowly folded the note, putting it into his pocket. He cried copious tears of frustration...why did she have to leave him now? He needed her! Then he wiped his eyes and sat at his computer. He typed in these words: " I was loved by something greater than life itself. I was truly loved." He saved it in his documents, then slowly shut down the computer and for the first time, allowed himself to feel the comfort she sent to him from above."

Clicking send, Sandy felt miserable. Going upstairs to her bedroom, she closed the door and called him. When he answered, she began to cry.

"No! We did this already! You are not going to do this to me anymore!" he announced angrily. She cried more, the tears touching him through the telephone wire. His heart broke.

"Ok, you leave me with no choice. Sandy, what I am going to say is going to hurt you, but I have to say it. .."

Sandy stopped crying long enough to hear it.

"Get your goddamned head out of your ass! So you're dying, so what? Do you think I care? Do you?" he was blunt in his drunkenness. "You have work to do and you can't do it if you're crying your goddamned head off."

There was silence at the other end. He was afraid that maybe she had hung up on him. "Are you there?" he asked.

Loud snuffle. Yes, she was. Good.

"Can you do that for me?" he asked, more tenderly this time.

"Yes, I can," came her weak reply.

"Good, because we have things to do. Sandy, I talked to your new publisher today."

Sandy gasped. What was he doing?

"I feel it's important that I know who you are working with, because when you're gone, I will be dealing with him."

More tears from Sandy.

"Hun, your books that you are working on are also our projects. I want to move them forward. I told him about your cancer..."

"You did WHAT?" Sandy asked. She wanted her work to stand on it's own merits, not because some publisher thought she was dying, and she told Brett so.

"I know that, it just slipped out," he apologized. In fact, it slipped out twice. He didn't want her to know either. "We talked for quite awhile, and I'm going to see him on Monday."

Again, Sandy gasped. Why was he doing this?

"Brett, you can't drive over there. No, I won't let you!" Sandy was worried that because he didn't have a license, he may be involved in an accident. Even if it weren't his fault, when the cops found out about his lack of license and who he was, he would end up back in jail, with time added on. "I'll take you!" she announced.

"You can't miss work," Brett began.

"I'll take time off. You are not driving and that's final."

"Ok. You can come with." Brett acquiesced.

Later, when he told Eva of his plans, her stomach plummeted. He was becoming more involved in Sandy's life. Eva wanted him to find a paying job, this had been her goal since she gave him the ultimatum way back last summer. Now he was helping an author with her books, making and selling the audio, which, although wasn't making money, they were just breaking even. Brett knew it was just a matter of time before they hit their market niche and the big orders would come in. He and Eva had several loud discussions about this. Eva should have been happy that he wasn't getting into trouble, that he was becoming more focused, but the old jealousy thing reared it's ugly head. He spent more time at the computer than he was with her.

He tried to bring her into his projects, but she shrugged them off. Why should he spend time with her, he thought? She showed no appreciation for what he did. With Sandy though, in her eyes, he could do no wrong.

One of their projects was a story about animals living on a farm. Although he had never written anything other than copy for radio stations, he gave it a try by helping Sandy edit the manuscript. She loved the silly ideas that came out of his head and applied them to her story. Once he suggested they actually visit a farm to get an idea of how things were run. Smiling, she agreed. He made an appointment and one fine Saturday afternoon in January, they left together. Eva didn't even see him to the door. She had thought the whole thing was ridiculous and showed her disapproval by her absence.

The time at the farm passed quickly. As they were making their way home, Brett suggested they stop in a little town and check into promoting her books. She pulled into a parking spot and they exited the car. The day turned cold and a soft rain fell, though it was only the end of January. They stopped in a book store, where Sandy spoke with the manager while Brett perused the selection of books and audio. Sandy returned by his side as he showed her all the subtleties related to the CD he was holding.

Smiling at his knowledge, they walked to the window and looked at the scenery. Though it was mid winter, the river just outside the window was still open in places.

Brett mused about the other times he had been in this town, then they stepped outside, standing under a canopy, the rain falling just outside of it. Sandy could not imagine being with anyone else. Not even Harry would do this with her. They still had their problems, but Sandy didn't care. She lived in this moment and didn't want it to end. Brett sensed her mood.

"Come on," he said. "Let's go get a drink." He named a place, and they stepped into the rain once again, soon entering a pub that was bustling with activity. They ordered their drinks, Sandy beginning to warm up. Sharing small talk, Sandy was surprised to see the time fly. Harry would be home soon, but he knew she was going to be out. She pushed it to the back of her mind. Brett placed another order, then went to the men's room. Calling Eva on his cell phone, he told her he would be home soon. She whined about having to make dinner, generally making him feel guilty about being out at all. He told her to get something from the deli, thinking of the times when she was out and he never complained. As he turned off the phone, he told himself he was going to have a good time with his real lady love, who was waiting for him at the bar.

Sandy anxiously watched for him, alternately turning her attention to the football game that was shown on the TV. When he finally returned, her heart glowed as he explained how he called Eva and she gave him a hard time. As they continued to drink, each became more free with the words and actions, twice Brett tweaked her on the breast. She leaned over to kiss him, rubbing his back. He positioned himself so that he could see the door, becoming worried. What if Eva suddenly walked in and saw what they were doing. She knew where he was. Looking at Sandy, he broached the subject. She jumped back as if she were prodded by lightning.

"Sandy, what we did before was a mistake. It never should

have happened. I carry the guilt around with me all the time." he began. She looked at him, tears welling in her eyes.

""I think about us doing it all the time. You know, had it been you that I met twelve years ago, we'd be together now. I am committed to Eva, for better for worse, till death do us part." To prove his point, he showed her the ring which was tattooed on his finger. Sandy looked at it, then back into his eyes.

"Oh, Brett, where were you 25 years ago? I was looking for you then, why did I find you too late?" Sandy asked tearfully, her Bloody Mary sitting untouched on the bar.

"I need you to do something for me. You must tell Eva that there is nothing going on between us. She is so jealous, she thinks there is. This is important to me! Sandy! Please!"

Sandy looked at him, put her head on the bar and cried harder.Brett got up and walked over to the napkin dispenser and pulled a couple out, handing them to Sandy.

"Sandy, please stop crying. People will think I'm abusing you. Stop!"

Sandy looked at him, taking the napkins and dabbing at her eyes. "When I die, there had better be a fucking throne lined in gold in heaven for all of the sacrifices I have made!" she exclaimed.

"Sandy, there is already. You're just adding to it," Brett said lovingly.

Sandy cried more, then nodded as he implored her beseechingly with his eyes. "I'll do it," she responded. This would be the hardest thing for her to bear. There would never be "Brett and Sandy forever after," only, best friends until the day she died. "I'll do it." The pain within her heart sluiced through her until she could hardly breathe. It cast a pall on the rest of the night.

It was after ten o'clock when they finally bid the bar goodnight. As Sandy drove Brett home, she listened in on his phone conversation with his wife, wanting to puke. He was kissing up to Eva big time and Sandy wondered why he even felt any gratitude to want to stay with her. What a wuss, she thought miserably. As she pulled into his driveway, he turned to her.

"I really don't want to go in there," he said. Sandy just gave him a weak smile.

"Then someday you'll have to grow up, and tell her off," Sandy thought. Instead though, she bid him good luck and watched as he walked up the driveway, shoulders sagging, defeat evident in every step. Shaking her head as she drove away, her heart rendered to smoke and ash, she cried.

Chapter 10

When Sandy returned home that night, she found her husband in a drunken stupor, her kitchen destroyed, as he threw everything he could lay his hands on. Slurring his words, calling her a bitch, a whore and anything else he could pull out of his drunken mind. Sandy was scared and hid in the bedroom, waiting for any moment that the door would be pounded down and he would hurt her. Shivering under the comforter on her bed, she knew her marriage was over.

He saved the most violent moment for two weeks later. It had been his week off at work and he used that opportunity to become falling down drunk. Finally, five days into his ordeal, he was ready when Sandy returned home from work. She was exhausted not only from work, but from her session of chemotherapy earlier that day. All she wanted was peace and quiet.

"How's the fuckin' whore tonight?" he asked her, stumbling his way towards her, his eyes bloodshot. She took one look at him, then tried to remain calm even as she tried to work her way out of this. It was over, she wanted to leave, or for him to leave. She couldn't go on like this any longer. There was no affection for him any more. When she didn't respond, he grabbed a box of her completed CD's and hurled them across the room. They fell to the ground with a resounding crash. Next came a skillet, hurled with great strength, it split in two pieces when it crashed against the back door. Sandy gasped as he backed her into a corner, then began to call her every name in the book.

"Where are the kids?" she demanded to know.

"Why? Why do you want them to witness this? Do you

want them to see what a whore their mother is?" he sneered.

"You're drunk," Sandy stated.

Harry grabbed her hair and yanked it hard. Sandy called out for one of her kids to call 911. She looked Harry in the eye.

"Let go of me!" she demanded. Harry let go just long enough to slap her face hard. Her head bounced off the refrigerator, pain blurred her vision as she thought of Brett. He would save her, she knew, he would also kill Harry to atone for this. Inwardly, she cried out for the hero who wasn't here.

"Quick!" she called out, "is someone calling 911?" she asked loudly, hoping that she was heard.

Immediately Harry once again slapped her hard. "I want to see you fucking dead and I'm the one who can do it!" he snarled. "And when your gigolo boyfriend comes to the funeral, I will kill him and his wife, too!" Sandy was stunned. She slipped out of his grasp and ran to the phone, quickly dialing 911. Before she could put the phone to her ear, he ripped it out of her hands. Sandy fled the house wearing only her clothes, into the cold night to a neighbor's house. Quickly opening the door, she barged in and slammed the door, locking it. Her daughter, there visiting with a friend, looked up in alarm.

"Call 911! Harry is on the rampage and he's looking for me!" she said, before breaking into tears.

Within minutes, the police were there, taking information and putting Harry into the back of the squad car. He was arrested. He would never hurt her again. Sandy would see to that.

That night she IM'd Brett, telling him what happened. His blood pressure shot up as he asked how she was. When she told him of the beating, he became incensed. His dearest friend, dying from cancer and now, dealing with this too. He didn't get too much sleep that night as he paced and fretted. Eva saw this and felt revulsion for the woman who had stolen her husband's affections.

Sandy made arrangements after Harry was released from jail to see to it that he never returned home. He was effectively banned from the house. Her heart broke over this decision, but she needed to protect herself. The feeling of freedom was overwhelming. No longer would she have to worry about what reaction he would give her. She could go to sleep when she wanted, wake up when she wanted. She was on her own now and determined to make the best of it.

The next few months passed quickly. The sales of the audio CDs took off, leaving Sandy and Brett busier than ever. Sandy worked, despite the pain the cancer was causing. Brett couldn't stand her misery as they worked together one day. He was talking to her when suddenly she grabbed his arm, looking at him.

"Brett?" she questioned, before passing out cold on the floor. Stunned, he bent over, calling her name. No response. His greatest fear was that she had died right there. He continued to call her, rolling her from her side to her back, he stood over her, hoping she would come to.

Sandy's eyes fluttered weakly. "What the...huh? Where am I?" she asked weakly.

Brett let his breath out in a whoosh. "What the hell happened?" he asked her.

"I don't know," Sandy said as she struggled to sit up. "I guess I just passed out."

"How long has this been going on?" he asked, his heart still racing.

"It never did before," she said. He went to get her something to eat, thinking that maybe she was hungry. Weakly, Sandy ate the applesauce he offered.

"I think that maybe I was just hungry," she said, rinsing out her spoon when she finished. He watched her warily, wondering what else he could do to ease her misery.

However in the next few weeks, when the episodes became more frequent, she finally confessed about the pain she was suffering. His heart broke. "That is the last thing I want to see, is for you to suffer."

"I have heard that marijuana is good for pain." Sandy offered. "My doctor won't let me take anything else."

"I'll get you some, " Brett agreed.

"Brett, you don't need to get into trouble for me," Sandy said with concern.

"It's no trouble, I still have my connections," he assured her.

The night before her birthday, Brett IM'd her. "The weed is in," he told her.

"It is? That was quick!" Sandy typed back.

"Come now," Brett demanded.

"Now?"

"Come now!" Brett insisted.

"Okay, I'll be there in twenty minutes," Sandy typed in. On the way to Brett's, she wondered about what Eva would say about this.

Pulling into the driveway, all was dark. As she walked by Brett's den window, she heard Eva's voice raised in anger. Stepping into the shadows, she listened as Eva berated Brett.

"We have been married for ten years and it's as if I don't know you!" she railed. "You never talk to me! You're never there for me!"

"You have never asked me to be," Brett said.

"Yet you do everything for HER!" Eva continued. "Goddamn it, Brett, I'm left out and I don't like it! Why did you get her weed? Do you realize that if you are caught, you *will* go to jail and I am NOT bailing you out this time, do you hear me?"

Sandy saw Brett turn away from Eva and she looked to see the computer screen on and tuned into to her instant message window. Oops, no wonder Eva was so angry.

"Why don't you just get into your van, take the camper and leave?" Eva demanded.

"Is that what you want?" Brett asked her.

When there was no response, he asked her again. "Is that what you want?"

Still no response. Eva just got up and left the room. That was when Sandy, her heart full of dread, went to the back door and knocked. Brett got up and walked to it, defeat in his shoulders. He lead her to the den, Eva nowhere in sight. The pain began to grip Sandy, she held her lower abdomen as the room began to spin. She knelt on the floor, but not before the pain had her passed out again. Brett panicked.

"Sandy...Sandy, come on, get up, come on," he called. Finally, she stirred as he helped her up. She looked at him.

"You just barely made it here," he said with sadness. He gave her the pipe filled with marijuana. She inhaled, the aroma filling her with it's calming influence. He pushed her to inhale again. Soon the pain subsided. Brett looked at her, tears coursing down his face.

"I love you, how could you doubt that?" he asked.

"I don't doubt it," Sandy replied. "I love you, too." she hugged him as he told her to take another drag on the pipe. She began to feel light headed. He drank from a can of beer that was sitting next to him. All he wanted was for Sandy to be comfortable.

"You're not driving back home tonight," he announced to her.

At once, Sandy felt happy, then miserable. How could she stay here with Eva here, as angry as she was. She didn't need the stress.

"I'll be okay," Sandy said, "Just give me a few minutes."

"No, you're staying overnight, no arguing. You can stay in the guest room."

Eva walked in then, over hearing the conversation. "She is staying," Brett said. "End of conversation."

Later as she lay in the bed, she overheard Brett and Eva in their room. She prayed hard that they wouldn't get amorous, she didn't think she could handle that.

Soon she overheard giggling. "Brett get off of me, you tub of lard!" Eva laughed.

Then Brett was overheard to say, "Yeah, right, whatever."

"How much do you weigh?" Eva asked. Sandy heard Brett's response. She never thought of him as having a weight problem. To her, Brett was perfect, big boned, sturdy muscles. Perfect.

The rest of the night, Sandy tossed and turned, at one point a cat walked in and jumped up on the bed next to her. Finally at 3:30 a.m., Sandy got up and wandered the house. She was uncomfortable being here. Every nuance in her screamed to just leave. But Brett would wonder where she was and she didn't want to worry him, so she stayed. She finally settled into a recliner chair in his den and dozed.

At five a.m. Brett woke up and went into his den, startled to see her in the chair. He sat at his computer, checking his e-mails, when Sandy looked at him, love in her eyes.

"When you see the deli lady, tell her I said hi," Sandy teased, getting up and stretching. Going to Brett, she hugged him from behind.

"I'm going to make you a breakfast," he announced quietly. "Happy birthday, hun," he said. He looked at her, then kissed her.

"Oh, hun, you're too sweet," Sandy whispered. "Thank you."

They talked in companionable tones until six a.m. when Eva woke up. Then the air was strained with tension, even after she left at eight thirty to go to work. Sandy felt like she was intruding and Brett didn't know what he could do about it. The breakfast was delicious, with eggs, hash browns and an English muffin. Brett always served more than Sandy could eat. He was concerned about her losing weight. She must have dropped thirty pounds in the last few months. She had been a pleasingly plump gal and now her body was more defined, the rounded edges gone, making her very attractive indeed. Although she still was able to keep up with her daily activities, she had a gaunt look about her.

Inwardly, Brett worried about her. He was torn between his wife and the best thing that had ever happened to him. If Sandy died… Brett couldn't allow himself to think of how devastated he would be.

Then came the day in early spring when Brett told Sandy that Eva was leaving town for a few days. Sandy's heart warmed at the thought of what could happen. She was helping Brett wash his prized vehicle, a 1979 Chevy van, hunter green with a pearl inlay and chrome everything. Brett taught her the proper way to wash a van, as Sandy carefully followed his instructions. The day was warm and sunny and she had the whole day off from work, it being Good Friday.

Then came the call after lunch from Eva. She was coming home from work early. Sandy's heart plummeted. There went that idea! Damn it.

"So, do you wanna stay or go?" Brett asked Sandy.

"Brett, I'm your friend, she can't just chase me off."

"She can be difficult, it may be best to go," Brett warned.

"I'm staying!" Sandy was adamant.

Well, adamant didn't work. Eva made Sandy feel so uncomfortable, at one point picking a fight with Brett right in front of Sandy. That made her feel even more uncomfortable. Eva was a very insecure woman, but also very controlling. Sandy didn't see how Brett could stand it!

Finally, Sandy made her excuse, she had to get out of there and away from the chaos. As she started up her car, Brett walked over. Sandy rolled down the window.

"I tried to warn ya," was all he said.

"Yes, you did. Take care, hun, I'll catch ya later."

"Hey, thanks for washing my van. It looks great."

"I had fun. Let's do that again sometime. Bye." Sandy drove off with Brett watching, then, shoulders sagging, he walked back to Eva.

Though neither implied it, being together while Eva was going to be away was a long sought after experience for both. Mentally, Sandy counted down the days in her mind.

On that fateful day, Brett instant messaged Sandy, saying he was trying to get Eva out the door.

"Why does it take so long to dry her hair?" he asked. "Now she's brushing her teeth!"

Sandy merely smiled. She was going to be busy that day, she had to work out a contract proposal with a business who was interested in her products. Brett was going to help her with it, that is, if Eva would ever leave.

Finally, he said she was gone. He called her, only to have the phone ring a few minutes later, he took the call on his second line. When he returned, he said, "that was Eva. She asked if I could make reservations for dinner for when she returns." Brett explained.

Sandy's heart plummeted, but she knew that this after all, what married people did. She wished it were her instead.

Later, Brett informed her that a friend of his had come over and they were sitting on the deck assembling more CD's. Sandy was happy that Brett had company, he needed a break. She wished him well, then hung up the phone.

The next day, when Sandy walked up the sidewalk to Brett's house, she heard raucous laughter, then noticed the back door propped open. Stepping into the kitchen she heard Brett's slurred speech as he bragged to his friend, who looked to be equally intoxicated, about how glorious his wife's shaved pussy was. Sandy merely hung back, listening, until she was observed by the friend, who pointed her out to Brett.

Sandy then went into the den to drop off supplies. Brett came in, catching her in a hug.

"I was so worried about you!" he exclaimed. "I tried to instant message you, but you didn't answer!"

"Yes, I did, I instant messaged you! Here, look!" Sandy said, going to his computer. As it turned out, his two computer screens both had messages, one from her and the other was his message to her.

"No wonder it got mixed up! We were on two different screens," Sandy held his waist, looking at him in love. She then turned to his friend.

"Hi, Brad," she said.

"Hey, can I have a hug like that, too?" he asked.

"Of course," Sandy said and gave him a hug. He put his arms around her and held her.

"Do you have to leave today?" Brett asked.

Sandy just looked at him, then became excited. "Why, no! I can stay, but I have to call in and let them know at work…I'll just say I'm sick, but I have to sound real convincing." Grabbing the phone, she made a plausible excuse to her boss, then hung up the phone.

"Good, we got that out of the way, have some of this," Brett handed her a glass of brandy. Sandy took a swig, feeling the warmth seeping into her body. Within a few minutes, she felt light headed and giddy, as if she was capable of anything. Taking another swig, she fielded Brad's advances, and when he asked her for a kiss, she gladly obliged. When Brett suggested that they go on and enjoy themselves, Sandy looked at him, stunned.

"Brett, are you sure?" she became worried. What man told his girlfriend to mess around with his best friend? Yet, here he was, doing just that. Sandy wasn't sure of this at all, she felt as though it were a betrayal. Going to Brett, she kissed him, saying it should be him.

"No, I want you to have a good time," he said, pushing her away. "You and Brad, go for it."

Brad was already peeling off his clothes when, suddenly feeling uninhabited thanks to the brandy, Sandy did the same. Brett then saw how thin she had really become as she lay on the floor, legs spread. Brad settled on top of her, kissing her clumsily before entering. All too quickly, she had an orgasm, then it was Brad's turn. Brett merely watched the proceedings, a smile on his face. As Brad untangled himself from Sandy, she cried tears of release. It had been so long since she had any contact with a man, and right now she wished it had been Brett who had taken her to those heights of ecstasy.

"Did you come?" Brett asked. Tearfully, she nodded. He got up from his spot on the chair, kneeling by her. "Are you happy?" he asked. Again she nodded. Going between her legs, he began to stroke her, his expert mouth so gentle that she had another orgasm almost right away. Sitting up, she kissed him full on the mouth, tasting her scent and savoring it.

"All right, tell you the way it is. I don't need Eva finding out about this," he began. "As soon as she comes back, we go back to what we had been, just business. But for now, we have this. Agreed?"

In her haste, Sandy agreed, knowing that she would savor every moment.

Brett needed more cigarettes, which Sandy bought for him. When she returned, Brett was sleeping, Brad sitting on the couch. He and Sandy had an interesting conversation about why men didn't leave their wives, no matter what.

"That's just the way it is. Brett will never leave Eva, and I'll never leave my wife. Sure it gets rough, but we do what we have to do." He talked until he was too tired to continue.

"Go in the spare bedroom and take a nap," Sandy suggested. "I'll go and check on Brett." She showed him where to go, then went into the next room to check on Brett.

"Take off your clothes," Brett said sleepily. Sandy, thinking he was still asleep, gladly stripped and got into the bed with him, stroking his body, encircling his shaft with her fingers, the first time since their first encounter nine months before. She was greedy as she climbed on top of him, rocking back and forth. He propelled her as she moved with the rhythm. In no time at all, a shattering cataclysm hit her, kissing Brett, she whispered her words of love.

The rest of the day passed with Sandy being laid out on

the pool table and worked over, taken naked onto the deck outside as the warm sunshine soothed her bare back, and bent over the kitchen sink as she was stroked to climax after climax. The day was sunny and warm and she was in love.

That night, Brett showed her to his bed and the time flew as they took complete advantage of the darkness. In the background, music played by Guns n Roses and Boston.

"You look so young," Sandy whispered at one point. "You look as though you're twelve years old all over again."

"I feel young," Brett replied. He cradled her against him, hugging her tight.

Sandy wondered about his friend, Brad, who spent the night on the couch. She knew she had been loud at times during their sessions, but she didn't let it bother her as together, they watched the sky grow from dark to light.

The next day Brett told her of a great place to have her nipples pierced. Sandy, still under the influence of all the alcohol she had been consuming, grabbed her purse, driving to the address Brett gave her. Shyly, she stripped off her shirt as Jamie talked her through the procedure.

"You'll feel some pain, and it'll be sore for a few days. Ready?"

Sandy nodded as she sat on the stool. She inhaled deeply when the first ring was inserted, the pain unbelievable. One down, one more to go. What had she done? After the second one was inserted, she admired her breasts in the mirror. She felt more feminine and daring as she paid the bill, driving back to Brett's house.

He and Brad were watching a movie as Sandy showed them her masterpiece. Brett nursed a glass of lemonade and was very quiet. Sandy could feel the difference in him right away, as Brad waited for his wife to come and get him.

Finally, Sandy agreed to take Brad home after hearing him argue with his wife on the phone.

"Brett, I'll be back in a bit," she said, guiding Brad out to her car.

All the way to Brad's house, he kept coming on to her, the brandy he had consumed making his words slur. Sandy just wanted to get back to Brett as she bid him goodbye in his driveway.

Walking back into Brett's house, she noticed once again how quiet he was. She wondered if he wasn't feeling regrets, knowing his wife would return the next day. Sandy had hoped he would resume his playfulness, but after dinner, he fell asleep on the couch, Sandy next to him.

About nine o'clock, he went to bed, with Sandy padding after him. She stroked him to firmness and they made love, but her newly pierced nipples wouldn't relent in their pain. She tossed a bit.

"What's the matter, Sandy?" he asked her.

"My nipples hurt so bad," she said, holding her breasts.

Brett got up and had a cigarette, then drank from a bottle of water next to his bed.

"Sandy, I'm uncomfortable having you here. What if Eva suddenly walked in?"

"I thought she was coming back tomorrow?" Sandy asked, looking at the clock.

"She might, or she might come home early. I don't need her catching you here."

It was twelve thirty a.m....Friday. Miserably Sandy got out of bed, gathering her clothes, suddenly feeling vulnerable. She had wanted one more night. It would not be. Getting dressed, she walked to the back door.

"Good night, Brett," she said, giving him a kiss. "Get some sleep, ok?"

Driving home, she sadly pondered the life of the other woman. Why did it have to be her?

The following week, she went to Brett's to bring him supplies for their CD's. He busily taped a letter to his wall, gathering up the words in his mind.

"Sandy, I have to tell you something, except this is personal, not business."

Sandy held her breath, her heart racing. Was he going to tell her it was over?

"Sandy, I love you, and I've decided that you won."

"I won...what?"

"Me, you won me over. I can't fight it anymore." Seeing the look of satisfaction in her eyes, he quickly added, "but I'm not leaving Eva, so get that idea out of your head."

Sandy hugged him.

"I suppose now that you've won the conquest, it's over. You girls always do that," he said, going to the kitchen and helping himself to a beer.

"No, quite the opposite. With me, it's the real thing." Standing on tiptoe, she kissed him deeply, feeling his arms around her. Pulling her away, he told her to go see the surprise he had for her in the bathroom. Walking in, she saw four vibrators of different sizes sitting by the sink.

"Oh my goodness..." Sandy felt a blush rising in her cheeks.

"Go ahead, help yourself, show me what you can do with it," he said, smiling.

Picking one up, she took it to the den, stripped off her jeans and began to pleasure herself. Brett sat for a few minutes, watching her, then walked over to participate in the fun. Soon, she was calling out his name as she soared. He smiled.

Spring evolved into summer. As Brett backed his prized Chevy van out of the garage, an idea formed in his mind. Calling Sandy, he asked her if she'd like to come over and help him wash his van. Smiling into her phone, she agreed.

The water and suds felt good on Sandy's fingers as she lovingly caressed the sponge around the grill. Brett took another swig from his beer can and watched, loud music blared from his CD player.

"I have good news for you," Sandy said. She pulled out a note from the lab that did her blood tests. He took the card from her and read it. It said, "results negative." He looked to her for explanation.

"It's over, Brett, the cancer is gone." She smiled at him. He grabbed her in a huge hug.

"Oh, hun, I'm so happy for you!" He kissed her, feeling lighter than he had in awhile.

"That means I'll just be around to pester ya for awhile, I'm guessing!" she teased.

"Good, now get back to work," Brett teased, swatting her rear with a towel.

"OK, now what would you like?" Sandy asked. Brett handed her a dry towel, showing her how to polish off the chrome so as to not leave water spots. He was a gentle teacher as Sandy took in everything he taught her. Grabbing another towel of his own, Brett asked Sandy if her son, Joe, could help him do a lot of yard work that had gone undone. In actuality, he dreaded the idea of doing all the hard labor himself and needed help. Sandy readily volunteered Joe, who at sixteen, wanted a job for the summer.

Eva was livid, however, when Brett told her the news that night. "Why does he have to come over here every day?" she railed at Brett. "What's wrong with you? Why don't you do something for a change?"

"I do work around here. Your lunches and dinners don't happen all by themselves, you know!" he shot back. "Besides, with Sandy and I now doing a radio spot in addition to our writing and CD's, this will give us a chance to get more done!"

Eva folded her arms and glared, then in anger, stalked out of the room. Brett shook his head, thinking of how Sandy had landed this job for them. It wasn't a paying job, but it would give him the opportunity to be heard on air and her was grateful for that right now.

The next morning when he instant messaged Sandy, he filled her in on Eva's tantrum.

"Tell her to get over it, you have a lot to do!" Sandy wrote. On her appointment book for that day was a meeting with an attorney to file divorce papers against Harry, something she hoped would convince Brett that she was serious about starting over, Brett being included on her plans as the main focus of that desire. Sandy liked the idea of taking Joe over everyday, it would give her a reason to see Brett more often now. "I have an appointment to get my divorce done!" she typed in.

"It's about time," Brett wrote back. "We can't proceed forward professionally or personally until you do."

Sandy beamed at that response. There was hope yet.

For his part, Brett was becoming tired of Eva's constant torture. Sandy listened to all of his rantings about her, wishing he would just leave. "Come to me," she always thought. "I'm here and I'll take care of you."

He first day she dropped off Joe, Brett showed him around, telling him what needed doing.

"OK, guys, I'm off to work," she said. "Don't get into trouble," she warned Joe teasingly. "Goodbye, Brett," she smiled.

Driving off, she hummed a tune, her spirits high.

It was about ten a.m. when a voice nagged at her. "Something's wrong, something's wrong," it chided her. She couldn't shake the feeling. Finally at ten thirty, she made an excuse to call. Walking to the break room, she dialed Brett's number. He picked up the phone on the third ring.

"Hey hun, what's up?" she asked.

"There's been a bit of trouble," he told her quietly. Immediately Sandy thought of Joe.

"What did he do?" she asked sternly.

"Oh, no, Joe is doing fine, a great job. It was me."

"You? What happened?" she asked.

"My PO came over today…" he began.

Sandy sucked in her voice and listened.

"Sandy, she caught me with two beers…"

115

"Oh no!" Sandy whispered.

"She is going back to talk to the county attorney but I may have to do time for this…"

"Oh God, Brett, no!" Sandy almost cried. She looked at the clock. Not even eleven o'clock and she had to work until four that afternoon. "Oh Brett, I feel so bad…oh no…"

"I'm sorry, Sandy. Joe witnessed it, too. I am so embarrassed that he had to see that."

"I'll see you at four thirty, I get out of here at four. Take care, hun…Did you call Eva?"

"Yes, she said to call our attorney."

"OK, kiddo, hang in there. I'll see you at four thirty. I love you."

"K," Brett said, hanging up sadly. How could his PO have snuck up on him? He was assigned a new one that his former PO said was a real barracuda. Brett had a sinking feeling about this and told Sandy as much when she picked him up from his last appointment. She had been doing this regularly for about four months and loved it. Anything to help him out. Listening to him, she assumed that maybe he just worried too much. Instead, it came true.

Brett had answered the phone that morning, checking the number on the caller ID, thinking it was an inquiry about his mobile DJ business. Instead, it was Linda, informing him she was right outside his back door. At that point, he had to open it and admit her in. Pulling out the breathalyzer, she asked him to blow into it. Closing his eyes, he did so, knowing he would fail.

He did.

"Mr. Pearson, I'm, going to have to alert the county attorney about this. You have a reading of point 33. You aren't supposed to have a reading at all."

"It was only a couple of beers," he admitted.

"Two beers do not give a high reading like that," she said sternly. Making a note in her book, she snapped it shut, waiting for him to say something, Joe watching sheepishly. He felt bad for Brett, thinking about what his friends' reactions would be when he told them.

"I had some mouthwash, too, before you came in…" Brett began, wondering what Eva would say about this also.

"Mouthwash, Mr. Pearson?" Linda questioned. "I hardly think so. You're not supposed to be drinking at all! You'll be hearing from me in about two hours." With that, she let herself out of the house.

Brett watched her go. "Better get back to work, Joe," was all he could muster.

As Sandy pulled into the driveway at 4:37, her thoughts were all muddled. Her friend needed her…what could she do to help? Stepping out of the car, she heard Brett's loud voice. Going to the backyard, she saw him piling twigs onto his firepit, Joe sitting with a can of cola on the deck.

"Fuckin' PO, why did she come 'round here anyway?" Brett asked no one in particular. Looking up, he saw Sandy. "Oh, hi!" Brett said slurring his words. Sandy knew he had been drowning his troubles, a can open on the table nearby.

"Oh hun, what happened? Have you heard?" Sandy was near hysteria.

"Yup, I'm going to prison!" Brett announced loudly, snapping a stick in two.

Sandy gasped, then cried. "Prison? For how long?"

"As long as they want me. They have my balls in a vise, ya know!" Brett was angry. "Quit your crying, it isn't helping me!" He strode past Sandy to drink from his beer can.

"Oh, Brett, I'm so sorry!"

"Two beers, that was all, just two beers!" He finished his can, crushed it and went to a nearby cooler, helping himself to another. Popping it open, he drank long, then burped.

Sandy went to Brett, hugging him. "Hun, why? Why?" she was at a loss for words.

"Don't hug me! Please, back off!" he said.

Sandy stepped back, her hands over her mouth. She felt

helpless.

"When do you find out?" she asked.

"I'll be getting a letter in the mail soon, she said," Brett replied. "Until then, I have no idea."

"What did Eva say?" Sandy asked.

"She wants me to hire our attorney, but I said I won't. I'll do this one myself." He turned on the radio, then walked to the front of the garage. Sandy followed, hugging him once more as she watched the tears form in his eyes. He fucked this up, too. Feeling her arms around him, he wanted to give in, to grab her and not let go. Instead, he pulled away yet again, walking to the radio, turning up the volume on the player.

"Let's just listen to the music," he said, sitting down. Sandy sat next to him.

Soon, "Sunset Grill" came on. The music pulled Sandy in as she watched Brett move his hands in time, as if he were playing an instrument. Her heart filled with love. He looked at her, mouthing the words to the music. She swayed in time, regretting when the song was over. How would she live without him for whatever time he would be imprisoned, she asked herself.

Looking at her watch, she realized she had better leave before Eva got home. Sandy didn't want to be there for that. "Come on, Joe," she said. He went to the car. Sandy walked to Brett, giving him a kiss. "Hang in there, kiddo. I love you, remember that!"

He nodded, watching as she got into her car, backing out of the driveway.

The next few days were hard on both of them. Sandy dropped off Joe early, leaving for work, then went back after lunch, enjoying the afternoons as Joe worked on his chores and Sandy worked with Brett on their many projects. The sales of CD's were holding well and they had a program on internet radio that Brett was editing. Sandy would find topics of interest, research them, set appointments for speakers, then Brett had fun doing what he loved. It wasn't a morning radio spot, but it was something, which was better than nothing. However, as Brett sat at his desk, headphones on, listening to an interview, frustration set in. Sandy looked at him.

"What's wrong?" she asked.

"This is so damn time consuming, and we're not even getting paid for this!" he said, drinking from his ever present beer can.

"But it's a stepping stone! It's giving us recognition!" Sandy said with excitement, hoping he'd feel it, too.

"I don't even know where I'll be in six months! What if they lock me away? Then what?"

"Then we'll have had something," Sandy began.

"Grrrrr!" Brett replied, putting on his headset once more.

He was still at it the next day, and the next. His zeal for perfection was his downfall. He heard every nuance that the average person probably wouldn't even address. He was almost finished with the long ordeal of editing on the third day, when all of a sudden, the power went out. He watched in dismay as his computer went dead. All of his hard work, days of it, suddenly lost!

"Oh, shit!" he said, starting the computer up, hoping it had gone somewhere, saving itself. Dialing Sandy, she answered on the first ring.

"Hi, love, what's up?"

"I lost it," was all he said.

"You lost what?' she asked.

"The radio show. It's gone."

"What?" Sandy asked.

"The power suddenly surged and went out. Everything I had is gone!"

"Didn't you save it?" she asked.

"No, I can't save till it's done. I was almost done. Now, it's gone." Angrily, he took a swig from his beer. What a friggin' waste of time this was, and not seeing any green for it either really sucked.

"Sandy, I'm done with his!" he complained.

"Brett...." she began.

"No, I can't do it anymore!"

Sandy listened, took a deep breath and, feeling his pain, allowed him this. "OK, tell you what. You're right. You have put forth a lot of effort. You've worked hard. I understand your pain. I knew you were burning out. I asked you to tell me and you said, just yesterday, that you were ok with this. But I knew, you're not."

Brett felt relieved. He thought she'd be angry.

"Let it go, hun. Just let it go." Sandy felt like a failure. She had begged the owner of this station to give them a chance, and now, it would be gone.

The next morning, Brett opened the conversation on IM cheerily. Sandy was surprised to see him so happy.

"How ya doing today?' she asked

"I'm feeling cheerio!" he typed back.

"Seeeee? I knew you were burned out and I'll bet ya feel way better. Admit it."

"Oh, absolutely!" he typed back.

Sandy smiled.

That afternoon was hot and it was Joe's day off. Brett called Sandy at work, telling her that he didn't feel well and to not come over. Sandy was disappointed, but agreed.

They spent the afternoon instant messaging, Brett sharing his songs with her as she downloaded as fast as her computer would allow. Then he called her, just to say hi. His call was interrupted three times by Eva's calling him also, each time he became more annoyed.

"Now what?" Sandy asked when he came back on her line.

"She said I sounded too drunk to help her friend move tonight!" he replied indignantly. "Do I sound drunk to you?"

"No, you're fine," Sandy fibbed.

"I oughta just not be here when she comes home! Fuck her!"

"So don't be. Come over here," Sandy teased.

"I think I will! What's your address?"

Sandy, surprised that he would actually do that, gave it to him. Writing it down, he said he'd be over in half an hour. Sandy hung up. He's coming over! He's coming over! She thought. Just then the phone rang.

"Hello?" she answered.

"Have beer ready!" he told her, then hung up.

Sandy raced to the liquor store around the corner, purchasing what she knew he'd like, then tore back home. She timed him on the clock, watching, waiting and hoping he wouldn't change his mind. Finally she saw his huge Ford van pull into the parking lot. Walking to it, she guided him to a spot, then greeted him when he opened the door.

"Here," he said, pulling the keys to the van off of his key ring. "No matter how many times I ask you, don't give them back to me." Sandy put the keys on her own key ring.

"Agreed," she said.

He looked at the other keys on the ring. "I have keys here to my aunt's house. I can go there if ever I need to," he replied. "The people who love me have given me their keys."

"Well in that case, here," Sandy said, taking her house key off her own ring and handing it to him. "If ever you need to, just come on over to me."

Brett took the proffered key and slid it on his ring.

Sandy felt a bit awkward as she shyly led him into the house.

"Where's my beer?" he asked. She opened the refrigerator as he groused about Eva's reaction when she would arrive home and not find him there.

"So, I guess that means I'm all yours," he said. "You can do with me whatever you want to," he said, holding his arms out to her.

Sandy smiled and stepped into his embrace, kissing him. Turning, she held his hand, leading him to the bedroom, locking the door and peeling off his clothes as he peeled off hers.

"I've sent you a lot of music," he said, looking at her computer. "How about turning on some?"

Sandy walked over and made some selections, then returned to Brett. In her mind, this was a dream come true and she had no intentions of not enjoying every moment.

She stroked his beautiful naked body, tasting, teasing, tempting, kissing, the tattoo of a Pegasus horse on his chest entranced her as nothing else did. Soon she was astride him, riding to glory.

"Atta girl," Brett said as she savored her orgasm, kissing him. She looked into his beautiful blue-gray eyes, not wanting to give up this moment at all.

"I need to have a drink," he said. Sandy jumped out of bed, throwing on a t-shirt and shorts. Padding downstairs, she reveled in the quiet house as Brett followed her. Her dog greeted them at the back door. Brett loved dogs and stroked the dog's ears as Sandy watched, handing him a cold can.

"Ya hungry?" she asked. He shook his head no, tossing back his head and gulping down a swig.

"So whatcha in the mood for next?" she asked.

"Let's go outside," Brett suggested.

They walked to his van and he got out a pack of smokes. His thoughts were on Eva, as he angrily tamped the cigarette on the van's hood.

"She had no right to torture me," he said to Sandy. "You look like you're seven months pregnant!"

"Who, me?" Sandy asked, confused.

"No, that's what she said to me!"

She absorbed his every word, secretly indulging in his anger. Good! Maybe he would finally see the error of living with her. Sandy wanted him to give her up, to spend the rest of his life with Sandy. She could make him so happy. She wanted to take care of him, to appreciate him for always, to spoil him yes, and help him to stay out of mischief.

"All I do is cook for her, clean for her, make her lunches. All she does is dog me about every little thing," Brett went on.

Sandy rubbed his arm. Slowly they meandered back to her townhouse and back to her room, her kids all at friend's houses. They had the privacy that Sandy yearned for.

Just as the song by Aerosmith said, Sandy stayed awake all night, watching the rise and fall of Brett's chest as she stroked the hairs on it. Rising up, she began to kiss him all over, taking in every plane and curve. He woke up and rolled her on top of him where Sandy came almost immediately. The night slowly turned into day, Sandy wrapped up in his arms, exactly where she wanted to be.

That next day, Sandy called into work sick, so that she and Brett could spend the day together. It started out with Sandy grilling steaks on the grill and making eggs and toast to go with. Proudly she served it, watching with a smile as Brett shared his breakfast with her two sons.

The rest of the day passed with Brett telling Sandy stories on the front porch, Sandy absorbing his every word as he drank can after can of beer. She wondered deep inside when this magic would end and hoping that it never would. At no time did Brett make any attempt to call Eva, his mind set on being angry and annoyed with her. That night followed the same pattern as the night before, with Sandy keeping him occupied. Finally at 3 A.M., she fell asleep in his arms, waking at 6 a.m. to get ready for work. Before she left, she kissed him, which resulted in his wanting more attention. She brought him to orgasm, leaving him with a smile on his face and a song in her heart.

However, while at work, she had funny feelings going through her mind. Not sure what was wrong, she couldn't wait to finally be done at work, racing home when it was her time.

Driving up, she noticed that Brett was on the porch, but not smiling at her. She kissed him on the mouth.

"Hi, hun, what's wrong?" she took a spot next to him, then got up to get a drink of water, sensing that something was amiss. Once inside the house, she noticed his things sitting by the door.

Going right back outside, she looked at him.

"What's up?" she asked warily.

"Sit down," he told her. Sandy obeyed.

Taking a deep breath, knowing how much this would hurt her, he began, "I'm going back home."

Sandy gasped.

"I called Eva earlier. She wanted to come and get me after I told her that you had my keys, but I said I would wait for you to come home."

"Brett, no! What about us?" Sandy began to cry.

"Don't make this harder than it already is!" Brett said, a bit strong. He didn't want to hear her tears or her pleas. He knew that he needed to make things right with Eva. As much as he loved Sandy, Eva was still his wife and he owed her his allegiance for the many times she stood by him during his many arrests. He couldn't hurt her, either. Damn it, why were things so complicated?

"Brett, please, stay with me. I love you! Don't go!" Sandy begged.

"Sandy, I have to. It's the right thing to do." Brett looked at nothing in particular, he felt like such an ass, first for running off on Eva and now, for doing the same thing to Sandy.

"I can't believe you're really doing this to me," Sandy said. "Fine. If that's what you want, then go, just go." Sandy got up, getting his things, she walked with him to his van, the tears threatening to spill over, but she held them in check..

"Can I have my keys, please?" Brett asked. Reluctantly, Sandy pulled them off of her key ring. Shakily, she handed them to him, then reached up for a kiss. He gave her a quick peck, then got into his seat.

"Brett, IM me when you get home, just so that I know you're safe, OK?"

He nodded.

Sandy stood back as he turned on the ignition, then with a slam of the door and a wave, he pulled away, Sandy stood rooted to the spot until she could no longer see his van. Going into the house, an overwhelming sense of loss assailed her as she fell across the bed, crying.

When Brett got home, he found a note from Eva, saying that she would come home immediately upon his arrival to talk. She was forgiving and loving, just wanting him back. Going to the computer, he typed in to Sandy, "home safe." He looked over the mail sitting there, finding a letter from the county with the date for his court hearing. He told Sandy about it as well as the note from Eva.

"I guess you both love me too much," he typed. "though I don't know why. I don't deserve it."

Sandy's heart sunk. Why did he have such a low opinion of himself?

"This letter from the county might as well say, "come prepared to be fucked over," he wrote.

"When is it?" Sandy typed back.

"Stirring the pot, are you?" Brett asked.

"No, just concerned is all, I do care about you."

"Late July," he typed back. "You might as well find someone else," he continued. "Why hang out with a felon like me? It's been a great year, time to move on."

Sandy, reading that, felt her heart sink even more. Brett was depressed and taking it out on himself. He walked away from the computer then, his mind preoccupied on what Eva's reaction would be shortly when she would walk in through that door.

When Eva got home from work, she went to Brett, hugging him, leading him to the bedroom, where they made love as she said over and over how sorry she was for whatever made him leave. He felt grateful for her acceptance as he guiltily thought of Sandy. What a predicament he had gotten himself into.

Chapter 11

Sandy didn't know exactly when the idea to do what she did came into her head, only that to her, it seemed the right thing to do. There was a movie producer who had been interested in maybe turning her books about Winston into a movie. She had sent him the stories, awaiting word. However, it seemed that because this was a small studio, investors for this type of work were few and far between. Sandy was hoping for a contract, if for nothing else, just to say she was somebody. As she sat thinking about it, the idea came to her to fake it when Brett brought it up in IM.

"So, what ever happened to that offer?" he asked.

"I'm waiting to hear back, should be any day now. They really liked the movie idea and are sure it'll be something wonderful." As she said it, she went to the website of a famous studio, copying and pasting their logo to her documents. Then, going to another website, she downloaded an official looking contract, pasting the logo on it and, adding her book's title, she included hers and Brett's name, along with an offer of money. It looked good, but how would she get away with it, she wondered. Brett really needed some motivation. It seemed lately, with his court hearing looming, that he was more focused on his problems than his goals. This might be just the thing to revive his spirits. She figured she could always say the deal fell through, if it had to come to that. Deals fell through all the time. A few hours later, dialing his number, she spoke eagerly.

"You'll never guess what I just got in the mail," she began in a sing song fashion.

"What?" he asked, chuckling over her enthusiasm.

"A contract!" she said excitedly, praying he would believe her.

"For a book?' he asked, sipping his beer.

"No, silly, a movie! Remember that producer I spoke with? Well, he's offering us what could be big bucks if we agree, what do you say? Wanna sign this contract with me?"

Brett was stunned. A contract? Sandy was going to share a contract with him? He couldn't believe his luck. Dollar signs floated through his head. Eva would be so proud of him!

"Sure, when do you want to bring it on over?" he asked.

"How about tomorrow?" she suggested.

"See ya then!" he agreed.

The next day, as he looked at the contract, he talked excitedly of his plans. He was so happy for this moment as Sandy held the pen. He read all the jargon, which seemed easier than he thought it would be, then went off on a tangent as he told stories of his life.

"Come on, kiddo, sign it!" Sandy said, handing him the pen. She was apprehensive, how much did he know about contracts? More important, she didn't want to leave a copy of it behind, Eva would take one look at it and, knowing her, bring it to work with her where those high falutin' lawyers she worked with would see through it in a heartbeat. No way, a lot was riding on this and Sandy did NOT want to blow it.

Finally, Brett signed it, then Sandy. She picked up a fresh can of beer, popped open the lid and, handing it to him, opened one for herself.

"To us, may we have a long and successful future," she said, tipping her can to his. "Congratulations, hun," she said, sipping on it.

"It's yours, you're just sharing it with me," he relied.

"But, we are partners, 50/50," she added, reaching up to him for a kiss.

As the summer wore on, Eva began to complain more and more about Sandy's visits at what she considered her house.

She tortured him endlessly about the fact that Sandy even drew a breath in her house.

"For God's sake, Brett, she's like your second wife, she knows more about you than I do!"

Most times, Brett would dispute it, saying they worked together, which Eva had her doubts.

"Working? On what? Where's the money, Brett? Do you realize that for all this time you have been "working," I haven't seen any checks? I don't trust her!"

Brett would merely walk away. He didn't need this conflict and hated her berating him. Of course, he would tell Sandy, which deep down motivated her to continue making up "projects" to make it appear as though they really had excuses to be together. As long as Eva was clamping down on their relationship, Sandy needed reasons to hang onto him. Plus, she was hoping that in time, Brett would see that Sandy could provide for him also and leave Eva.

Brett often thought of that too. As much as Eva had been there for him in the past, her constant nagging was wearing him down. He thought more and more of just packing his bags and leaving her. He felt so torn between his loyalty for Eva and his love for Sandy. It consumed him day and night.

His court hearing came. Standing before the judge, she handed down a sentence of three weeks with possible work release. Breathing a sigh of relief, he and Eva went out to dinner.

Meanwhile, Sandy paced and fretted at home, waiting for word. Finally at eight o'clock that night he let her know.

"Well?" she typed in.

"All systems are go," he wrote back, explaining the time he needed to do. He actually seemed relieved that it wasn't more. Sandy was so happy, but sad about the fact that he had any to do at all.

"So, we'll plug away at what needs doing before I have to turn myself in in November."

"It's almost August. We need to hustle," Sandy said.

"We will, never fear." Brett reassured her.

By now, Sandy had Brett believing they had four contracts with movie studios based on the work they did with their audio productions. She was very careful to never let on more than he needed to know, which infuriated Eva to no end. She wanted details and when they weren't forthcoming, her suspicions became more aroused.

"How do you know she isn't taking advantage of you?" she demanded to know one day when Brett was IMing Sandy.

"Because I trust her," was his reply.

"Well, I don't!" Eva said.

"You're just jealous because you have a job you hate and have to answer to "the man." I answer to no one."

"It's more than that and you know it," Eva said with a flounce in her attitude.

Brett realized that he'd better settle her down or there would be no living with her in her present state of mind. He teased her, making her smile, then caressed her shoulders.

"You know, my guy is feeling lonesome, maybe you and he ought to get acquainted realll soon," he suggested.

Turning around, she hugged him.

"Oh, Brett, I hate it when we fight so much," Eva whined.

"So, don't. You're the one bringing all this shit up, not me. I just work here."

"All I am asking is, where's the money for all this work you do?"

"Sandy reimburses me for beer, cigarettes, you name it."

Dropping her arms, she glared at him. "Like I said, a second wife." Eva went to her bedroom, slamming the door.

Brett sighed. There would be no winning this round. His mobile DJ business, which he had to give up when he had jail time the previous year, was awful quiet, despite Sandy's involvement in creating a website and contacting possible venues, as well as lots of word of mouth advertising. She even helped him at a couple of shows, mingling with the crowds and really getting into it. Brett was happy to have her along.

Eva wasn't and said so. Still, there were no solid leads in acquiring more business through that. In a way, he was relieved. He had put in so many years and was literally burned out. In another, it was an easy six hundred bucks, just play what the people wanted and bullshit with the best of them. Only, Sandy made it more fun than Eva did when she accompanied him. Once again, his thoughts turned to Sandy.

Slowly she crept into his thoughts more and more. He thought of nothing else. He was becoming distracted, which wasn't helping their business any. He had wanted to record another CD, but every time Sandy was around him, all she wanted, with his blessings of course, was sex and more sex. The woman was starved for it! He hated being clung to, but she had a subtle way about her that made her irresistible. Other times he would take her to his finished basement where a large stereo sat, waiting to be used. Brett would pick out music and, with the sound blaring loud enough to rattle the dishes, in Eva's words, they would dance in time, Sandy being so thoroughly uninhibited, which made Brett continue. He was a master at this and told her so. Still, with his jail date looming, he had to concentrate!

It was 1:30 a.m. as Sandy sat at the computer, typing up a story that she and Brett were to use on their "contract" with a major studio. Sandy felt so torn. Why had she begun this? It was extremely frustrating, keeping up the charade, yet she knew she had to. One, she wanted Brett all to herself. As long as he thought he had something coming, surely he would leave Eva... eventually! Two, she wanted to build up his confidence level. He needed something to concentrate on other than his impending jail time. She wanted him to have work release also and what better way than to have work to do? Suddenly the orange blinky light came on. It was Brett.

"Well, the cat's out of the bag," he typed in.

"What do you mean?" Sandy asked back.

"I told Eva about all my other 'girlfriends.' I need sex, a lot! She's fine with it."

Sandy thought he was being ridiculous! "You mean she's fine with it, as long as it isn't ME...right?" Sandy wanted to know.

Brett realized Sandy was right. Eva had said he could fulfill his desires with anyone, as long as he didn't fall in love. God, what a mess. He loved Sandy too much to let her go.

"Yes," was his only reply.

"Well. See? We're still back to where you began," Sandy replied sadly.

It didn't help that day that Brett had more than his share of Bloody Mary's, so that by the time Eva came home from work that evening, his lips were extremely loose. She happened to look at the e-mail he composed to Sandy about a gal she knew who was willing to meet with Brett. She went into a rage, calling Sandy.

Sandy, seeing his number on her caller ID, picked up the phone.

"Hello, sweetie!" she sang out, thinking it was Brett who had called.

"I'm not your sweetie!" Eva spat out.

Sandy's heart plummeted, but she sailed forth.

"Oh, you can be my sweetie, too!" she chuckled, hoping for brevity. What now, she thought.

"What is this, you're finding a girl for Brett?" Eva demanded.

"What? What are you talking about?" Sandy faked a lie.

"Don't give me any shit! I know what's going on and I'm not going to put up with it!"

The next sound was a click, followed by dial tone. Sandy's heart beat in double time as she looked at the phone, then hung it up. What the hell did he do now? She wondered.

She paced and fretted, watching for the indicator light on

her computer to go on, but all was still. Suddenly, the phone rang. Looking at who it was, Sandy cautiously answered. It was Brett.

"Didn't I tell you a long time ago that I belonged to Eva?" he asked.

"Yes," Sandy answered quietly.

"We could have gotten away with this forever, but I spilled the beans to her. She knows about us. I'll be finding out what you went through with your divorce from Harry, because I think she's planning one now for me. Everything I have will be gone."

"Brett, I don't know what to say…" Sandy said with remorse.

The sound of a dial tone became the only sound she heard next to her own heart beating. Why did Brett blame everything on her? He was a willing participant also! It took two to tango, after all.

That night she tossed and turned. Sleep was not an option. Getting up, she turned on her computer monitor, only to see that Brett was instant messaging her. Only it wasn't Brett.

"If he loves you as you say he does, then why is he still here with me?" came Eva's question. "You care about yourself and Brett and nobody else. You've lied and deceived me. I will NEVER forgive you for this. You just couldn't leave him alone."

"Eva?"

"What?"

"I am so sorry for all of this, but I do love him, and he loves me. We tried so hard to keep it to ourselves, to deny our feelings, for so long. we tried so hard to just "keep it business." Both of us never wanted to hurt you. It was all he said, and I told him that I really liked you also and I didn't want to see you hurt."

"Really? so why is he still here?"

"Because he said that he wanted to stay with you, he never had it so good with anyone, that it's the house and everything he did with it, the level of financial comfort you provide, he has it so good with you, the only thing I can provide him with his my heart. He wanted so much for you and I and him to all get along, to be together in harmony and love. That was what he was striving for. I told him I could live with that. He kept saying he didn't want to see his marriage to you break up, but that he also loves me too much to give me up. I was willing to be the second fiddle, because I didn't want to give up even that. Eva, I do love him, yes, but I do also care about you. Hard to believe but true. I don't want to see you hurt. Yet hurt is what happens in this cruel game. Are you still here?" Silence… "I am so envious of you, because you have him and I am given only what's left. I would walk thru fire for him, and I have. I have defended him to everyone, including to the judge, his PO, the people he used to know at his old radio station. I put my own reputation on the line so many times for him. I would do it again in a heartbeat. If I could sit down with you face to face, it would be so much easier than all of this typing. I mentioned that to him not too long ago, that we should all just talk this out. He said no. He was so embarrassed that you knew about all the girls he was doing. He wanted to run away that one morning. I begged him to stay and not take that easy way out. He did and was able to talk to you about it. Eva?"

"STOP!!"

"Then would you talk to me? Yell at me- something!"

"Sandy, Have you lost your friggin mind?"

"Who is here now? No, I haven't lost my mind."

"ME!"

"Me who ?"

"ME! Get some sleep!"

"I can't… too much on my mind. I slept for about an hour awhile ago."

"Sandy… Deciphering your rendition is a bit tuff right out of the gate. Your thoughts and mine need to be considered individually."

"I'm here. I'm listening …" Sandy thought once again

133

she was typing to Eva. "I would do anything for him, you should know that, but...I would also do anything for you, to the best of my ability."

"Sandy, I'm mad at you right now."

"I know you are, accept your anger. I am willing to work with you and that anger. I don't wish to humiliate you."

"We gotta stop or I walk." Brett was adamant. Eva was harassing him big time, waking him from a sound sleep to torture him for Sandy's response.

"Stop...?"

"ALL! I mean it, ALL!"

"Please, don't walk," Sandy begged. She couldn't bear the thought of losing him. What had happened?

"WIYEP is done! BYE!"

Sandy gasped.

"Your CD's, comp and anything else you consider yours is available when Eva is here to deliver it. Unlike others, I fulfill my end."

"What? please...no! Don't break this up!"

"I have had to make a choice, Sandy."

"Brett... not that." Tears coursed down her face.

"THE END!"

"Please, I beg you … everything we were on the edge of …"

"Sandy, I'm not strong enough to defend myself.. Ya gotta go, kiddo."

"I can't …" Sandy felt as though a truck hit her. "Please, don't make me! Our contracts? How can they be fulfilled now?"

"Lose all or lose everything....what would you do?" Brett was torn, but the desire to hold onto all the material possessions he had acquired through Eva over the years won out.

"Hun, please," Sandy begged. "Why? I can't do this!"

"I can still work for these people if they pull their heads out."

"I need you to work with me as well! You said you loved

me, my kids…"

"WHY? Scroll." Brett felt like such an ass for putting Sandy through this, but Eva was standing behind him, watching every transmission that came through. Her mouth was filled with such a bitter aftertaste as she watched Sandy squirm in print. The little bitch just couldn't accept no as an answer, could she?

"How do I tell them?" Sandy continued. "I can't lose you! I so don't want to lose you! please....don't do this...I did so much for you. I gave up so much for you!"

"STOP!"

"Without you, I am nothing. You have given me my life. I fought my illness because you gave me the motivation to do so." Sandy didn't know about Eva's presence or she would have been embarrassed about how much she was carrying on.

"Yer welcome."

"I can't lose you now! we are too much alike! Brett, please...don't cut me loose. I am no one without you. With you I could do anything. I can't do these mall shows without you!" A plan that Brett had to promote their work was to set up a display at upcoming mall shows for the holidays, working with Sandy. "There would be no point. Please, don't leave me hanging this way! What about your work release? This will change that now. I never wanted that to be affected. You don't deserve to just sit in jail. Here's the deal. without you, I am not doing mall shows. There will be no SSB, why? What's the point in that, or Ricky, SD or MI?" All work they had been producing, now, up in smoke it would appear. "I have nothing to work for. The movie contracts? I am informing them we are done. I will not adhere to them." Sandy was really reaching now out of desperation. There were no contracts, but she needed a reason to hang onto Brett and this was the only plausible one right now. "I feel no anger in all of this, only sorrow. Sorrow in that we are letting so many other people down. Yes, one person's life changes so many others, for good or bad. I will pick up the CD's and stuff, or you can give them away at Halloween. as you see fit."

It was quiet now on Brett's end, yet Sandy continued on, like a truck with no brakes. "I do NOT want this business to end. You have been a big part of it, without you, it would be nothing. You know that. So many have depended on us and the world is now crashing down. My own world is crashing down. Hurt? yes, I am hurting, in a way that no cancer or liver pain can even compare. You say you are not strong enough to defend yourself? Neither am I. I can't go on. I choose to not go on. When my sister died, it was horrible. This is worse. Harry will be loving this... he wanted me to fail so bad. I guess he has his wish now. Please, reconsider the business at least. You worked so hard to just throw it out now...you earned it, you deserve it. What will you do now? This is your legacy too. Our work had so much potential....I swear to you, I will keep it strictly business if only you would tell me that WIYEP will not quit. I beg you this. Please. Let's finish what we started on the *'Circle of Life'* story yesterday. Remember that story I started way back when? *"Because of Friday,"* now has an ending. A sad ending."

Tearfully, Sandy backed away. It was 3:14 a.m.

"So why quit your business?" Eva demanded to know. She had dollar signs as well as an agenda of her own. She wanted the power of being the talk around the water cooler and having Hollywood connections appealed to her. "Just tell that bitch that you're my property and to keep her hands off. Otherwise, you're throwing away a lot of money from your movie deals. You're a damn fool if you do that!" Eva dictated.

Brett fiddled with a pen, clicking it rapidly. "You can handle that?" he asked her quietly.

"BUSINESS only, or I'll destroy it with my bare hands. Clear?" she assailed.

"OK. Business it is." Brett sat defeated.

Eva readied herself for work, but the wind was completely taken out of her sails. Sitting on the steps leading to the bedroom, she was deep in thought. Why? Why was that little vixen interfering with her life, her husband, her marriage? Eva hated her with a passion as she hated nothing else. Brett denied that anything had happened, that he did not sleep with her, but something deep inside Eva screamed betrayal.

Walking into the den, she confronted Brett once more.

"Do you mind telling me once more what she meant by the fact that you just stay with me for *my* money? Would you PLEASE explain that one?" she yelled.

"Oh, fuck! She said it in anger or confusion or something! Why would I just hang out for your money?" Brett was incensed. It just never ended! This whole affair had cost him dearly in trouble and torture.

"*You* tell *me*! You have no real source of income. Maybe she's on to something. Maybe I ought to just kick your dumb ass out and see where that takes you, except that I won't give that BITCH the pleasure of moving you right in to her clutches!" Eva stormed out of the room.

Brett looked at the clock. "You're running late," he reminded her.

"DON'T tell me when I'm late, you bastard. I do what I please...just like you!" Grabbing her purse, she stomped to the back door.

"Don't I get a goodbye kiss?" Brett asked quietly.

"Ask HER for one!" Eva screamed, then slammed the door. A cat who was napping on the chair jumped up at the sound, running upstairs and hiding under the bed. Brett shook his head. Women!!!

After she completed her morning work with the kids in her care, Sandy went home, heart hammering away. She couldn't stand it any more. Grabbing her keys, she drove to Brett's house. Finding his back door locked, she went to where she knew he had a spare key. Fitting it into the lock, it turned and she looked at Brett apprehensively. He glared at her.

"Thanks so much for telling Eva I'm just here for her money. That made me look real good. I'm getting some beer from the liquor store. You can come with or stay here, it's up to you."

Sandy went with and plead her case. Brett was so angry at her as she cried.

"Quit the crying! Eva conceded and said we can work together, WORK and nothing more. Ya got that?" He turned into the liquor store parking lot and got out. Sandy waited in the car.

Sandy nodded, praying with relief that it wasn't completely over. Yet a part of her selfishly wanted more and she wondered how she could deal with the close proximity and not fall apart.

"I knew that as I was writing it," Sandy typed in the next day. She was referring to Brett's creativity. It was 3:44 a.m. "Wanna know why? Cuz even last summer, when I barely knew ya, I was running ideas past you on air and you were helping even then. You have the soul of a writer within you."

"How ya figure?" Brett asked back.

"Because you have the creativity to accomplish great things. You know what you want to say and how to say it."

"I am not allowed to be around you." Brett typed as a reminder. Sandy was surprised he was instant messaging her at all. "Eva is quite bitter right now. If we behave and let her cool down, she'll come around. I can't let you do the Maplewood shows all by yourself, however. That isn't fair." Brett was wondering how that would work out, the show was two months away, as was his incarceration. The world was closing in around him.

"I still miss you, you know," Sandy typed wistfully.

"I think we spend quite a bit of time together still."

"Yes, but we're not supposed to be "that way" and when we do spend time together, you are questioned like a murder convict or something."

"Can't be helped, I guess." Brett responded. "sux bein' me."

"Sux being both of us. I am on the outside looking in... that hurts, too."

All too soon it was time for Sandy to go to work. Later that afternoon, Brett opened a letter handwritten to him. Reading it, he felt his heart thump double time.

"If you think you can protect Sandy, think again. Her days are numbered. When I am done with her, you're next."

Shaking, Brett dialed the police, explaining the note. Who was it from? Harry? Was Harry jealous now that the divorce was finalized? After the police arrived and made out the report, taking the letter as evidence, Brett called Sandy.

"I got a letter in the mail today," he told her.

"Oh?" Sandy asked, feeling a bit rushed. The kids were racing around, yelling.

"Sandy, it was a threat." He told her the contents. Sandy gripped the table she was standing next to. "Oh my God, oh my God," she uttered over and over.

"Sandy, is this from Harry?"

"I don't know, what was the writing like?"

"It was a typed letter, but the envelope was hand written. I gave it all to the cops. They'll be getting in touch with you."

"Brett, I'm scared! What if...?" Sandy asked.

"Don't worry, hun, I'm here," Brett said. "Just be careful. Let me know what happens, okay?"

"OK, thanks, Brett. I love you."

"I'll talk to ya later." Brett replied, not responding to Sandy's reply. Eva walked in just then as he hung up.

"You'll talk to who later?" she demanded to know.

"Sandy. I received a letter in the mail, I called the cops. It was a threatening letter that I think her ex sent here."

"Her ex? How would he know where we live?" Eva demanded. It had been a hard day at work and she didn't need this now, not from that bitch anyway. "Great! We're moving! I'm NOT staying around here waiting for every asshole to find us!"

Brett got a can of beer and drank most of it in one gulp. It was going to be a long night...again.

"I got quite the reaming for that same thing." Brett typed in early the next morning in response to Sandy's comment about being a prisoner in her own home.

"I didn't even clean the office." Sandy typed back. It was yet another job she took on to make up for the lack of income she had since Harry left. "I woke up an hour ago and there was that same car parked outside that I saw a few nights ago, so I said, fuck it, the office will have to wait. Someone is waiting for me." Sandy stopped typing long enough to read Brett's words. "What now, hun? A reaming for what?"

"For us being holed up as prisoners. Call the cops and report the suspicious vehicle." Brett was scared for her. One more thing to worry about. His problem child, he often thought.

"I did, then I went back to bed. I am not talking to anyone... BTW...the cops never did get back to me here last night. My level of protection is zero. I am a walking dead person."

"Would that be the sequel?" Brett teased. "Sandy, Dead Author Walking." He chuckled when he wrote it.

Sandy was not laughing. "Hun--go places, do things... he is after me, and as long as I'm alive, you're safe. I can only imagine what happened at your place last night."

"Yup, torture again. Eva may not be safe, though. I can see him going after her just to say....see how it feels."

"NO! He only will do it to me, he is jealous of you but is only messing with your mind. He wants only me and will do so to show YOU how it feels. When I am gone, he will back off. He is vicious. He wants for you to feel the pain of my absence. Better for you to live the rest of your life without me, than to also be gone and not feel that pain of loss. He is pissed off that we have done all of our work together. He wants all of it erased and to do so, he will get me out of the picture. When it is daylight, I have to get going. I can't just sit here all weekend. I'll take that risk only because of the things I must do for our business."

"So, how do you figure he found me?" Brett asked, ticked off that his security, which he valued so highly, was compromised.

"Maybe he pumped Joe for the info." Sandy suggested.

"Sandy, Joe wouldn't know my address."

"Joe hasn't been around all night, he was at a friend's house and I sent the other two away. I don't want them here if there is a confrontation. I'll do this myself. I don't have your addy written anywhere and I certainly have NOT given it out."

"I'm thinkin' that was part of the reason for him rummaging through your room." Brett said, referring to the night not too long ago when Sandy came home from work to find her things gone through in her room.

"Rummaging...who? Joe? As I said, it isn't written down. I tell no one nothing about you. Not any more than they need to know. I give out only your phone number or email addy. Only what is already on the web site."

"Then the only thing I can figure is he followed you over here. Is that car still out there?"

" I was JUST thinking that too and because white Tauruses like his are so common, I didn't pay attention. Seems we are followed everywhere, you and I for different reasons. I am so sick of it! I'll check." Sandy carefully looked out the window. "Yes. Raining too, now. They have their stereo loud, I can feel the banging from here."

"Not real bright, regardless who it is." Brett said. "I just opened my window. It was closed all night. 63 out."

"64 here." Sandy said, checking her computer. "Do you want that monitor today?"

"I have mine open to hear for mischievous activity. Yes."

"I am thinking let's wait til maybe Tuesday, maybe things will calm down a bit by then," Sandy suggested.

"I need it now," Brett said.

"Well, where should we meet?"

"Up to you."

"This is so stupid! Clandestine! How about at your grocery store in the parking lot?" she asked.

"ok," Brett agreed.

"What are you driving?"

"The Escort."

"OK, I'll be there by 8:30..."

"OK, you gotta look into a cell phone, too. For your protection."

"I have been checking plans already. I am pissed, Brett. He will NOT do this to me! I will survive! I figured that he would sign the divorce papers, then get even.

"Yep, ya did. One sick puppy that guy is."

"My fear is that he will make it slow and painful, just like all the torture he gave me in our marriage, like the last encounter we had. Two hours of following me around the house, hitting me, yelling, destroying things. It was horrible! For what? *For what???* Just because I am his...a possession he can no longer have! He always said he owned me. I was never his wife, I was his possession!"

"Lincoln abolished slavery, or hadn't he heard?"

"I often said that. I got hit for it, so I quit. There are so many things I never told you about my marriage to him. I didn't want to set you off. It was awful. But Teri knows."

"Nothing I haven't figured out already," Brett said, feeling her pain, as well as remembering the e-mail Sandy's daughter sent to him, in which she told him how she heard her mother crying in the night.

"She wanted him out for so long," Sandy went on. "I was never strong enough to do it. Now that I was and am, he still has a vengeance thing going. Do you think the last few months have been easy? The stress level has me set so high...it's no wonder I don't sleep."

"We are contacting our realtor on Monday." Brett said, angry that his life was upset. " I am constantly watching, because I am being watched."

"I am sorry you have to do this, Brett. Look at what has happened since you first met me. I feel so responsible and bad."

"I needn't look. Eva made an evening of pointing it all out."

"Again, I am sorry." Sandy felt miserable for him. "I can just hear her words. It must have been awful for you to hear it, too"

"Hard not to let her be mad. She should be. I sure have fucked up a lot. One man's life...yada yada yada."

"All I wanted to do as to write. I never thought it would end up this way."

"That's just it...you haven't. He has."

"But hun--it affects you. and anyone who has anything to do with me, like a ripple in the water, it goes on and on... now you're moving out of a beautiful house because of all of what I stand for. "Why?" by Annie Lennox is playing thru my head."

"I got the recorder out of the box and set it on the table. You should see this manual....eeek!" Brett said, referring to a new recording system they had for their work.

"I'm surprised that you are still "allowed" to be able to do this. I was waiting for that phone call that said, come get it, I can't use it."

"Nah."

"Why when we are on the precipice of something good, does someone have to louse it up?"

" I need this for more than just our stuff."

"Oh really? Like what?"

"Anything else that may develop."

"A lot, I hope!" Sandy tried to sound optimistic. "Shit, someone is at the front door. Hang on." She got up to scc what the fuss was about. "Now someone is yelling, dogs are barking. I have the cops on the phone."

"Yeehaa!"

"I am not answering it. Oh here, this is good. They will patrol the area , but won't just "come out.' Wonderful, protect and serve WHO? Assholes!"

"Who do ya think is at the door?" Brett asked, feeling helpless that he couldn't do more. "I'll just go and find out. Stay here," She returned shortly. "They ran away when I confronted them. From my bedroom window, of course! I didn't answer the door."

"Get a glimpse?"

"It was some guy, he got into that car and drove off finally. I demanded to know who sent him and all he said was, "you think you have problems now, it'll just get worse." Great. Find me a bridge. Nice, find me a lead weight, too!"

"That would be like letting him win."

"I guess the problems will still persist. HA! papers...what papers. I thought I'd be free, freedom has a price. How much am I worth to you, Symba?" Sandy asked, using Brett's on air nickname.

Brett laughed sardonically. "Trick question?"

"No. I said, freedom has a price, how much am I worth to you?"

"I have no idea how to respond to that inquiry."

"Give me something to shoot for! I need a reason to stay mad, stay focused, hang in. He is messing with my mind. You see what he is doing here, you know. He wants me to give in, to do something stupid. and in my present state of mind, it's working. I need to get rid of the emotional part and take this bastard out. They say the pen is mightier than the sword. They also say fight fire with fire.

"Tuff to do both."

"Then help me, Brett, to light that match I need to stay focused here, and he is weakening me as we speak."

"Why haven't you gotten another gun?"

"Why? because I don't want to give him an arsenal. He already has one, and it has been used against me."

"You can do better than that."

"Hun, I can't shoot at what I don't see."

"You need to be able to protect yourself. Everybody is on high alert. Calm down, Sandy. Hope for the best."

Sandy took a deep breath. "ok, just let me get this out, it's like a poison. excuse me, this'll hurt, but I need to do this... shit fuckpissgoddamnittmotherfuckinghellbastardeyesmotherfuckers on-of-a-bitchcocksuckerwhoremongerasshole. I wish he would burn in hell forver! There. Deep breath, and another. Now the tears." Sandy was crying.

"Such language from a lady," Brett said, understanding her frustration. "But you know what? If it festers inside, it'll hurt even more."

"I feel a bit better," Sandy admitted.

"I'm printing, burning, labeling, stuffing, loading, packaging & attempting to console you while keeping at Eva at bay....all at the same time. I'm supposed to be reading that manual for the new studio.

" OK, OK, I get the picture. I understand." Sandy took a deep breath. "I feel for you, I really do."

"As I do you, kiddo." Brett really felt for her. "The frustration level over here is at an all time high. 3 DWIs never got this house in such an uproar."

"I'm sorry, hun, what can I do?"

"I'll talk to ya tomorrow."

"k. thank you for letting me bomb earlier. I had to do that."

"Understandable."

"Thank you for being there. I mean "there" not there... you know? well yeah there, too…"

Meanwhile, Eva spent the afternoon quizzing Brett on every nuance of his relationship with Sandy. Finally, he couldn't handle it. Going to the phone, he dialed her number in anger.

"Hello?" Sandy answered.

"We're through!" Brett barked into the phone.

"What?" Sandy was shocked. Now what had happened?

"I mean it! It's over!" The only sound after that was the dial tone as Sandy held the receiver, wondering what she was going to do now. She felt numb inside as she walked slowly upstairs to her bedroom. Sitting at the computer desk, she couldn't move or even think. The phone's ringing jarred her to her senses. Picking it up, she heard Brett's voice.

"We need to talk. I can't take the scrutiny any longer."

"Brett, why do you want to quit?" Sandy asked.

"That's not important. What's important is that you tell Eva here how you will keep it business and why you keep hounding me even after I tell you we must just be about business."

Sandy felt a lump in her throat. So, it had to be this way then. Humiliation at it's worst. She swallowed her pride and spoke. The speaker phone was on and Eva was listening.

"Eva? I'm sorry I hurt you. I won't take Brett from you. I was mistaken and I promise, you have nothing to fear."

"Didn't I tell you that I was Eva's and that I wouldn't leave her?" Brett impatiently asked Sandy.

Boy, he was playing it to the hilt, Sandy thought. She felt it would be easier to go along with it, just to keep the peace.

"Yes you did and I refused to listen. Boy, do I have egg on my face now," she replied.

"So, you thought you could get away with funny business?" Eva demanded. " I have nothing to say to you. I don't trust you!" was her hot reply. Sandy felt small.

"I apologize," was all Sandy could offer.

"I don't want or need it! Brett, why are you putting me through this?" Eva wanted to know. This is ridiculous!"

"Because you need to get this out. I'm tired of you dogging me about shit! Talk to Sandy and work it out!"

"There is nothing to work out! Can I go now?" Eva asked, getting up from her spot on the ottoman.

The room became silent.

"She left," was Brett's reply. "I gotta go. I'll see ya in the AM," Brett said.

"Bye, hun, good luck," was Sandy's quiet reply before the phone line went dead.

"Sorry kiddo. I have to defend and protect myself. Self preservation, if ya will. I knew it was hurtin ya. So sorry." Brett had defended himself well after midnight before Eva finally gave up and went to bed. His was not an easy life, but he felt he deserved it for everything he had put her through and felt grateful that Eva even stood by him this long!

"Hunny--" was Sandy's initial reply.

"Bunny."

"You need to tell me and I need to know..."

"k..."

"Do you love me?" She waited, holding her breath. Well, that silence must be the answer then...

Brett smiled. "Hang on." He typed in, "Had to go ask the boss how I can feel. She says I can love you, but I can't say it or show it.

"Oh really? is she still up?"

" Just kiddin', kiddo!

"So....then? your answer is...and no kidding around anymore, hun."

"First bit of peace I've had in days."

Sandy wouldn't relent. "Well?"

"I do."

Sandy's heart warmed. "Yes?"

"Ya know I do."

Not giving up, she went on. "Are you IN love with me?" tick...tick...tick...tick..."

"I'm just here...that is all I can be."

"I understand. Self preservation and all. I just want you to be happy. Please, just be happy. If I have to stand on the outside looking in, all I want is your friendship."

"I never had to fight for a friend. This has been soooooo hard for me."

"I know, hun. Fight FOR a friend or fight to HAVE a friend...? You shouldn't have to make a choice like that. Everyone needs friends."

"Lucky to have even one friend these days." Brett laughed sardonically.

"Brett? you will always have me, I will not leave you, no matter how many times you shitcan me. True unconditional love is that way. I have never judged you, never trashed you, I hope I haven't tortured you. The stories that you have shared, all of your "secrets" I have never told."

"The secrets we must now contain," Brett reminded her.

"It seems trite to say it, but I do love you. A year ago, when you quit your radio station and you were cutting ties with everyone who just wanted to use you, you also said to me, "if you want to leave me, I will understand." At that time, I said I wouldn't leave you, why would I? Friends stick by each other. I hope that I have with you."

"U have."

"I have been right there with you. I have never held anything over you. You have been there for me. So, together we walk into the sunset. Not too many times in anyone's life can they look back and say that."

"This whole thing has been exhausting. Eva's fighting for me & you understand why."

"Remember that e-mail I sent to you about friends being either a reason, a season or a lifetime? You are a lifetime friend for me. I'll always be here for you, no matter where you move to. Ain't no mountain high enuff. Of course I understand why. I did it when my asshole ex husband was holding his torch for his G/F. All us women do that! Why? Cuz we are fools in love, I guess. Hopefully she'll back off a bit so that you can relax."

"That was the purpose behind the call. I just wanted you two to have it out and leave me alone for five minutes."

"Every word you utter will be scrutinized, however. If last night was an indication, you're living with a prosecuting attorney!"

"Ten minutes would've been even better. She wonders why I drink so much."

"I tried to have it out and she kept walking away. Yet I held back so much because I don't want her to torture you. if I could have, I really would have spoke my piece, but then, you would not have survived it. When she asked about us, I bit my tongue to not say...well, how about a three way? cuz that's what would make him happy. See? Just be happy, hun."

"Knowing how she feels about you, that was wise not to say that. But I would love it."

" I know, sweetie! Thank you also for saying I made you feel special. That warmed my heart."

"Of course, she chopped that one up," Brett typed in, wishing Eva would grant him this just once, that he could have a friend without all the justification.

"But I still felt special. I don't know what tomorrow will bring, or next week or next year. heck, I look at what has happened in the last year. but just know that I will do my best to keep us working together and of course, I'll just be here. you know that."

" I do. TY"

"Hugs, hun." Sandy felt a bit better, knowing it was she and he against the world. She realized then that she would have to step up her efforts to win over Brett. Eva had set the parameters and Sandy was prepared to fight also...at any cost.

Chapter 12

As time went on, Eva relaxed a bit in her attitude towards Sandy, after hearing Brett go on and on about the potential money they would earn on this new contract that Sandy had secured through a movie studio. In actuality, it was a trumped up excuse on Sandy's part to be with Brett as much as possible. Eva bit her tongue and bragged to her friends about the Hollywood influence her husband was divulging in. Only Sandy knew about the deception and as every day ended, she mentally kicked herself for the day when her house of cards would all come crashing down.

She noticed that Brett was quieter in IM, his depression level was increasing as he counted down the days to his incarceration. Sandy tried to brighten his spirits, but even in person, Brett was hard to console. If it were possible to chain drink, Brett did, one can of beer after another. Sandy had never known anyone to down an 18 pack in under 5 hours and still function as he did. She worried and fretted.

"I'm sorry you couldn't secure work release," she said as she helped him to cut peppers for a wonderful recipe he invented. He was preparing to go camping later that day and needed something to dwell on other than the stress level that was building. As soon as Sandy walked in the back door that morning, with her beautiful smile, Brett took her small hand in his large one, escorting her upstairs where he peeled off her clothes. He traced the tattoo on her pubic bone, one word which read "Symba," his nickname. Sandy wore it with pride and savored it every chance she saw it. It was worth the pain she endured stoically to have it inscribed. Making slow and deliberate love to her, she whispered her words of love to him, noticing how quiet he was. Brett hugged her to him, wishing his life could always be like this, sharing passion unhurried and sensual, before dressing to resume his cooking activities.

Sandy sat at his computer, coming up with a storyline for this supposed blockbuster movie, but ideas wouldn't happen. Brett's mind was on other things and he apologized for not offering assistance.

Brett could no longer handle the scrutiny of his probation officer constantly monitoring his activity. That thought figured heavily in his mind that day as he tried to come up with a plan to avoid her. He told Sandy that later that afternoon while she was at work. He called her, his words slurring. She felt for him, but became alert when he said he would call his PO and tell her to back off.

"Brett, no," Sandy said. She knew it would take just that one phone call, his PO would hear the alcohol in his voice and have him arrested on the spot. "Let me call her."

"Tell her I'm out of state. I know I have an appointment with her next week and I'll be back for that. That's all she needs to know."

"I'll do it for you, hun. Don't worry. She'll back off."

"Thanks, kiddo. I love you," he replied.

Dialing the number Sandy was given, she listened to the recording, checking her watch. The officer was gone for the day. Sandy left her message, embellishing it as she went, hoping to impress her. "Brett is in LA meeting with producers about our upcoming movie. He is aware of your appointment with him next Tuesday and he'll be there, have no fear. Thank you." Sandy then hung up, her heart beating loudly. All she needed was for the PO to call and verify her story. The cat would be out of the bag and the shit hitting the fan big time. Sandy was on borrowed time at this point.

Linda Studdard listened to her phone messages the next

day. Hearing Sandy's, she pursed her lips together, feeling the frustration rise. So, the high and mighty Brett Pearson had his business partner covering for him, eh? She pulled out paperwork, filing a motion for a court hearing. Won't he be surprised come Tuesday, she thought, as she signed her name on the violation of probation sheet. Failure to contact PO about leaving his residence for more than three days. Failure to inform PO of permission to leave town. Failure to return phone messages. Oh yes, Mr. Pearson, you will be seeing the inside of jail for a loooonnngggg time!

When Brett showed up for his appointment, she was waiting.

"Mr. Pearson, why do you have your business partner calling me, telling me you're in LA? Are you aware this is a violation of your probation?"

"LA?" Brett asked, surprised. He had to fake it, realizing then and there he was in deep shit. Sorry, Sandy, he thought…I have to fight this one on my own. "I wasn't in LA." he said with shocked surprise.

"Then, where were you?" she demanded to know, crossing her hands in front of her.

"I was in Wisconsin, helping my uncle."

"Why is she even calling me? This is your probation, nobody else can do it for you." Linda told him.

"I'm aware of that," Brett said.

Linda handed him a pink form.

"What's this?" he asked.

"It's a copy of your violations. You will be receiving a letter from the county attorney shortly."

"For…what?" Brett asked.

"You will be facing the judge. You're going back to jail, Mr. Pearson!" Linda said gleefully.

Jail? Shit! Brett was sunk. In his efforts to evade Linda's scrutiny, he played right into her hands. And what was with this LA shit? Sandy told him she said out of state! Damn it, anyway!

Eva waited for him in the car. She looked at her watch, wondering what the hold up was. She needed to be at work and still had to take him back home first. Brett strode out to the car, angrily getting in, clutching his papers. "Let's go!" he said.

"What's that?" Eva asked, merging into traffic.

"I'm going to fucking jail," Brett replied hotly.

Eva slammed on the brakes, nearly hitting another car. "For what?"

"Because Sandy told her I was in LA. She thinks I was gone."

"Why would Sandy do that?" Eva demanded. That bitch again, always horning in!

"I told her to get Linda off my back. I didn't think she would do this!"

"I told you to stay away from her! Now what? We get the attorney involved, *again*, which costs money, money I shouldn't have to spend. God damn it Brett, where's your fucking mind?" Eva shook her head, as she clutched the steering wheel.

"I don't want to talk about it! Just go!" Brett said.

Eva drove him home, dropping him off, tearing down the street. She was more than late by now.

A few minutes later, Sandy pulled in. Going into Brett's den, she felt rather than saw his mood. Giving him a kiss on the side of his head, she asked what was wrong. He told her.

"Oh, Brett! It was to get her off your back, not to cause more trouble! I'm so sorry!"

"Where did you say I was?" he asked.

"I said out of state, just like you asked," Sandy lied, covering her tracks. She didn't want to hear the fallout.

"So why would she think I was in LA?" he asked.

"I don't know, maybe she was leading you into a trap," Sandy offered.

"I am not accepting responsibility for any of this. It's all your fault. You will accept the fallout for this, you got that?" he spat out. He would not jeopardize his freedom. He was tired of jails and had seen the inside of more of them than he cared to admit.

Surprisingly, Sandy agreed. "I'll do what it takes to get you out of this, even if I means doing time myself," she said.

Brett was surprised then, but realized that she was so unselfish, she would do that time for him. He relaxed. "It's OK, hun, I did ask you to go to bat for me, but I was so drunk, couldn't you have agreed with me, then just not called her?"

Sandy shrugged. "I always do what you tell me!"

"I know, and I appreciate it. But this one time, it's costing me. Why do you always have to listen to me?" Brett pleaded.

"I'm sorry, hun." Sandy began to cry. "I only wanted to help you and I messed up!"

Brett hugged her to him. "I'll be OK. It's just that now I may have two jail times to do instead of one."

Sandy cried harder, thinking about that. His sentence for the two beers incident was in only two weeks. Sandy couldn't bear the thought of it.

"OK, get to the keyboard. We're writing a letter to my attorney." Brett said. Sandy blew her nose with a tissue and settled in the chair.

As soon as the letter was written and mailed, Eva called Brett. He informed her that Sandy just composed a letter to their attorney. Eva blew up.

"WHY? She got you in that mess, why do you have her writing letters now?"

"OK, tell you what," Brett said to her. "I'll go to the mailbox, get the letter and rip it up, then I'll type it out myself and mail it, how's that?"

"She does everything for you!" Eva said hotly. "She got you in trouble to begin with!"

"Have it out with her then and quit bitchin' at me!" Brett shot back.

"I fully intend to!" Eva yelled back.

Sandy sat listening to this exchange, feeling utterly

miserable. Brett hung up, looking at her. "Don't be surprised to find a note in your e-mail. It'll be from Eva."

"I heard," Sandy replied.

Brett got up from his chair, pacing. The mall shows were coming up and he had nothing done to prepare for it. Eva was laying the smack down also on his even being present with Sandy at them. Why were these two women fighting so hard to keep him? He didn't feel as though he deserved either one! These fights were killing his motivation level also. Even with Sandy there, she was so distracting, he wanted her all the time and she did nothing to prevent it! GRRR!

The day of the first mall show, Sandy went to Brett's house to pick him up. She was excited about this, promoting their audio CD's that Brett recorded of everything she had written with Brett's collaboration. This was a four day twelve hour per day event and Sandy knew it would be tough. She hoped her episodes of passing out could be kept under control. In the weeks leading up to this, she endured liver pain, an unwelcome leftover from receiving chemotherapy. She even had Brett smack her hard on her bottom, closing her eyes to the pain and allowing her mind to take her to a higher level, so that the pain became nothing more than a mild annoyance. Brett hated seeing her pass out, and though he would turn away when she went down, inside he was torn apart.

Finding their booth, Sandy set up as Brett went back to his van, retrieving their products. He was setting up a display for his mobile DJ business as well, a beautiful canopy of a Pegasus horse on a black background, ten feet across and suspended over ten feet in the air. Sandy loved it, feeling a sense of pride in the business they shared.

Once everything was set up, Brett turned to Sandy.

"Well, I'lll catch ya in a few hours," he said hurriedly, hating himself for his.

"A couple of hours?" Sandy's eyes narrowed. "What do you mean? We're doing this together!" She rubbed his arm.

"Sandy, you sell better when I'm not around. I'll come by around 11 with lunch." An idea occurred to him. "I gotta go home and record! You want product, right?"

Sandy nodded.

"Well, product won't happen if I'm sitting here for twelve hours! I'll bring you lunch."

"But, Brett, I'll miss you! I don't want to sit here all by myself!" Sandy began to panic, unsure why. She had done shows similar to this, although not as long, all summer and into autumn. Most were successful.

"Hun, I can't waste valuable time," Brett pleaded. "I will call you and check on you. Don't call me, I'll be recording. I have to do this, we're behind already and I only have nine more days before I have to go away." He looked into her eyes, his blue-gray ones begging her to understand. He didn't want to leave her, but he sure as hell didn't want to stay here all day. He hoped she would understand. Tears formed in Sandy's eyes. She was hoping they would spend quality time together.

"Let me finish recording, then I'll come back, OK?" He looked so convincing, Sandy nodded.

"I promise, I'll bring you lunch. Take care, kiddo and good luck." Brett gave her a quick arm squeeze, then strode off.

Sandy watched his back recede until she couldn't see him anymore. Heart heavy with sadness, she straightened out their table once more and put on the happiest smile she could, but inside she felt like mush.

Brett called at one thirty that afternoon. By now, Sandy's stomach was growling from hunger, she had to use a bathroom and she was annoyed beyond belief. Only one sale had been made and she wasn't happy.

Her cell phone rang. She snatched it up, seeing his number. "Hi, hun, missing you here."

"Sandy, I had recorded chapter 13. I was editing it. I had only about a minute left. Then my computer acted up and I lost it, everything!" Brett wailed. He sounded miserable.

"What? Oh, sweetie, are you sure?" Sandy felt so bad now, her problems were minimal compared to his.

"Sandy, I have checked and I can't find it anywhere! It disappeared!" he flipped through any and all folders, just in case it may have went into one of them with no luck. He knew Sandy must have been starving, but he wanted to finish up. "Tell you what, I'll keep looking, but I don't know if I am gonna have any luck. I'll talk to you later." His line went dead.

Sandy ended the call, looking at her cell phone. Setting it down, she looked around. No customers in sight. She used that chance to run to the bathroom, getting a bag of candy from the vending machine nearby. This was really fun, whoopee-ding! She thought. Why did she let Brett talk her into this? Four hundred hard earned dollars to secure this spot and there had better be sales to break even, she thought miserably. She walked back to her spot, seeing nobody that she missed and sat down, waiting.

Soon a familiar visage appeared and Sandy's heart thumped. Brett! And he had a cooler. She jumped up, smiling. That smile made him feel even worse. He literally abandoned her to do his recordings that didn't go right either.

"I hope you like yogurt," he said, pulling out a container. Sandy looked at it hungrily, pulling off the lid. He also had a rice side dish, some turkey and a fortune cookie. Sandy laughed at that one, picking it up.

"Remember, whatever it says, you have to add, 'in bed' at the end." he told her.

Opening it up, Sandy read the saying. "You will be complimented on your creativity...." she read..."in bed," both she and Brett finished. Laughing.

She ate the cookie while he went to the railing, looking down at the activity below them. He felt so bad for the failure that morning. "I'm just gonna do it to get it done," he said to Sandy.

Her brow furrowed. "What?" she asked. "That doesn't sound like the Brett Pearson that I know and love. Do it just to be done? Whatever happened to that perfect, anal side of you?"

"I fucked up! I just want to get done with this!" He scowled.

"Fine! Fine! Be done with it! There goes our reputation! So why am I even here then if all you're gonna do is mess up all the hard work you've done before?" she was taunting him and she knew it. He needed to hear it.

He continued to scowl. "Fuck it, I'm leaving! I ain't stayin' here!" he turned away. "Enjoy your lunch, maybe I'll see you later, maybe not!" He strode away.

"Brett! Brett! Wait!" Sandy called out.

He heard her call out to him, but ignored her. He felt like such an ass as he kept right on walking. Sandy stood forlornly, the food no longer appealing to her. Looking around at the people milling by the other vendors, she realized she had better put on a professional face, but inside she felt like hell.

It was three hours later when her cell phone rang. Looking at the number, she answered.

"Hello?"

"Hun, first I want to apologize for being such an ass. I shouldn't have left you that way."

Sandy was quiet, listening.

"Sandy? Did you hear me?" Brett asked her.

"Yes."

"I really am sorry."

"Brett, I know you are. I love you."

"I love you, too, hun. But guess what? I redid it and I think it sounds even better than the first one I did!"

"You did? Really?" Sandy's heart warmed. He *had* been working!

"You'll love this!" Brett sounded like an eager kid.

"I love anything you do, you know that!" Sandy replied.

"I don't know what happened or why, but maybe it was for the best," Brett said. "You never told me the dog dies in this chapter."

"I wanted you to see it as it happened, to catch the emotion of the moment. I know you don't preread anything."

"Well, it had the effect you wanted. Boy, you sure know how to kick ass! You're a great writer!" He meant it, too.

"What happened to you happens to me, too, when I'm writing," Sandy said. "I just growl and go on. What comes out second is usually better than the first attempt."

"I'll be by in a bit, I just want to put this away. What do you want for dinner?"

"Anything. I just want to see you," came Sandy's response.

"I'll be there. Hang in. Any business?"

"No, it's been very quiet. It's only Thursday, maybe tomorrow will be better. I have four more hours here and believe me, I'm watching that clock!"

"K, see ya," Brett hung up. No business?? This wasn't good! Poor Sandy must have been bored out of her mind by now. He looked a the clock. Eva would be home soon. He wanted to get out of the house before she came home. He didn't need her scrutiny of why he had to go back and check on Sandy. Putting some food in the microwave, he added some beer cans into the cooler, a travel mug, then the food. He fully intended to spend the rest of the day with her. To hell with what Eva thought, he owed Sandy this.

When Eva pulled in the driveway, Brett's van was gone, as was Sandy's car. So, he was with *her*! Eva felt her blood boil as she entered the house. No note or anything. She perused the mail, then checked the computer. It looked as though he finished another chapter in the narration he was doing. Eva felt that everything Brett did with Sandy was a waste of time. These were Sandy's books, why did Brett feel as though he needed to promote them with her?

When Brett approached Sandy, she was deep in a conversation with someone about her latest book, along with a CD project Brett had done for her.

"...and the story on this CD is in production right now with a movie studio, we're waiting for a release next summer,"

Sandy told her. The customer seemed impressed, but walked away without buying anything.

Not even the bit about the movie deal was hooking them! Sandy thought. Good grief, it was almost Christmas, one would think people would be lining up to buy their kids books!

Brett smiled at Sandy's sales spiel as he unpacked his cooler. Kneeling down behind the long tablecloth, he poured a can of beer into the travel mug. Sandy smiled back at him as he screwed the lid on, handing it to her.

"You look as though you need this," he said.

Sandy drank long and deep, covering her mouth with a polite burp.

"Thank you, hun. I missed you!"

"I did awesome!" Brett bragged. "I got that chapter done and edited. I can't wait for you to hear it, you're gonna love it!" He drank from the mug, handing it back to her. "I need a refill, it seems."

Sandy knelt down and opened another can, pouring the contents. Screwing the lid back on, she took another sip, then handed it to Brett. He gave her a plate that was wrapped in a towel. It contained a rice and chicken hot dish, which Sandy devoured gratefully.

"This is soooo good, thanks! I was waiting."

"Did you think I'd abandon you?"

"Well, maybe a little!" she teased. "Was Eva home when you left?" Sandy asked, looking at her watch.

"No, I got the hell outta Dodge before she got home. I didn't need her torture." Brett said.

Sandy just raised her eyebrows, but continued eating. Brett went to talk to the vendor next to them, returning a bit later. Sandy had a letter about upcoming mall events, which she handed to Brett. He read it, then was going to fold it, when an impish look came over Sandy's face.

"Hey kiddo, know how to make a paper airplane?" She looked over the railing behind their booth, where shoppers milled about, unaware of the show upstairs, it seemed.

"Yeah, I've made some, why?" Brett said, watching her reaction.

"Make one and we'll fly it," Sandy smiled.

Brett folded the paper, showing Sandy how to do it.

"Where should I aim it?" he asked. They both looked once more over the rail.

"See that spot right there?" Sandy pointed out, "right there."

Ya sure?" Brett questioned.

"Go for it…what are ya, a wuss or something?"

That alone set Brett off. He hated being called a coward. Symba, Airwaves Warrior, that was him.

"OK, here goes," he said, aiming it. He drew back, letting it sail. It did a loop, then straight for the gal at the information desk it sailed…and landed! Brett and Sandy ducked behind their Pegasus canopy as Sandy covered her mouth, giggling like a schoolgirl.

"Oh, Brett, did ya see the look on her face? 'Where did it come from?' She wanted to know…hahahahaha."

Brett loved Sandy's enthusiasm. Where was she so many years ago? She made him feel so special.

Soon it was time to close up for the night. Brett carried her things to her car, then suggested a beer. Sandy slipped her arm into his and together they walked in the bitter cold night air to a restaurant that also served liquor. Brett told Sandy to order a Bloody Mary for him as he went to the bathroom. She sat and smiled at him, his heart swelled with pride. She was so beautiful!

Coming out, Sandy joked that when she told the bartender she wanted two Bloody Mary's, he told her he'd make one, then give her another when she was done, thinking that they were *both* for her. She said she had a friend with her who was to join her shortly. Brett laughed.

As they sipped the drinks, he regaled her with stories,

of which it seemed he never ran out. Sandy leaned into him, not wanting to miss a word. She loved his tales. He ordered a beer, urging Sandy to get one also for herself, which she did. All too soon, It was almost eleven o'clock, yet Brett didn't want to leave. He enjoyed Sandy's company and said so.

"Gonna be a busy day tomorrow…and the next day…and the next…" Sandy said with less enthusiasm. Brett walked with her to her car and she started it up, wishing it to warm up faster. As she pulled out of the parking lot, he looked at her.

"I wish Eva was out of town," he said. "Then you could just stay with me."

"Me too," Sandy smiled, thinking of the possibilities.

"It's late, I don't want you driving all the way home. Stay the night." Brett said.

"Brett, I can't. What about Eva? She hates me already! She doesn't want me there. I wouldn't feel comfortable."

"I'm not taking no for an answer. You're staying, got that?" Brett told her.

"Brett…"

"No, you're staying."

"What about Eva?"

"I'll deal with her…you're tired, you're staying. End of subject. Will you?" he looked at her.

Sandy considered it. "OK, if you're sure…" How could she resist his plea?

"I'm sure. Good, it's done then."

Sandy pulled into his driveway, walking into his house with trepidation. All was dark and quiet. Brett lead her to the couch, waiting until Sandy lay down. He turned on the space heater fan, adjusting it so that the heat would warm her. It was only fifty eight degrees in his den! Covering her with a warm blanket, he looked at her. "Goodnight, get some sleep."

Sandy gazed back. "night, kiddo." She fell asleep almost right away.

She woke up at one thirty to use the bathroom. Cautiously,

she stepped into the light in the kitchen, listening for sounds. Going up the stairs, she was shocked to see Brett in the guest room, sound asleep. "My goodness, what was that all about?" Sandy wondered. She studied his sleeping form, resisting the overwhelming urge to go in and kiss him all over. She performed her duty, going back to the couch once more, dozing again.

At three thirty she woke up, for good this time. Walking to the kitchen, she got a drink of water, then heard stirring from upstairs.

"What are you doing?" came Eva's angry whine.

"Getting up," Brett said sleepily.

"Well, get up, then!" she groused.

"Good grief, happy lady," Sandy thought, staying in the shadows to avoid being seen. She wasn't sure if Eva knew she was there and didn't want to find out. Suddenly she heard Brett's voice, "Quit bitchin' at me!" He was now in the bedroom.

"How am I bitchin' at you?" Eva asked.

"You always bitch at me. I hate it. I only have today, tomorrow, Sunday and one day next week, then this mall shit is over. I hate them, I just do it to make money."

"All I wanted to know was why she can't do a few hours and then you a few hours. Why do you have to be there together?" Eva insisted.

"Because she needs to use the bathroom, walk around, she can't just sit there for hours on end."

"So, you go there, tell her to go home, then come back a few hours later and you come home. What's the problem"

"The problem is," Brett was so tired of explaining it to her, "the problem is that she is the AUTHOR! She HAS to be there! Who else will sign those books if not her?"

"So, why do YOU need to be there? Let her sell her own stuff."

At that point, Sandy had heard enough. She wanted to leave, to check on her kids and dog, to be in peace. How could one guy handle all that torture?

163

A cat stood by the back door, waiting to be let out, one was outside waiting to be let in. Sandy did both, then left quietly, getting into her very cold car and driving off without even warming it up. All the way home, she mentally cursed the woman who held Brett in a vise grip so tight, he couldn't breathe without permission.

Walking in her house, she noticed wet towels all over the bathroom floor. Obviously, the toilet had overflowed. The dog was very happy to see her, she showered, changed and saw the kids off to school before returning to Brett's house. Eva had left for work, Brett was sound asleep in the guest room bed. Walking to him, Sandy kissed his mouth gently, then with more insistence. His eyes opened and, seeing Sandy, his heart thumped in anticipation.

"I know what you like," Sandy said suggestively, stroking him over his jeans.

"What?" Brett asked lazily.

"This," Sandy said, unzipping his jeans and taking him into her mouth. Soon that wasn't enough. She stripped off her sweater, unzipped her own jeans and climbed onto his swollen member. The silky feel was exquisite as she rode him, gazing at his adorable face, memorizing his features, achieving an orgasm that was so sweet. She continued to ride him, whispering quiet words as his movements became more insistent until he, too, came.

"I'm hot," he said as Sandy rolled to one side, then off of him.

"Wait, I'll clean you off," she said, swiping her warm tongue around him, licking and sucking until all traces of her scent and taste were gone. "There, all done," she said with a smile.

Brett got up, removing his shirt and replacing it. He was quiet as Sandy got dressed. He felt guilty that he gave to her what by rights, should have been Eva's alone. Sandy always caught him at his weakest sometimes and sleeping was one of her favorites. He wasn't going to complain, however. He craved sex all the time and in his mind, first come was first served. Or was it first served, first come?

The next few days passed the same, Sandy sat alone most of the time, going home alone, returning alone to face another twelve hours of boredom. This was a disappointment, she was counting on Brett being with her. On the last day, Brett came by to bring her lunch, saying how Eva was pissed off that he even did that. He took out a cold slice of pizza wrapped in plastic and gave it to her. She missed him terribly and told him how she'd almost lost her mind, she just wanted this to be over. The only thing that kept her busy was writing down ideas and plotlines for her next novel, *"Because of Friday."*

"You'll never have to do this again, I promise," Brett said. He was finishing up the recording of Sandy's newest book about Winston, and still had to burn the CD's and package them. He had a long week ahead of him.

That night he came back to help her pack away her things. They celebrated the fact that Sandy survived by going back to the same restaurant as before and drinking beer, sharing stories. Brett became teary eyed as he recounted how his Big Brother would no longer have anything to do with him.

Sandy was shocked. "Why?" she asked.

"Because of my drinking. He said he couldn't handle it anymore, that after almost thirty years there was nothing more he could do for me." Brett's eyes misted over as he toyed with the napkin next to his beer. Sandy wanted so much to hug him and erase the pain, but he hated clinginess, so she rubbed his thigh, silently wishing she could remove the pain.

He looked at her, wiping his eyes. "I tried to call him when I got out of jail last summer. His wife answered the phone and said she'd give him the message, but he never returned my call. Maybe I ought to call him again, but what would I say?"

"I don't know," Sandy said.

Brett dabbed his face with the napkin, smoothing it out on

the table afterwards.

"I'll never leave you," Sandy reassured him. "Thick and thin, that's us."

Brett took her wrist, looking at the time on her watch. Nine thirty. Sandy's heart felt heavy as she realized it was time to go. Slowly, they walked to their respected vehicles, she in her car and he in the van. Climbing in, he looked at her.

"OK, make it quick, it's cold out here," he said.

Sandy leaned in. "Thank you, Brett for your help this weekend. I love you." She kissed him, then backed away.

"I'll see you tomorrow," he said, starting the van. She backed away as he closed the door, driving off. She watched until she couldn't see his van anymore, the empty parking lot seeming so desolate as she got into her own cold car and drove home.

Chapter 13

Brett counted down the days until he had to report in to jail. He worked feverishly getting Sandy's latest audio release ready. Then it was four days before doomsday. Beautiful, sunny and 50 degrees, unusual for early December in Minnesota. His depression getting the best of him; he instant messaged Sandy:

"Eva contact you tonight? I went to bed early. Dreams of cuntslimewhore were runnin' through my head. Must be the XX-mess season. 96 hours & counting.... BTW...no more measly dollars with huge deadlines. Without the dollars, I do not want to be pestered! Basically we're making twenty cents an hour split in half....what a joke. I can make more in prison and like it. Ya know what???? I been thinkin', You've got a great spring board here with all these studios. Let's let you go and make all ya can. I don't want anything. Anything at all. Glad I could help and I wish ya the best....happy trails. You can use my van for Saturday and then we're done. I know you've done everything you can to help me. The pressure of the state and the biz is too great. I can't stand it any more. I thank you for all you've done. If you want to return this recording studio, just say so. I won't be using or needing it any time soon, so why pay for it. You can cancel my website and if anyone asks about that guy...tell them I died. Simple enough explanation & they'll more than likely have sympathy enough to buy something. Good luck. BTW, I won't be doing any of the voiceover or narration on any of work that the studios wanted. Kissin' cash bye-bye. It's time to start behaving....behaving like the felon I am. No soup/success for me. I'll be watching to see your movies come out. I'm sure they'll be hits."

Sandy quickly read through his transmissions, feeling her heart sink. Uh-oh, what now? He was an extremist, all or nothing and right now he was doing both. She had been through this before. Looking at the clock, it was 12:37 a.m.

"...we are NOT through! no way, man! you have been the reason for me being the success that I am! please...don't quit on me now! Don't quit on yourself, either!

"How could I have fucked it up so bad...grrr? starting over." Brett typed back. "Say what ya want. I quit. You are and always will be a success. Ya don't need me, you have the shit to make life happen. I am just shit. You need to go forward on your own. I can only hold you back. Stop telling the studios... Brett's doin' this or Brett's doin' that....Just get shit done and stop allowing me to hold you back."

Sandy realized that her plan to keep him motivated was failing also. Damn it, what would his reaction be when he found out, IF he found out? "Bull!" she bluffed.

"Whatever. I'm done. Got all this stuff packed up. Hope ya got room."

"You're not done. please don't... we can do this... I NEED YOU!"

"You can do this," Brett said, feeling sorry for himself as he drowned his sorrows in beer.

"No, I can't. Who made me what I am? Gee, I think it was you!"

"You need me like a Tabasco enema."

"No, please, don't quit on me! Will Randy even take that stuff back with out the boxes they came in?" She was referring to the studio, which he never did figure out how to use, beyond playing CD's.

"Nope," came Brett's swift reply.

"Gee thanks," Sandy thought. "Leave me stuck with a three thousand dollar studio that I can't use or return. Way to go!" She felt annoyed at his attitude but persisted. "Of course not. Yer being foolish."

"Just tell me how much I owe ya."

"Oh, yeah, like you can just write a check for it," Sandy thought bitterly, "and I'm sure Eva would love that, too." To Brett, she typed, "It was $2788.00, plus $168.00 for the monitor." She hoped that amount would wake him up. "I can't believe you're cutting me loose. You felt bad when your brother shitcanned you, how do you think I feel? Please, don't shitcan me."

"I am not shitcanning you due to anything you did. This is all about me. When I do my thumbs thing, which direction are my thumbs?" Brett asked, referring to the way he pointed his thumbs at his shoulders whenever he did something really cool, giving himself his due.

"At you, as they should be," Sandy said. "I need YOU, not the business! I need your friendship."

"Sorry."

"Sorry? For what?"

"Gotta go. Need & want are a lot different."

"Selfish bastard," Sandy thought. She was getting tired of his infantile rantings by now. "But I always want you, too," she typed back. "I have always appreciated who you are. Why are you doing this to me?"

"I'm burning up as many supplies as I can to give ya a runnin' start."

"Brett, I beg you, don't give up our friendship." Sandy was beginning to think he got off on her begging him for anything.

"You will have a ton of stuff to keep ya in business for quite a while. Up to you to maintain your stock."

"Fuck the business a minute! Listen to me!" Sandy wanted to throttle him! "Don't give up on US! It was our friendship long before the business even was a memory."

"Our "Friendship" has nearly destroyed my marriage. I will not lose Eva ever. Ever."

Sandy tried to not let this information rattle her. She knew by now she was just number two and had felt him pulling away from her in the last few weeks. He had been bragging about how

Eva was performing more and better in bed, mostly due to the fact that she felt Sandy was cutting in to her territory. Sandy knew all about that from when her own husband had an affair years before. She did the same exact thing. "You had mentioned 'Pearl Harbored.' You have just PH me!"

"I've said this before...nothing....NOTHING lasts forever."

"This is how you've lived your whole life. When it gets too much, cut loose. I should have been taking notes, I guess."

"I don't want any money from any of the adventures. It's all yours to do with as you see fit."

"Oh how generous of you!" Sandy thought bitterly. To Brett, "I know what you're doing. You're trying to make it "easy" on you to have me think you have dumped me. Or easy on me... whatever."

"Not. Way wrong."

"I'm sure Eva will be happy to learn you have quit WIYEP."

"Not gonna argue with ya."

"I'm not arguing." "Yes, I am," Sandy thought.

"She'll be ecstatic."

"I am trying to make sense of what is happening ."

"I am nothing again and that's exactly the way she wants it," Brett thought bitterly of the string that Eva kept him on. Yank that string, he wanted to tell her now.

Sandy felt really bad about this, but then again, why didn't he stand up for himself? "So why give in to her? Why? *why?* Your radio show...you had said you would NOT do that again... give in...and yet you are once again! just when the big bucks will be rolling in."

"Too tired of fighting," Brett felt weary.

"I know," Sandy sympathized. "I hear ya. I care too. Really. I'm sorry... so sorry that you always have to cede to *others* instead of yourself. YOU are #1, yet you give in to others! Tell you what..."

"You are so wrong ..." Brett began.

"I will put everything on hold," Sandy continued. "You think about this. I'll be here when you get out of jail." She knew that's what was going through his mind.

"Sandy."

"Yes?"

"I am not drunk." Brett lied. He had in fact, been drinking all night.

"I never said you were," Sandy typed, "though I sure think you must be to be carrying on this way," she thought.

"I know what I'm saying and will not back down this time. I can't live like this anymore. Take the money & run kiddo."

"And you...you'll look back on this and realize one day, once again, how foolish you are! IF you back away from me again I will tear up all contracts.

"Oh well."

"I will NOT allow myself to take credit. Everyone can go to hell because, don't you see, It's not the $$$...it was what we could do together!"

"Hate to break it to ya, but YOU are under contract and will be forced to comply and receive all dollars thereafter."

Damn it, he wasn't giving in, but then again, neither would she! "Fuck that shit! Without your creativity, it will all go in the trash anyway, so why even try? It was all about YOU because I wanted it that way! *The Chase?*" she asked, referring to a story he wrote on his own, "all you."

"Thanx, but, oh well."

"NOT oh well."

"Very oh well."

"Molly Hatchett .You know what I'm saying."

"Yes."

"Dreams I'll Never See."

"Yes."

"Don't give those up," Sandy admonished.

"Long gone, hun. You can say whatever you think is what

you should be saying."

"I'll say this. I'll always be here for you. You know how to find me. I'll not give up on you. Whatever I can do for you, it's all yours. You know that."

"Best thing you can do for me is, don't let our work die just cuz I ain't around."

"But it will fizzle out," Sandy reminded him. "This was always a 50/50 effort. As I told Linda, without you, I can't do this. Perfect song right now is 'November Rain'...Nothing lasts forever. I'm in shock here. You had said just last week you would see this through."

" I did."

"And? You want to quit on me now. I beg you to not do that. You are a human capable of thoughts, dreams and desires. See those through."

"State proposed. Sandy, stop and think about this."

"Listen. If it was a day, a year or ten years, just tell me that we will run together again as we have been."

"You say ya don't care about the money, but if you play yer cards right...its all yours. Why let me have jack when you do all the work?"

"You have done a lot of work and been the inspiration. Sorry, but that counts a lot in my book."

"I am the definition of ball & chain. The sooner you realize that, the better off you'll be."

"Fuck that! You are not a ball and chain! You have given me wings to fly and I have soared with you!" Sandy fought so hard for him, the effort was wearing her out.

"Now ya know you can fly...all on your own."

"No. I need you to continue to show me the way!"

"In the story, Sarah did it all on her own." Brett typed, referring to a story they wrote for the "movie" he knew they had going on.

"This is not a story, this is real life," Sandy reminded him.

"That is our story," Brett gently reminded her.

"Josh never gave up on her. NEVER ! He stayed with her till the end. The bitter end! You are needed by me just like that."

"Now it's my turn to say...this is real life. Not a story."

"Please know you will always have a place beside me. I am NOT shit canning ya, I never will."

"The cloud awaits & I bet I'll be the one waiting. You can slug me in the shoulder when ya get there."

"You'll always have a #1 place in my heart."

" Thanx. See ya Friday."

"Wait! Please, don't go!"

"Look at it this way. ... *Because of Friday* has an end to it now."

"No hun, please, let's at least finish *'Chase'* for now."

"I have finished it. The rest is up to you."

"I'm stupid, I admit it, I need a second brain to work it! God, how dense am I? See? If not for you, I'd a been a success before I met ya!"

"If I died right this minute, you would finish it."

"But you haven't and neither have I. I promised you I'd fight my illness because of you. You gave me that reason to fight."

"Keep on keepin' on..... Bye."

"I love you. Now, clear your goddamned screen! Take note: I will NOT say good-bye this time! Hey,"

"Rhubarb," he joked.

"Kiddo, let's be civil. This is turning into a kids' fight."

"I don't wanna fight."

".. really…"

"I ain't fightin'."

"Me neither, so let's just be who we are."

"My decision is final," Brett said.

"You are giving up so much."

"Actually, I'm giving up nothing."

"Really? So, you consider me nothing?"

"This ain't about you."

"What is it, then?"

"I am attempting to maintain my sanity."

"I know that. I have always known that. You know what, though? When the chips are down, that's when you gather your friends around you and hang on for dear life. You don't cast them aside and go down with the ship."

"Nice theory."

"Fact, kiddo. Yer my business buddy, ya lout."

"..grr. Not! Won't, so there!"

"One thing you need to know about me. I am tenacious."

"I'm an extremist. All or nothing."

"That's why we work well together." For twenty minutes all was silent. That was because Eva walked into the den to see what Brett had been up to all night. It was now almost four A.M.

"I told Sandy I'm quitting WIYEP," Brett announced.

Eva's eyes narrowed. "Quitting? Why?" Not that she cared, but the money from the studios beckoned her greed.

"Because I don't have it in me to continue."

"You're walking away from money...? God, what an ass! So what do you intend to do, let her have all of it?"

"I told her that, yes. She worked hard for it, she deserves it."

"Brett, what are you drinking?" Eva picked up his now empty can. "Or should I say, how much have you been drinking?" She went to the refrigerator, opening it. The beer was gone, all twelve cans that were there before she went to bed. "Just as I thought. You get back online and tell her that you're not quitting, do you hear me?"

No answer.

"I asked, do you hear me?"

"Fine, whatever," Brett reluctantly agreed. He really didn't understand where she was coming from. First, she bitched because he spent time with Sandy, then she bitched because he quit. No wonder he drank!

"So, whatcha up to now?" Sandy typed in, waiting.

"You win. Eva won't let me quit either. GRRRR! I'm sick of bein' a pawn."

"A pawn in what?" Then Sandy couldn't believe her eyes. "Eva won't let you quit WIYEP? Yer kidding! Well, It 'tis Xmas...a time of miracles. I'll have to thank her. You know, I really do want to get along with her. When I passed out on yer deck right in front of her, I remember her concern. I was touched. You're right though about something...you ARE all or nothing... it drives me nuts sometimes. But that's what has made us who we are...your drive for perfection, and for that, I thank you. But you use it against what you are up against, too...with not so good results. You tend to want to give up. I'm not like that. I just give it more of what I have. My 'Try Me' attitude. it's why I worked so well at the kennel and why I gave 26 years of my life to Dickhead. I haven't died yet either, or hadn't you noticed? I just don't give in. It's how I survived my childhood. This is me."

"I give up on shit when it becomes more of a hassle & problematic than its worth. I had to fill out a sheet in court stating my job/position & income. I had no idea of what to put down."

"You are partners with our business, executive producer."

"I can always find another route for a living. I've done it before & I will do it again."

"Income?" Sandy queried. "I'll know more by month's end, but it would be fair to say you've made about five grand so far this past year."

"They wanted a weekly income."

"Yes! but it all went to beer, cigs, and other things you wanted me to get for you. OK, divide $5000.00 by 52 weeks."

"Executive producers don't make the $300.00 I wrote in."

"$300.00 a week?"

"I had to say something, we're a fledgling company. No.

$300.00 per month."

"Hey, that's $1200.00 a month, pretty good income if you ask me." Obviously instant messaging had it's downside, too, when it came to math.

"$96.00 dollars a week is what breaks down to," Brett calculated.

"I make about that much at KC. Say $300.00 a week. I'll cover that. If anyone asks...sure he makes 300 a week. Can you change it? Put down an IOU amount.."

"I originally wrote, 'income varies.'" Brett busied himself burning CD's.

"You know, this is a baby business, it takes a while for it to start producing money. We're so on the edge." Sandy was hoping beyond hope it would start raking in the dollars. "We are self employed."

"Once again...all they care about is the money."

"I have to pay expenses, too. Of course...what can they get from you is all they wanna know. I'll do what I can to cover John's expenses, too. You don't need to do that alone. It's my fault you're in that mess." Sandy was remorseful, yet glad that Brett was no longer mired in self pity. He had quite the load on his plate and she wished she could make it all better.

"Not."

"Eva asked me to, no...*told* me to! Well, strongly urged me to, actually! She sent me a letter yesterday."

"I told ya she would."

"I wasn't offended by it. I know she's suffering, too."

"We all are." Brett was exhausted. He was up all night. "Nap time, kiddo."

"ok...take care kiddo."

"See ya around 9?"

"Yes." Sandy was glad the storm was over...for now... again!

"Beer?" Brett asked.

"K," Sandy smiled. "bye."

"lots of it!"

"You betcha."

"Thank you, tata."

"Hugs, hun."

When Sandy arrived, she brought in the case of beer, then going to him, she reached up for a kiss. Looking into his eyes, she said sadly, "don't you *ever* shit can me again!"

Brett's eyes welled up.

"I can't handle it when you do that! Promise me!" Sandy pleaded.

"I don't know what the future holds. I was tryin' to make it easier on ya," was his reply. He put the beer in the refrigerator.

Sandy hugged him from behind. "We'll get through this, just don't think I'll leave you, because I won't."

Inwardly, Brett wished this whole thing was over with. As it was he still had the hearing in January to look forward to. What a mess!

Eva told him she had made reservations at a restaurant he really liked. This was after giving him grief for wasting time chatting with Sandy on IM. He wasn't happy as he told Sandy that Eva was off his visitor list. Sandy wished he would include her on it, but he felt that jail was no place for her to be. Sandy's heart was torn.

"I'll call you, though and you write to me. That I will enjoy!" Brett told her.

Sandy promised.

On the day he was to check in to jail, Sandy paced and fretted. She looked at the clock at least a thousand times. In her mind, she pictured Brett wrapped in a day-long sexcapade with Eva and there wasn't a damn thing Sandy could do about it. He had been drifting away from her for awhile now. Sandy didn't know what to do, even with the charade she had going on about the alleged contracts. She came so close to 'fessing up, but knew that would be the end of everything she held so dear. It was a weight she carried about.

Her one big mistake was making up a news story on her computer, then sending it to Brett's e-mail. Eva was checking Brett's mail when she saw it. At first she was flattered and excited, until she went to the link and couldn't find the story. Her suspicions were raised. She immediately e-mailed Sandy, asking her about it.

"Oops!" thought Sandy. Busted! She then made up a big elaborate story about not finding the link either and how maybe she was the victim of a hoax. Eva wasn't buying it. She had her own doubts, thinking that maybe Sandy was making the whole thing up just to keep Brett with her. Now she had evidence. It was a matter of time before Sandy was history.

Twenty days dragged so slow. Sandy sent Brett letters every day, and finally one week later received several from him, which she read many times over. She missed him with an ache that was almost unbearable. Her phone company wouldn't allow phone calls from the jail he was in, so she had to be content with the letters. She dreamed about him every night, only imagining what he must be going through.

For Brett, it was just as difficult. His canteen had been misplaced, so he had to wait for his supplies. When he finally received them, he had a stub of a pencil that he needed to use to write scripts for Sandy. His hand cramped many times over. He walked the track as many as ten miles a day out of boredom. He looked at the food they served as being slightly better than the last time he was in. He waited for Sandy's letters. oh! How they were welcome! He called Eva every night, wishing also he could speak to Sandy, to keep his spirits up. Eva told him she had a hotel room reserved for the night he got out. All he wanted was a hot tub and peace and quiet.

Finally, day 20. He was out by 5:30 a.m. He went home and became reacquainted with his cats and the peace of home. He checked his emails, then IM'd Sandy.

"Howdy Rowdy!"

"Brett?" Sandy typed. "Is it you?"

"Yepper!"

"How do I know it's you?"

"Tilapia sounds mighty good right about now!"

Sandy's eyes became teary.

"I thought you were going to a hotel," Sandy typed in, wishing it were her who was going to a hotel with him. But, he was married, after all.

"Later. Checkin' on stuff right now," he replied. "So, how are things going?"

Sandy filled him in. God, it felt so good to be doing this again.

"It was weird not yapping with ya," he said.

"I missed you, too."

Eva watched him at the computer. "Soon, bitch," she thought, remembering the e-mail Sandy had contrived. "Your days are numbered." As soon as Brett found out what Eva knew, he would ditch Sandy forever! She would see to that!

"Thanks for the letters. They meant a lot. The other guys were jealous that I was getting something every day."

"A few of those letters were returned. I just sent them right back out!" Sandy said, feeling that frustration all over again. She detailed the problems she had with their contracts. Reading over his shoulder, Eva wanted to hurl. Instead, she retreated to her room to finish packing for the overnight hotel trip. She had every intention of rocking Brett's world, then she would dump the truth about his precious writer on him. Wouldn't he be surprised!

"See how necessary I am?" Brett asked Sandy.

"Yes, I saw it every day I couldn't talk to you!"

"So, I went on this 'vacation' thinking I'd lose weight... guess what?"

"You lost 12 pounds."

"Nope."

"You lost 84?"

"No, I gained one pound, lost the fat and gained muscle. Lots of walking! I would walk, then stop and write, then walk some more. Just seemed the right thing to do as I was going along."

They discussed some more ideas, then Eva strode back in the den.

"Are ya gonna yak it up wih her all day?" she asked, none too happy.

Brett looked up. "Just catchin' up," he said.

Eva scowled. "Well, I'm leavin'. Yak if ya want."

"Gotta go," Brett said apologetically to Sandy.

"NOOOOOOO!" Sandy whined. "Oh, OK."

"Catch ya later." Brett pushed away from the computer.

"Here, take this." Eva said, handing him a bag.

"What are you so grumpy about?"

"I'm tired of sharing you, that's it! Just plain fed up!" Eva walked to the back door, securing it. Brett did a quick head count of cats, to make sure they were all in, then locked the door behind him.

Finally the day arrived when Sandy could see Brett. It had been a long month. All the way to his place she was rehearsing her speech. She wanted to admit to him about her deception, to spill the beans. She was fully prepared for his reaction.

He would hate her forever.

She knew that.

Her stomach quaked at the thought of losing him, yet her mind could no longer tolerate the many lies she had to remember.

Yet, as soon as she knocked on his locked door and saw his beautiful face in the window, her heart and resolve melted. He took her up in a big hug, kissing her as she hugged back, holding onto him as if her life depended on it.

"Every moment is so precious," she thought. "I won't have him much longer."

She couldn't do it. As much as she wanted to, she couldn't do it. He took her in the den, pulling her clothes off. He pulled his pants down and Sandy feasted on him, savoring the taste, the feel of him in her mouth, the pure joy of seeing him writhe, of hearing his rapid breathing and feeling him explode in her mouth. He sat back in his chair, thoroughly spent. Smiling at her, he wished her a merry Christmas.

"I have missed you so much," Sandy said, kissing him once, twice.

He clicked on his e-mails, then typed in a response to Eva's query about what was for dinner. Sandy burned inwardly as he replied, adding "love ya, hun," but she didn't let on. She wished for the millionth time it was her and not Eva he was committed to.

Brett put Sandy to work packaging CD's as he worked at the computer. Inwardly, he questioned what Eva had harangued him about all weekend, that Sandy was making up the whole movie deal scenario. The night before he instant messaged Sandy about how an entertainment news show was talking up their movie, just to see what her reaction would be. When Sandy saw it, she knew that Brett was doubting her claims. That was the reason why she wanted to confess, yet after seeing him once more, it was beyond her to do so. He had waited, hoping she would spill the beans. Or something, *anything* to prove Eva wrong. Oh, how he wanted to prove Eva wrong! He couldn't believe that Sandy, his sweet girlfriend, would deceive him in such a way. He trusted her with everything had, all of his thoughts, secrets and stories. What would she benefit from lying, other than what Eva had said, that Sandy saw it as a way to keep him.

Brett talked about the movie, his ideas, what the producers plans were. Sandy gave him answers that sounded convincing. Eva was wrong, she had to be! Jealousy maybe rearing it's ugly head? Soon, it was time for Sandy to leave. Brett saw her to the door, kissing her goodbye. After she left, he was deep in thought.

When Eva arrived home, she immediately quizzed him on all that Sandy said and did. Brett answered her questions, but Eva persisted.

Finally, he couldn't stand it any more. "Why must you be so sure she's lying?"

"Have you talked to these people that she speaks of? What do you know about them? These contracts, has a lawyer looked at them?"

"Sandy had a lawyer look at them, yes." Brett defended.

"So *she* says. How do *you* know?"

Brett shrugged his shoulders.

"I asked, how do you know? You don't, do you? See? More lies!"

"Goddamnit, Eva, I really wish you'd back off!" Brett couldn't imagine Sandy being so callous!

"Goddamnit, Brett, I wish you'd get your head out of your ass and smell the coffee for once! *THERE IS NO MOVIE DEAL!*" Eva stormed out of the room to get out of her uncomfortable work clothes.

Brett checked on dinner. He didn't need her hassling him. He had the court hearing on Friday to think about. More time in the gilded cage.

Chapter 14

Sandy was thinking about Friday too. Because of Friday. Everything that ever meant anything to her with Brett happened on a Friday. She first met him on a Friday, made love to him on a Friday, the outdoor classic car shows they were to attend together to sell their products were on Fridays, and now this. She had to be in court also, seeing as how it was she who called the probation officer in the first place. It was Brett's attorney's idea.

Friday dawned dark and dismal. Sandy instant messaged Brett, who was subdued as he put together the CD's for Sandy's latest book, *"Summer School Blues."* Sandy tried to give him a pep talk, to no avail.

"You need to come and get me," he instant messaged. "Eva can't bear to see this again."

"I'll be there by eight o'clock."

"Make it eight fifteen."

"K."

Brett got out of his chair for some coffee. Eva wandered in, looking at his IM screen.

"What did you tell her this for?" she demanded, pointing to the message on the screen.

Brett hated that she was always looking at every little thing that he did. "Because, I didn't think you'd want to go."

"Why not? Jesus Christ, Brett, it's as if we're not even married anymore! You have her do everything for you!"

"Well, do you want to go?" he asked, unsure of where she stood on anything anymore..

"John asked me to be there when I talked to him last

month, or had you forgotten?"

"What good will you do? You're not taking the stand or anything."

"Right. That little bitch got you into this mess. I want to see her squirm her way out. I've already told you what a great liar she is!"

"Eva, don't start..." Brett brushed past her to take a shower.

Eva went to the computer, typing in, "don't come for him. John wants me there, so I'll take him." Stupid bitch! Eva thought as she hit send.

Sandy saw the message as she walked in from her shower. Looking at it, her heart drooped in dismay. "OK," she typed. There went her idea of keeping him company, she thought ruefully.

On the drive to the courthouse, Sandy had a premonition that this would be the episode that would change everything about her relationship with Brett. She was scared as she pulled into the parking lot, then proceeded to the courtroom to wait. She looked at her watch at least a dozen times, wondering where they were. Finally she saw Eva, with Brett following. John came in, shaking hands, then took them all to a conference room, explaining what the perceived outcome would be.

"I need to speak with the prosecuting attorney to see what her plans for you are. Because they feel you have committed violations about your whereabouts, being out of town and not returning your PO's phone calls, they may want to toss the book at you. I'll be right back."

Eva glared at Sandy, then asked Brett once more what happened during those two days his probation officer was looking for him. "Amazing, you were home, you did nothing at all, and you'll probably have to do time for it!" Turning in her seat, she addressed the woman who was the cause of all of her grief. "Thanks a whole hell of a lot," she said to Sandy.

Sandy felt bad. She was prepared to tell the judge that Brett *was* home the whole time and to throw the book at her instead. Brett was innocent.

John walked back in. "OK, I have her down to giving you a 14 day sentence. How about it? If you don't fight this, you'll actually get off pretty easy. But if you choose to bring this to trial, you may have the whole time to serve. What's it to be?"

Brett thought about it. "Oh damn it, maybe I should just do the two weeks and be done with it!"

"But, honey, you did nothing wrong!" Eva protested.

"It all hinges on where you were, did you really go to LA, as she says Sandy told her?" John queried.

"No, I was not in LA," Brett stated adamantly. "I was in Wisconsin helping my uncle." Though not even that was true, but he had to cover his tracks as to why he didn't return Linda's phone calls.

"OK, I'll go back and see what your probation officer knows. She just walked in." John excused himself.

"Sandy, why didn't you lie and say there were no phone messages?" Eva demanded. Looking to Brett she asked, "and why didn't you two get your stories straight? I told you two to do that!"

The door opened. John looked worried now. "Linda said she has the voice mail message from Sandy that states you *were* in LA and she can prove it. If we protest this, she has evidence that will lock you up for a long time."

Eva stood up angrily. "I knew it! That's it, I'm outta here!" Brett watched her go.

"Oh fuck it, I'll take the two weeks and be done with it! Just get me out of here and be over with it. I ain't fucking playing her games anymore!" Brett said hotly.

"OK, if that's what you want. You know, I'm not telling you what to do," John advised.

"Just get it done."

Sandy looked at the ground. "She's bluffing," she said quietly, feeling so horrible that Brett had to do any time at all. "She doesn't have that message saved. She said so earlier."

Brett got up. "I need a cigarette," he said, walking out, looking for Eva.

Sandy was pacing the floor when Eva came storming back in. "You just *had* to call her...why? Why? Half the time Brett doesn't remember when he tells you to do things! Now he's doing time for it! Why did you say he was in LA?" she railed, her brown eyes blazing. She was petite, but her attitude made up for what height lacked.

Sandy felt lower than a crumb as she stared at the floor.

"The judge will see us now," John said, poking his head out from the courtroom. Brett walked in, followed by Eva and Sandy.

"Mr. Pearson, I told you before I didn't want to see you again and yet, here you are,"
the judge said, shuffling papers.

Brett said nothing as he stood before her, shoulders sagging, hands folded in front of him.

Sandy felt for him. "What must be going through his mind?" she wondered. Eva sat in the bench in front of her, rigid as stone.

John did a lot of fast talking to both the judge and the probation officer, as well as to the prosecuting attorney. The judge looked past him, waving a letter.

"Ms. Malone, I don't want to receive any more letters from you in support of Brett, do you understand?"

Brett winced inwardly, he had told Sandy to not contact the judge this time, it would only make things worse.

Sandy's stomach fell through the floor, her heart racing so fast, her head spun.

"May I see that please?" John asked. "This needs to be introduced as evidence. I had no idea there was a letter."

The judge handed it over. "Brett is perfectly well aware of what his responsibilities are concerning probation," the judge went on, looking beyond him once more at Sandy. "He doesn't need you intervening, is that clear?" Sandy nodded from her spot on the bench.

Eva seethed. Always, always, always interfering! That's what she tried to impress upon Brett, that Sandy was always interfering. Nobody needed to know their business. NOBODY!

"This letter is not incriminating in any way," John replied. "I see no problem with it. My client has agreed to doing the 14 days the state imposes on him. He will begin his sentence within the time allocated."

"Fine. If he wishes to also do Sentenced to Serve, I will deduct two days off from his total time in," the judge agreed. The papers were signed, then set to one side.

"Agreed," John said.

"Two days, big whoopee deal," Brett thought. "Just let me get this shit done." At no time did he mentally curse Sandy. It was his fault. He was so drunk from wine those two days, he was saying and doing all kinds of things. Hell, he even sent Sandy home so drunk because Eva was due to arrive home shortly and he had to get Sandy out of there. This was after Sandy had vomited all over him. Of course, she had had two huge glasses of wine herself, on a dare from him, of course. She was so paralyzed from intoxication, she couldn't even move from her position on the couch. Brett had used that opportunity to take complete advantage of her, watching her writhe in satisfaction.

Although Sandy couldn't move, she could see, hear and feel everything happening to her. The music was loud, Brett's expert hands bringing her to orgasm time and again. But then Eva called, giving him her estimated time home. He panicked, looking at Sandy's bleary eyes. He offered her coffee, helping her to dress. Her words were slurred, she couldn't put two words together as Brett walked Sandy to her car. She could barely see straight, let alone walk without stumbling.

"Hun, I hate to do this to you," he had said, "but ya gotta get outta here. Tell you what, go to the grocery store parking lot and rest there until you feel better." Brett gave her credit, she was such a trooper. However, he was concerned she'd get into a car wreck. His mind spun out of control, why had he let it get so out of hand?

Which is what Sandy did. She passed out cold in the front seat, just seconds after she pulled into the lot, tilted the seat back and tossed the keys on the floor. She was unconscious for two hours. The setting sun chilled the interior of the car, bringing Sandy to her senses. Shakily coming to, she then drove home, taking all the back roads.

Eva pulled in the driveway only minutes after Sandy had left. That was too close a call for Brett. He felt so bad that he sent Sandy off that way, e-mailing her when she didn't alert him through IM that she had arrived home safely. He worried that maybe she had an accident, laying dead or unconscious somewhere, or worse.

Now, standing before the judge, he realized that today *was* his fault, for telling Sandy the day after that incident to call his PO, making up lies to save his ass. Look where that got him… two weeks in the gilded cage. He had spent half his life in jail, since he was eighteen. What a life.

Eva stood up, walking out of the courtroom, totally ignoring Sandy. She instead made small talk with the attorney and paid him cash, as Brett talked to Sandy. She knelt before him as he sat on the bench in the lobby.

"Brett, I'm so sorry you have to do time at all. And about that letter, I had to do that, let her know that I support you…"

Brett smiled at her. "I know. You meant well. It'll be OK. I can do two weeks. Don't worry."

Eva was ready to go. She held the door for him as they all walked out. Brett and Eva got into their car, driving off. Sandy passed them on the highway. Again, she had the strange sensation that today was going to completely change their whole relationship. If only she had a crystal ball, she would have known that she was right!

Chapter 15

Brett searched for the paperwork he knew he had to prove he didn't need thirty days per year of home alcohol monitoring. Eva buzzed about, her mind full of acrimonious thoughts. If not for Sandy, she wouldn't be out fifteen hundred bucks that she paid to John. If not for Sandy, she wouldn't have to share Brett. If not for Sandy…the list went on and on. Brett didn't need her harassment, but she vowed that before the weekend was over, he would know the full truth about his "bestest delilady."

The next morning, Sandy and Brett chatted through IM. He seemed quieter than usual. Eva spent the night quizzing him on what he knew about Sandy's involvement with the studios, putting doubts into his head. He, too had questioned Sandy's evasiveness whenever he'd asked her for phone numbers and contact information. Now that he'd thought about it, she always changed the subject or sounded like she really knew what was going on. There was that time this past summer, he thought, when he asked her for a phone number and she gave him one, which had turned out to bc bogus. In his drunken state at the time, he instant messaged her he was through with her, he refused to answer the phone when she had tried to call him, yet told her in instant messaging that he loved her, why did she have to embellish what wasn't true? Sandy maintained that it all was true. Because he was drunk, he finally passed out, completely forgetting that episode, until now.

Until now. Until Eva kept watering that seed of doubt. Finally he backed away from the computer, ignoring Sandy the rest of the morning.

"When are you going to check about that supposed movie deal?" Eva nagged.

Brett sat at the computer, dread in his heart. Please, Sandy, he thought, let me prove Eva wrong! He set up his microphone, adjusting volume levels.

"Well, what are you doing?" Eva asked.

"I'm gonna record this conversation. If you're wrong, we'll know. If you're right....." he let that thought hang.

"We'll know," Eva said, feeling vindicated already.

Dialing the number to a bookstore that Sandy had said hosted a filming session two months before, Brett spoke with the manager. He explained that he was looking for a particular CD title that Sandy had told him she sold ten copies of to the manager.

The store manager seemed confused. "No, we don't have that title here," she said.

"Did you ever?" Brett asked, closing his eyes to the growing pain that enveloped his heart.

"No, we didn't."

"Well, I was told that a movie was being filmed at your store," he said, giving her the date.

"No, nothing happened here that day," she confirmed. "I'd have known if it did, I work long hours and I'd know if something like that happened."

"Thank you, you've been very helpful," Brett said, preparing to turn off the microphone.

"Is there something that I can help you with?" she asked.

"No, I was fed a load of bull and now I must deal with it accordingly," Brett told her, anger sluicing through him. "Goodbye."

He shut off the microphone, saved the conversation to mp3 format, then wrote a quick e-mail to Sandy, "can you explain this?" Hitting send, he sat, numb, uncomprehending.

Why? Why did she feel the need to lie to him. The walls came crashing in.

There were no contracts, no movie deals, no money rolling in, he was what he always had been, Brett Pearson, major fuck up. This was his chance to redeem himself. Instead, he had let himself get so involved with Sandy that he fell in love.

The sad part, the heartbreaker of it all, was that he really truly loved her, as he had loved no one else.

Not even Eva.

Betrayal, pain, sorrow, anger, heartbreak. All these emotions roiled within him.

Then came Eva's voice.

"See? I told you that she was lying, but did you listen to me? *Noooooooo!*" she gloated as Brett clenched and unclenched his fists, the big meat hooks that had caressed Sandy, entering her and bringing her to spasms of joy. Now he wanted to use them to hurt her. Eva continued on with her bragging, the words sailing over Brett. Crow…he had to eat crow. He waited for Sandy's response.

Sandy saw the e-mail message come in, checking it. The subject said, "interesting conversation." She wondered what it was about as she downloaded the audio. Listening to it, her stomach quaked. This was it. The moment had come. She was now through.

She stared woodenly at the keyboard. A thousand thoughts ran through her mind. What could she say in defense? Nothing! It was her fault. She made up stories to keep Brett in her life. Well, Eva had said, keep it business. In her quest to see Brett, she made up business. Lots of it! Why? Greed. Selfish greed, plain and simple! She was so afraid of losing him, she did the one thing that destroyed their relationship, she created doubt. Slowly, she typed out words to try to save herself, tears nowhere in sight. She was numb with grief.

-------------- Original message --------------
From: Sandy Malone

how can I answer this…

191

you already know.

as you so eloquently said, "nothing lasts forever...
NOTHING!"

it just seemed easier to go on, even long after everything
fell apart. It was not anything against you.

I was always amazed by what you could do.

I wanted to work with you.

what we have done so far has not been a waste.

Seeing a deal fall apart, then another...if I said yet another
deal went down, it would have appeared that I was a loser.
I no longer wanted that title anymore.

I tried so hard to succeed. It became more and more
frustrating.

How could I tell you that?

I didn't want to jeopardize YOU. It was never you. It was
me somehow. So, I lead you to believe that we still had
something. But I was determined that I "protect" you. the
question in the back of my head was always..."How ya
gonna tell him when ya keep embellishing what no longer
is?"

So, if you wanna quit, if you wanna tell me to get the hell
out of your life, take all my shit and go, I'll understand.
I'm not even going to use the platitude, "I never wanted
to hurt you." That's lame.

spell it all out for me...I deserve that much.

all I ask is that you look past my failures to the successes
we did have with our projects.

She ended the missive with, "If you tell me to go to hell,
I'll understand, but please forgive me and hear what I
have to say." Pressing send, she sat, unmoving.

"What did she say? What did she say?" Eva was fairly
bouncing as Brett tried to read the note.

"Can you go find something to do? I need some peace here!" Brett was at the breaking point. Eva slunk out of the room, anger welling up inside of her. The little bitch was through... yippee!

Brett typed out a letter, the words coming so fast. When he was done, he instant messaged Sandy:

"Come get your shit...NOW!"

Sandy saw the orange light blink on her computer. Clicking on it, she read the message. Her heart plunged.

"No, I can't." she typed. "I have a five o'clock appointment."

"Read your E first," Brett replied.

Sandy opened the e-mail and read it.

"Sandy... I have a million things I want to say. None of which are good. I trusted you. But the single word, SELFISH is the real truth. I will not be vindictive. I know what your mind was doing and I know you knew better. Your judgment however, was way out of whack. Keeping this in mind, here's what's going to happen... You nearly destroyed my marriage and jeopardized my freedom. I know that you had your own agenda, but come on... how did you think this was going to turn out once I found out the truth? You knew I would find out eventually. This has to be the stupidest thing anyone has ever done to me ever. No One can hold a candle. I would like to say thanx for the things you did do that were on the up & up, but right now it ain't happenin'. Did you notice when I was runnin' the show and made the decisions, things actually worked out or at least were for real? I gave you the opportunity to have a successful life and now look at you. I want back all the SOH & T4T CD's. They are now mine and rightfully so at this point. Make sure, (& I want this in legal writing) that those 2 releases belong to me and me alone. You will have the credit that stands on them, but that will be it. How can I ever save face amongst all my friends and people that once respected my work ethics? You can keep the Winston CD's to do with as you see fit. Maybe give them to Harry to throw away. I will give you

all the Winston stuff I have before I delete all that unnecessary information from my computer. As yet another lesson for you to continue to learn from, I will keep the recording studio that you can pay off and try to save my name if that's even possible. Close my DJ website too. There is no need for that any longer either. The bank account under OUR name will be dissolved. I want and expect legal documentation. As for the taxes on all this, once again, you dug this hole. I have no pity for you. I am so pissed at you for misleading me for so long, the damage you've done is absolutely irreversible. The WIYEP card needs to come out my name if it's on there at all. I don't know cuz I don't know what to believe out of you. People I knew were so proud of what I never really did. I feel so empty, worthless, used & mostly made a fool of, I literally wanna scream at the top of my lungs. I certainly hope you enjoyed yourself in all this, because I can only imagine what you feel like right now. The balance is not nearly equal enough to benefit from all the lies and misleading stories you've made up. Now ya have an ending to, *"Because of Friday."*
Brett"

Sandy read it, feeling so miserable. She was paralyzed by shame, disappointment. Why? Why did she think that having an affair, of being "the other woman" would be so easy? Because she wanted Brett all for herself. She had pictured him leaving Eva for her. Then she remembered what he had said after they made love that first time, "I will never leave Eva, I belong to her…"

I belong to her…I belong to her…I belong to her…it ran through Sandy's mind. He was her possession, for all the shit and sorrow he put her through. He knew it, she knew it. Sandy had wanted to rescue him from it, but without success.

Now, because of Friday, it was all done. Her marriage, her kids' respect for her was gone. They knew of her affair, when Brett had spent those days with her. Not once, but twice. So did the neighbors when they heard Sandy scream in ecstasy, her bedroom window wide open!

It was over.

Early the next morning, Sandy was sitting at the computer when the orange light came on. It was Brett. Numb, she clicked on it.

"Your things are ready, come and get them," he said.

Realizing that she couldn't put it off anymore, she told him she'd be there in a while.

The drive out was not filled with the anticipation she always felt when she went to see him before. The shame welled up inside of her. Pulling into his driveway, she dimmed her headlights, seeing the boxes of equipment piled high by the garage. Turning off the car, she quietly got out, taking box after box and stashing it into her car. At one point, she passed his den window and peeked in. He was there by his computer, a cigarette in hand, looking at his security monitor that she helped his friend install. He was obviously waiting for her to go, then went to the back door. By then, Sandy was in the car, preparing to leave. Brett's only words to her were to open the passenger door as he put in a boxes he had missed, then turn and walk away. Sandy wished he had looked at her, said something along the lines of, "hey, let's talk." Instead, he went back into the house, locking the door.

Sandy backed out of the driveway, turning for home. On the way, she composed an e-mail in her mind. Once at home, she went to her computer and typed out a letter for Eva, detailing every instance that she and Brett were together. It was vile and vicious, just the thing to put that woman in her place, Sandy thought, sending it to her work e-mail box. Then she instant messaged Brett once more.

"Now that I have what is mine, there are some things that you need to know. Hell has no fury like a pissed off Aries! On Monday morning, Eva will see a letter from me that isn't very pretty. Your PO also will be getting a letter, detailing everything that you have done to avoid her."

"Not wise, I don't take threats," Brett typed back, the hurt digging it's way deeper. When he saw Sandy pull up in his driveway on his monitor, his heart went out. He wanted to grab her, to shake her, ask her why she had hurt him so bad. Instead, he let her drive off. Now this.

"I don't make threats, I make promises. You ever see "Fatal Attraction?" Don't worry, your cats are safe. I don't hurt animals, only people's feelings, you asshole!"

"Don't do something that you'll regret," Brett typed back. "While you're stewing, remember, I didn't do all this shit. I wonder what you will have gained through all of your vindictiveness. You have to live with yourself, you know. It wasn't enough to shatter my dreams, now you have to literally destroy my future, too."

"You killed off your dreams, you and your all or nothing attitude. All about the money, you know. All you had to do was to forgive me my one faux pas. But no, you had to push it to this! I said I was sorry, I can't undo what happened."

"Face it, it's over! This is Eva. There isn't anything that you can write to me that I don't already know about! You have lied so much I don't believe a word you say! Why would Brett be attracted to you anyway? Have you looked at yourself in a mirror lately?"

"Way to go!" Sandy furiously typed back. "When confronted, a woman always attacks what she knows best: her visage in a mirror!"

"Oh, ouch! That really hurt! You're a piece of work!"

"Eva, I'm done. I have destroyed three lives already. The wild oats have been sown. I was looking for irresponsibility, but the fun is gone. I want stability in my life. Time to finally grow up. It's over, finished." Sandy backed away from the computer. She felt dead inside.

Eva was not done. "Keep it coming, we're finally seeing the real side of you!"

196

She looked at Brett triumphantly. He felt so sick inside. Eva didn't understand that Sandy was truly the light in Brett's life. She assumed that Sandy had just been what all the other women had been in Brett's life, one night stands that meant nothing. Eva had put up with his affairs just as she had put up with his drinking, his trouble with the law. She merely took care of it and went on. He owed her so much and she was determined to make him remember that as long as he lived.

Brett spent all that day ruminating in his mind about Sandy. He had to tolerate Eva going on and on about how it was over with him and Sandy. No more never again, did he understand? It was like being harassed by a mother. Early the next morning, he checked his IM, seeing Sandy's few transmissions, he typed in what he could try to comprehend. Sandy seemed contrite, as she apologized for her words of hurt.

"No one else holds a candle to you. I want us to keep working together, please?" She waited, hope being all she had right now.

"I want you to understand something," Brett began.

"Yes? Any thing!"

"I was not the one that began the abolishment of this. Eva had been hounding me for days on the whole movie deal. I wanted to prove her wrong. Instead, I had to eat crow. BTW...it tastes like chicken!"

"Crow...chicken, I get it," Sandy had to chuckle in spite of the situation.

"I did not go running to her, she kept on me. I have suffered through so many disappointments in my life, that's why I never get excited about anything anymore."

"I know. Beat me, torture me, I deserve it," Sandy replied. "I can't bear to know that I hurt you so bad. I'd crawl on broken glass to apologize to you."

"I'll get over it, I have new direction now."

"Can we please work together as we once did? I promise I won't blow it this time."

197

"You know what sealed it? When I decided to stop the madness due to nothing of my own doing and you had said you were going to send a note to Eva and another to Linda to make sure my doom was sealed. I was going to be divorced if you had your way, go to prison, lose my house. I can't be involved with these motivations."

Sandy's mood dropped. When Eva saw that e-mail, she was doomed. Why did she have to always act on impulse first? Damn it! "I spoke out of anger," Sandy typed back. "I never meant it."

"I know you were mad, but you took it out on me. I'm sorry, Sandy, but the damage has been done. Put yourself in my shoes, would you deal with someone who said those things?"

"I know about damage, I also know about healing and moving on."

"I wasn't as angry as you think. I am an extremist. You know that. I also am all about the money. You know that, too. Can't pay bills on compliments and testimonials."

"I tried like hell to get you more money."

"I know you did, maybe too much."

"Is there still a chance, Brett?"

"Quite simply, Eva will not allow it."

Sandy let this sink in. Once again, Brett was that puppet, held in place by the strings controlled by Eva. It made Sandy so sick to even see that in print. "So it's over then?"

"I literally have no choice in this anymore. All that vindictive stuff that you said killed off any opportunity that we may have had. I'm sorry, Sandy, but I have been taken out of the mix on this deal. Lucky to have my home and my freedom as it is. As you review the last couple of days, I haven't been mean or said anything to hurt you."

"I know and for that, I'm grateful."

There was no other response from Brett after that. Sandy looked at the clock. Eva was probably up by now and Brett played it cool, Sandy supposed. She needed to get ready for work anyway.

Brett was receiving the third degree from Eva. He just bowed his head as she went on and on about how he was never to contact Sandy again.

"Ya got that? I don't need to see you chatting with her, you have nothing to talk about! I mean it!" She went upstairs to shower. Brett wondered when the fire would finally go out from her spiteful nature.

When Eva arrived at work, she checked her e-mails. There was a letter from Sandy, right there, as promised. Eva read it, horrified. Immediately she called Brett.

"You two went to Wisconsin? She was with YOU?" Eva knew Brett went there, but she assumed that Sandy was at home, after contacting her through instant message that very night!

"Eva…" was all Brett could say.

"You asked her to find you girls? Having a three way with Brad?" Eva was about to hurl. She was so mad! Brett would pay dearly for this humiliation! She contacted her supervisor, telling him she had to go home, an emergency came up. He never saw her so angry as he told her to go. First though, she wrote to Sandy, calling her a slut, telling her that she had no respect for her at all. Slamming the send button, she grabbed her purse and left the building.

Brett knew the end was here. Eva would divorce him now, he'd have no money, no home, no place to go. Angrily, he typed an IM to Sandy.

"You just had to do that shit to Eva, didn't you?"

Sandy saw it, playing dumb. "What shit?"

"Telling her all about our history! Thanks for nothing!"

Sandy denied it. "What are you talking about?"

"Me asking you to find girls when she goes out of town next month. Going to Wisconsin. Brad. Real cool of you!" Brett sat, waiting for the inevitable- Eva's arrival.

Sandy didn't bother to respond. Brett was angry and rightfully so. Sandy wished once again that she hadn't acted on impulse. It was too late now.

Eva drove home in a fury. Pulling into the driveway, she stormed into the den, where Brett was.

"Get up and out of my way!" she demanded. Brett stood up, watching. Eva went to the computer, removing the instant message capabilities from it. She then placed a call to the phone company as she reached for Brett's red address book. He wondered what was next. She was so pissed off, he didn't question anything!

Eva explained to the phone company representative that she wanted several numbers blocked from her phone, giving him Sandy's home, work and cell numbers.

"Oh, shit!" thought Brett. "Now what?"

When it was over, she turned to him. "Explain. Now. Everything. I'm waiting. And don't lie."

Brett helplessly looked around the room. It was so bare now, devoid of spindles of finished CD's, written testimonials that he so proudly taped to the wall, Sandy's written books were gone from his bookshelf. It was bare and cold and empty. His life was over, he decided, might as well come clean. He told her everything. Eva felt sick, horrified that everything had gone so far beyond her control. She thought she had him figured out. She had called him several times each day to check on him, she e-mailed him, she made sure he was behaving, he assured her of this and yet, it felt as though her world came crashing down. She paced, standing in front of him as he sat, then paced some more.

Brett watched her every move, cursing Sandy. Why? Why did she do this? He wondered what would come down from his probation officer also. It just didn't end!

"You have humiliated me for the last time. I can't go on like this anymore!"

"What are you going to do?" Brett asked.

"Do? DO? What the goddamned hell should I do, Brett? I can't trust you! You made a fool of me! I ought to just toss your dumb ass out, but that would be too easy! No, you owe me. You

200

owe me *big*. I'll let you know what I'm going to do!" With that pronouncement, Eva went to the bedroom, slamming the door.

Brett quaked inside, feeling the tears well up. When he first met Eva, he had nothing. He was sleeping on his ex girlfriend's couch while he heard her being humped by her new boyfriend in the bedroom. Talk about lower than low, Brett had been there and done that. Now it looked as though he would be there again. He shook his head, feeling utterly defeated.

Sandy noticed that Brett was offline, assuming that Eva had shut his computer off as she had it out with him. It never occurred to her that Eva went that one step farther. Sandy could only picture in her mind what was happening, and it was nowhere near to what had actually occurred.

Chapter 16

The cold war continued. Brett did everything he could to stay out of Eva's way. Finally two days later, she finished her argument.

"You can stay on one condition. You are not working with Sandy. Ever! She is evil and I don't ever want to see her, hear of her, speak to her or anything. Understood?" Eva came to the conclusion that she could forget this time also, if she tried really hard. She did it before, she had to do it again, she had to! She needed Brett. She hated to think of everything she'd have to do on her own otherwise. She could overlook this, many wives did. She didn't want to know about his involvement with Sandy anymore. It hurt too much.

In relief, Brett agreed. He had done a lot of thinking also. Despite what Sandy did to him, he still cared about her, although he was also still very angry at her as well. He also had decided that he was going to do his fourteen days as soon as possible. He needed to get away from everything that was happening to him. He was so on the verge of mentally and emotionally falling apart. His mornings seemed lost to him, he missed not yapping with Sandy. Instead, he'd wake up, have a cigarette, sit at the computer, staring at the keyboard. What was she doing now? What was she thinking? Did she enjoy the misery she'd heaped on him? Looking at the shelf over the computer, it still sat empty, as was the wall next to him. He felt stark, alone and vulnerable. Going to jail would actually be a blessing. He would tell Eva that he was turning himself in.

For her part, Sandy was miserable. Time and again, she'd lay awake, wondering about Brett. She still loved him so much.

Every time a song came on that they listened to together, she'd cry, buckets of tears cascading down her cheeks. She remembered those days when he'd play his monster stereo in the basement, rattlin' those dishes, just because Eva had told him not to. He'd look at her each time "Hearts" came on, tears in his eyes as he mouthed "I love you," to her. The emotions of that song always got to her as well. As she sat at her computer a few nights later, an e-mail with his name on it came through. Heart pounding, she shakily clicked on it.

"I know you never wanted to hurt me intentionally, but trust & honesty is all we really had and you gave that up due to cowardice. What a shame. I don't know what ass kickin' I'm gonna get around the next corner, but I'm even tougher and less trusting now than I was before. Probably not a good thing. Good luck. I really do hope that you've learned something from all this. I know I have."

Sandy read it over and over. Summoning up her courage she wrote:

"What was I gonna do if I died and left you holding the bag? How often did I ask myself that?
Time is short, that came up so much.
I knew you'd be upset...what a legacy for me to leave behind! Your reaction, of hurt, anger, and everything else running thru your head is just the tip of the iceberg, and to be expected. Things that I deemed failures due to some loose end on my part... what could I have done to avoid it? I lost the Winston movie, it seemed to not want to take off.
I needed and wanted you to be successful, not me. I didn't want recognition, or glory. It was no feather in my cap to go to those craft shows and tout my stuff. It still isn't.
As to what to say to everyone who holds you dear, put the blame on me. I'll take it.
I'm done with everything myself. que sera sera. An apology seems so trite, yet I have nothing else to offer you. I do apologize. You

said I was selfish. In spite of the hurtfulness, there were many times I dropped what I was doing to come to your aid, and I did it willingly. Not gonna be trite and name it, you know all of it anyway. All I ask now is that you move forward...
I never wanted it to turn out like this. Friends forever is what I wanted. I'm so sorry. You have been kicked in the ass so many times by people...you're wondering when it will end, I'm sure. There are no more words that I can say... except to quote what I've heard you say a few times... you only hurt the ones you love. Though I never set out to hurt you. I never had it in for you, not for any reason. You never gave me one."

Sandy was tempted to add, I love you, but felt that admission would be laughed off, by both Brett and Eva. She was sure that he had made some sort of peace with her if he was still sending e-mails. She left the note as it was and hit send.

Then came Brett's next missive:

"Sandy, Sandy, Sandy...   I have done quite a bit of homework since the questions started coming up as to the validity of all your claims regarding WIYEP. I'm sure your heart was in the right place, but you have to understand the difference between reality & wishful thinking. Wishful thinking is what did WIYEP in, or at least my involvement. I have found no record of anything made for WIYEP from anyone. I still have more investigative work to do to be sure I will not be held accountable for something along the way. Whatever hole you've dug, you need to stop digging. I am now at a loss for words and do not understand what you thought was going to happen. The fact that you made up so many stories of work that needed to be done right now...with deadlines, and elaborated so incredibly much on so many planes is mind boggling. There's your next story. You could call it, "How to build hopes & dreams and then crush 'em!" #1 seller I'm sure.

"We are done, Sandy. It doesn't matter to me what you say to my friends, acquaintances or business people, I will stand on my own as a real, (non-fictionary individual) for as long as I breathe. I do admit I have problems of my own, but they are my own problems brought upon me by me. That I can handle. I don't need any more help creating problems. I just listened to "Hearts" & for the first time I didn't shed even a slight tear. I figure its due to the callous temperament I've been left with. Thanks. None of this matters anymore. The thrill of success is gone, to say the least.

"I have to go, Sandy. Please understand that what was is exactly that...past tense. I realize I will have to fight through all the Linda stuff you've gone out of your way to provide for me, but that's just another part of the torture you are so willing to provide at ultimate cost. Thanks again. I harbor no ill feelings towards you regardless of whatever you try to do to me. I am comfortable with me the way I am. I have given you the world on a string. Use it & PLEASE leave us alone. Sandy, I was a major loser with a small amount of talent the day I called you. I am still that same loser and getting worse as the days go by. All I ask is that I can save face amongst those that appreciated me for me. Stop helping me. At all costs, Please Stop Helping Me!! Note: From here on out... use my address on a send checks only basis. No other contact is necessary."

Sandy read it with a sinking feeling. It was over. She sent out one last message:

"Brett,

"one more explanation.. I'll make it brief, simple and to the point.

"You were extremely depressed when you left your radio station. I wanted to build you up.

"We had our CD fun, then came SOH. The big seller...it was way awesome. But, there was still that empty spot inside of you--you seemed to yearn for more...and I had my own yearnings. I yearned so much to be accepted, to be loved, to be noticed. Not for money, but to be loved by you. I thought that if you loved me enough, you would be all mine. Selfish, yes, but that was what I wanted.

"The Winston movie deal WAS true. But it fell thru. We were so excited that something I had done could maybe be BIG.

"So, I made up a white lie. Which, as we all know, grew bigger and larger. I wanted to have you all for myself. I wanted acceptance at any cost. NOTE: ANY cost. So it became more elaborate. I needed reasons to be by you, to see you, to call you. I couldn't be without you. You were my drug and I was addicted.

'Steel Destiny' is a book deal in the making. As is Ricky, the llama story. I intend to see them through.

"Yes, I did try to help you, to give you confidence in yourself so that you'd go on and do greater things than what you did. Thus the things that I did and now regret...and will live with that regret all of my life.

"You will not have to worry about dealing with me any more, as you said, past tense. I have my memories. I failed you so horribly. I am sorry.

"Thank you for what you have done for me, namely, giving me the confidence to go on. To know that I don't need to be accepted by anyone except myself.

"I imagine then, that you'd not want your name on SD when it comes out..? yes...no?
As for SOH...you may not want me to sell them for you. I think you can and will do a fine job on your own. If ever something cool comes up because of that or any of the work we did...then I guess we're just lucky!

"As I said, it perpetuated because all I wanted...was to build you up and keep you by me. It was so sweet being the "other woman," but I wanted so much to be "THE WOMAN!!" You didn't see it that way, however. I was always number two in your eyes. But I had fun and will rejoice in my memories.

"This will be my last email to you. You will not hear from me, or see me. Thanks for the memories, kiddo.

"I really did love you. I still do. Sorry for screwing up your life, and my own as well.

I took it hard, because I knew that I had failed you so bad. Being the other woman has it's disadvantages too. I always knew that what we had was on a limited time basis. Thus the reason why I "fought" so hard to keep you as long as I could...by creating excuses to keep you with me as well as providing a reason for you to be so proud of me. Again, apologies seem so trite. Remember when you sent me home so drunk? I couldn't see straight, let alone drive straight. Thanks also for Wisconsin and for letting me wash your van, mow your lawn, for all the coffee I drank, and for the beer, both real as well as recycled. I'll never forget that. ahhh, the memories.

"Oh well...farewell. Maybe when we meet on that cloud, you'll knock me down a peg or two. Thank you for everything. Mostly, thank you for being who you are."

Sandy sent it on it's way, then put her head into her hands and cried.

Brett needed to send her one last one. Everything inside him screamed to let it go, yet he couldn't.

"Just do your thing and rejoice in your memories. We don't ponder in depression of the losses we endure, we rejoice in the knowledge that they ever were."

Tears welled up inside of him. Jail time loomed yet again, only this time there would be no letters from Sandy, no anticipation of helping her with projects, only walking that godforsaken track and getting his time over with. Looking up, he didn't see Eva anywhere around.

He allowed himself to cry. Huge gulping sobs that wracked his body. He loved her, truly loved her and it was all gone now.

Sandy spent the rest of that month just trying to keep as busy as she could. She worked to promote her books, as well as at her current writings. Yet, there was a void in her that sliced deep in her soul. Brett was her soul mate, through and through. Whether or not he believed it was another matter. She sensed that he was in jail and hoped for he best. The nights were so long, however. She woke up, then realized she couldn't instant message him any longer. A song from their past would make her cry. She cried deep sobs, clutching her pillow, wishing she could just forget those blue gray eyes and his wonderful sense of being.

For his part, Brett spent his jail time walking until he was exhausted. Yet the dreams at night were nightmares. He thought of Sandy, willing himself to be angry, to stay focused on not thinking about her.

For all of his efforts, it didn't work. Fourteen days dragged. He called Eva every night, the only thing he had now to look forward to. Try as he might, Sandy was a thorn in his side that he could not let go of.

When he was finally freed, he tried to get back into a routine. He was once again merely Eva's pet. He cooked, he cleaned, he made her lunch, he looked at porn on the internet. When Eva was preparing to leave town for a business trip, she'd admonished him for days beforehand to NOT have any contact with Sandy. He tried to reassure her that would not be the case.

The day of her departure, Brett e-mailed Sandy.

"It's time to remove the extra CD's from my pool table. Make it happen."

Sandy looked at that. Well, what was this? Just as she thought that maybe she could make it through a day without tears, this came in.

She sent him a quick reply, letting him know that she didn't have cash on her to buy off his supply.

Then came his reply:

"Why? Why did you do all this to me? Don't play dumb either!" He sat back, took a drink of beer, tears running down his face. Oh, God, Sandy, I miss you so much, he thought.

Sandy quickly typed out a reply back, sending it.

"I'm not playing dumb...I accept full responsibility for my actions. My heart is broken thinking of what could have

Because of ... Friday

been...Wish I can go back and start over...hindsight 20/20 and all. I'm so sorry. why...because I wanted to be accepted by you 100%.. that's it in a nutshell. I wanted you to be so proud of me. I wanted the adulation from you. I never had it...I wanted to be thought of as so special, and now I am nothing but crumbs under your feet. I cry...a lot. I heard 'November Rain' tonight coming home from work and I cried so hard.

why? a three letter word can cause so much havoc. I'm so sorry, Brett, truly I am."

Brett saw it, knowing then that she was at her computer. He thought about it, then resisted. He had promised Eva. But he had to call Sandy, he wanted to hear her voice one more time. Dialing her number, he waited.

Sandy looked at her caller ID, then quickly picked up the phone. "Brett? Oh God, Brett, I miss you so much! I am so sorry for what I did!"

"Why? Why did you hurt me?"

"Brett, I didn't mean to, and now I'll live with this for the rest of my life! I just wanted your acceptance. I wanted to have you all for myself. It's that simple." Sandy cried, big tears falling down her face.

"I'm not happy, and you're not happy..."

"No, I'm miserable all the time. I cried tonight on the way home from work."

"So, what should we do about this?" Brett was on shaky ground and he knew it.

"I need to see you, just this once. I have to apologize to you in person."

"No! I'm only calling you because Eva is out of town. She'd never agree to this call if she were here, you know that!" Brett said adamantly.

"I know," Sandy said, "but just for ten minutes, please. Give me ten minutes, to look into your eyes and apologize. I have

209

to do this!"

"No! I can't let you! Why do you need to? No, it's wrong. I told Eva I would not even contact you. She was afraid of this very thing."

"Just ten minutes, I beg you, Brett please!"

There was silence, then Sandy heard Brett's breath exhale in a whoosh. "Ten minutes? No more?"

"Yes, please! I promise, you'll never see me again, just give me this." Sandy could not believe her ears. She just sold herself out. Never to see him again? It was suicide.

"This is it? Never again?" Brett asked. "OK, but you're not staying here, we'll go to a hotel."

"A hotel?" Sandy thought, "I just wanted to apologize, not make out, but OK," To Brett she said, "I'll be there in twenty minutes."

"Bring me beer and cigarettes," Brett told her. Just like old times.

Sandy quickly gathered up some cash, then told her kids she had to go take care of a friend. She ran out the door into the bitter cold night air, driving the route that was all too familiar.

Brett tried to call her back; he chickened out. Not getting her response, he hung up. Damn it, now what had he done? He ran upstairs and quickly showered. This was a mistake, yet to be able to see Sandy once more, his heart soared.

Sandy saw him through the window and smiled as he unlocked the door. Stepping in, she was met with his angry admonishment.

"My marriage just ended right there," he said, pointing at the spot she was standing on. "I told Eva that I wouldn't do this, and here I am, doing it."

Sandy ignored his rantings. They were all too common. Once again, the mighty Eva reared her ugly head. "I need a tissue," she said, walking to where she knew he kept them. He gathered his things as they left, but not before he took a head count of cats.

"Did you bring me beer and cigs?" he asked, not seeing her with any when she walked in.

"No, I forgot," sandy replied lamely. "We can stop and get you some on our way." They both entered the car and drove to the gas station, then a liquor store, then off to a hotel.

Checking in, they walked to their room. Brett immediately filled a tub of hot water, taking off first his clothes, then Sandy's. Climbing in, then out just as quickly, he exclaimed, "It's hot!" Sandy turned on the cold water, swirling it around the tub until the temperature was comfortable. Brett slapped her on the rear once, twice, then climbed in the tub, Sandy right after him. She kissed him on the mouth, then went lower and lower until she was at his crotch. Taking him into her mouth, she suckled.

"I can't believe I'm letting a woman I hate make love to me," he grumbled, then allowed the sensations to take over.

Sandy let his words roll right off of her, understanding his hurt feelings. She continued with her ministrations.

"You've missed this, haven't you?" he asked tenderly, looking down at the top of her head. She had just had her hair cut and colored that morning, which Brett found to be completely attractive as he gently stroked her head.

"M-m-m h-m-m-m," Sandy replied. She did, too. He had a taste and scent that she never tired of.

"Let's go into the other room to warm up," he suggested, walking in and grabbing a bottle of beer. Popping off the top, he drank some then offered the bottle to her. Sandy gulped it down, as Brett watched. "Lay down," he told her.

She lay back on the bed.

"Hold on to your ankles," he told her, pushing her legs back over her head.

She did what she was told. Carefully, he poured the beer into her. Sandy lay, relishing the cold feel of it.

"Stay like that, don't move," he told her.

"What you need is a straw to drink it up with," Sandy said.

"No, you'll absorb it, just give it time," he replied, watching her. He then took the bottle, handing it to Sandy. Lifting her head, she drank the rest of the beer, giving Brett the empty bottle back. He tossed it into the wastebasket, then climbed on the bed.

Man, she was quite the woman! This is what he missed, the way she could take whatever it was that he dished out. None of this discussion, "let's try it this way." She just did whatever he wanted, no questions asked. He wished once more that he could always have her like this, completely free and uninhibited.

Laying back on the bed, Sandy kissed him on the mouth.

"Turn around and get on me," he instructed her. Sandy did, taking him in her mouth once more as he also kissed her, licking her to heights she only dreamed of. She groaned while sucking on him, until a shattering sensation took over. Brett felt the stress of the evening slowly ebb as he closed his eyes. Sandy, seeing this, covered him with a blanket so he that wouldn't chill and lay next to him. She was reminded once more of the song by Aerosmith, about staying awake just to hear him breathing. If this was the last time, she wasn't wasting a minute of it, not a precious minute.

Soon, however, need overtook her as she stroked him to hardness, then climbed on him once more. He opened his eyes, and looking at her, took her face into his hands.

"I love you," he said. "I love you so much."

Sadly, Sandy looked at him. It was too late for that, she thought as she slowly undulated her hips. Was he serious or setting her up? She chose to not reply.

"You are the greatest thing that happened to me," he said into her eyes. Sandy smiled at him, kissing his mouth, whispering her words of love. Once more, she came. She continued on, she wanted to feel him come inside of her also. He did a surprising thing instead. It was as if he finally realized where he was. He pushed her off, causing Sandy to lose her balance as she fell onto the floor. He showed no mercy as he told her how angry he was at her.

"Get over here," he said. Sandy picked herself up off of the floor, standing by him at the foot of the bed.

"Lean over," he said.

Sandy did, as he caressed her pubic area. Just as she relaxed into the feeling, he slapped her hard, causing her to cry out. Again he caressed her, the stinging sensation hurting her as once more, he slapped her hard. Sandy fell forward.

"Back to where you were," he told her angrily.

Sandy stood up, looking him in the eye, daring him to say something.

"I'm mad at you," he said. "Look at me!" he glared at her. "You didn't think it would be easy, did you?"

"No, I figured it wouldn't be," Sandy admitted.

He leaned her over the bed once more, slapping her hard several more times. Sandy bit down hard on the quilt, stifling her cries. He then went over and drank some more beer, lighting up a cigarette. Sandy sat on the bed.

"I'm naked, you're naked, we're here and completely vulnerable," he said, sitting next to her. "I want to know why you did what you did."

Sandy looked at him, stroking his arm. The regrets assailed her once more.

"I wanted you all for myself. Plain and simple. Just you." She looked down at the rug.

"I didn't block your phone number. Eva did. She made me get rid of everything that had anything to do with you. Everything! The books that you signed, all of it."

"Why didn't you tell me that? I thought that you were ignoring me!" Sandy said with relief. "I still have those books if you want them back someday."

"Eva disabled the instant messaging, she monitors everything I do. You were begging me to unblock the phone, I couldn't." Brett said sadly. "You realize I almost lost my wife, my life, my home...I had to tell Eva everything after she saw that e-mail from you. How do you think that made me feel?"

"I'm sorry, Brett. Really."

"I put thirteen years into that marriage. When I met her, I had nothing. Still have nothing if she makes me leave. I worked hard for what I do have. I have no intention of giving it up."

Sandy felt so low as he said that. Of course, he told her that from the beginning, she just had notions of her own and refused to listen. Now, as he ranted, she continued to stroke his arm, getting up to kiss him, loving the look of the Pegasus horse on his chest. She never tired of him, not even now. He turned on the television, flipping through channels.

"I can't believe that people watch this crap," he said, settling on some old movie, then relaxed back on the pillows.

Crawling under the covers, Sandy snuggled next to him. He held her close, then dozed off. Sandy finally allowed herself to doze as well, waking up about half an hour later when the needs of the bathroom called to her. Carefully, she disengaged herself from his grasp, then returned and snuggled in once more, looking at his face. Quietly she kissed him, whispering soft words.

"Oh Brett, I do love you so much. I wish I could tell you now, so that you'd understand. I love you and I will forever." She kissed him down on his chest, over Pegasus, then back to his lips.

Brett kept his eyes closed, but he heard everything she said. His heart broke. He didn't want to be so hard on her, but he had to teach her a lesson, too. He let her lips roam across him, then opened his eyes. Sandy climbed on top of him once more.

"Let's put you where you belong," she told him.

Slowly she rode him, feeling everything and not wanting this moment to end. It did, however, as Sandy once again took him into her mouth. She so wanted him to have his satisfaction also and was disappointed when he didn't allow himself to yet. Moving her position, she looked at the clock. Twelve thirty seven a.m. Their last meeting had occurred on…Friday.

Brett once again fell asleep with Sandy snuggled in next

to him.

"You better get what you want, because soon it will be over," he told her in his sleep. Sadly, she knew it would be true.

The rest of the night was spent in talking, sharing beer, tears and laughter. When it was daylight, Sandy opened the curtain.

"Hello, world!" she exclaimed.

"You said that on your second interview with me," Brett said quietly.

"What?" Sandy asked.

"Hello world. You said that on your last show with me."

"Hello, world, down under, up over and everywhere in between!" Sandy said sadly. So he remembered that, too.

He handed her a cup of coffee and asked if there was a paper outside the door.

"Well, I'll just have to go and look," Sandy said with a smirk.

"Naked?" he asked.

"Why not? Has nobody seen a naked person before?" Sandy dared. She opened the door, carefully peeking out. No one in sight. She slid the paper in, then closed the door.

"Anyone see you?" he asked, loving her free spirit.

"Nope." She handed him the paper. He looked over the headlines, but nothing appealed to him. Sandy became pensive. It was almost check out time. He knew it too.

"You promised me," he said. "Eva can't know about this. If you say anything, you and I will have words."

"I promise, I won't. I mean it. I want to redeem myself. I want you to look back and say, 'Yup, that Sandy, she fucked up, but she finally did good, too.'" Sandy downed the last of her coffee, tossing the cup away. She cleaned up the stray beer cans as Brett picked up his clothes. Sandy was surprised to see him put on underwear.

"What's with that?" she asked. "You never wear under-wear."

215

"It's been so cold, I want to stay warm," was his reply.

Sandy found her clothes and got dressed.

She sat on the bed afterwards, where they chatted about the books Sandy was working on. Then he stared into space, lost in some memory. Looking at Sandy, he asked the inevitable, "are you finally done with me?"

The words sliced through her heart. This was it, then. Over. She considered it. "Sadly, yes."

"You have everything?" Brett asked, getting out of his chair. Sandy replaced it, looking around for anything left behind.

"Yes. Brett, thank you," Sandy gulped down the tears that were on the verge of falling. She wrapped her arms around his neck and kissed him gently on the mouth. "Thank you. I will never forget this," the last words came out in a whisper.

He returned her kisses, looking at her sadly. Why had he agreed to never seeing her again?

Together, they left the hotel, Sandy let Brett warm up the car while she checked out. He drove to his house, Sandy getting out of her warm seat to drive.

"Remember what I said, you promised," Brett reminded her. He was so desperately afraid Eva would find out.

"I promise. Good luck," Sandy said with a watery smile, feeling none of the spirit behind it.

The drive home for Sandy was sad, heartrending, grief filled. Never to see him again, never to call, to e-mail, to instant message. It was over. The world was an empty, bottomless pit and Sandy was freefalling deep within it.

Winston greeted her when she returned home, tail wagging. She petted him, thinking, "I wish I'd never lay eyes on this dog! Why did I have to write that story? Why did I have to meet Brett? Why does love have to hurt? Why?" Tears falling, she buried her head into his fur. He squirmed, then licked the tears off of her face. Looking into his soulful brown eyes, she made up her mind.

I am a survivor. I have to do this, too. I can do this.

The next days dragged. Sandy looked at the clock, the calendar. "I promised, I promised, I promised," she kept telling herself over and over. She wanted to e-mail Brett and tell him something, anything! Remembering her promise, she didn't.

It was now Valentine's Day. What a difference a year made! Sandy couldn't stand it any more. She went online and selected a cute e-card for Brett. Writing from the heart, she said simply, "I am keeping my promise. I miss you. PIP"

She choose PIP because in the paper she had read to him at the hotel there was a story about a winter summary with a PIP rating, PIP meaning, "pain in the posterior." Brett chuckled over that. He had given Sandy the pet name of PIA, "pain in the ass," and thought PIP was cute, also. She knew he would find it amusing.

Brett had an equally hard time concentrating. Eva came home from her business trip in a foul mood. He knew what she was after as she asked him questions, hoping to trip him up. He kept his voice calm, giving her answers that he had rehearsed, glad he had told Sandy they were to meet at a hotel. Eva was not stupid.

He went to her, expecting a hug. She rebuffed him, using the excuse of exhaustion, she did not want her groin anywhere near his until she could prove he had been worthy while she was gone.

The next few days dragged for Brett also. He thought of Sandy, the way she made love to him. He only wished he had allowed himself release. Just as when they first made love, the last time left him wanting. Sandy tried, she wanted his release as well, but he wouldn't allow it. He was so distrustful of her at that point, what if she turned on him again? He didn't need her screaming rape to the cops or his PO, so he held back, although holding back took a supreme amount of effort. Now, seeing her e-card, he immediately found a cute one, sending her a reply.

"Hope you're doin' OK. Thanks for keeping your promise.

217

Makes it easier day by day, to be sure."

Sandy saw it and smiled.

As the days went on, Eva's suspicions of Brett gnawed at her day and night. She berated him, withheld sex, even went online and checked his e-mails. Sandy had to e-mail Brett about the book they co-wrote. It had been accepted by a publisher and she needed to know little details concerning the cover. Brett tried to keep his responses to a minimum, but Eva questioned even those.

"It's business!" Brett yelled at her.

"You two are not working together anymore, remember? I want you to have nothing to do with her, NOTHING!" Eva screamed back.

Brett hated her anger.

Later that night, he stole into the den, sending Sandy a quick e-mail, telling her that Eva was on the warpath and for Sandy to keep her e-mails to the absolute minimum. He didn't want to cut her off entirely. Though she had hurt him deeply, he was capable of forgiveness and still loved her. His life wasn't a perfect one either; he couldn't hold her in judgment.

Eva saw him at the computer. One thirty a.m., it figured. She hid in the shadows as he came up the stairs, going into the bedroom. Eva then went downstairs, sitting at his still warm chair. Brett always kept his computer on, so it was easy for her to go into his e-mail account. Damn! He already deleted who he had sent his last message to. Pushing away from the computer, she went back to bed, where Brett was already snoring.

"Who did you just send an e-mail to?" she demanded.

"Huh, what?" he asked, uncertain of where he was, then realizing that Eva just woke him up.

"I asked you who you just e-mailed!"

"Nobody, get over it! Go to sleep!"

You're up to something, I want answers!" Eva was adamant.

"I gave you one, now go to sleep and quit bitchin' at me!"

Brett turned over, hoping she would give up.

The frustration made Eva want to scream. She fumed, then got up to feed the cats, who thought the conversation meant that it was breakfast time and were setting up a meowing storm. After she left, Brett finally was able to relax enough to fall back asleep.

The following next couple of weeks Sandy kept as busy as she could so that she would not be so conscious of the pain that Brett's absence caused. He still sent her little e-mails querying her on the design of the book cover, when it was due out, where a certain DVD was that they had watched together and other odd things. He wished he could send her the e-mails he used to and found that she was sitting at her computer the same time each afternoon and the rapid responses was for him a lot like when they instant messaged each other. He took small comfort in it.

The question from Sandy came up about her house key's disappearance.

"It was on my key ring when you went to warm up my car while I ...ahem...checked out..." she asked, keeping the message as innocent as possible, just in case Eva accessed it.

He replied, "I didn't see your key and have no need for it."

Sandy knew he had to have it, it was on the ring the night they checked in at the hotel, but he had grabbed the keys that night and didn't return them. She only noticed it was missing when she returned home and was locked out of the house. It warmed her heart, thinking that if he had it, he probably had good cause to have taken it. She wasn't worried.

Eva, snooping on Brett's e-mails from work, also saw that transmission. She called Brett immediately, asking him what it meant.

"What the hell are you talking about?" he asked. Great! Now Eva had access to his e-mails from work! He had no privacy at all! None!

"It says here that you had her keys while she checked out. From where? Where were you?" Eva knew he was playing around! He was still seeing Sandy while Eva was out of town, after she told him not to!

"Eva, she's stirring the pot is all," Brett defended himself. He hated dumping the blame onto Sandy, but this was a matter of survival. Without Eva, he had no house, no life. She provided everything he needed.

"Stirring the pot? Then why did you respond that you didn't have her key? Why are you playing into her hand?" Eva was certain now that he was lying.

Did the woman never work? Brett wondered. She was always torturing him. He was tired of her dogging him and said so.

"Well, you give me cause to. You still e-mail her, don't say that you don't!" Eva was so angry now. "I want you to know that I hate her for everything that she has done. You obviously don't care about my feelings!" Eva slammed the phone down.

Brett looked at the receiver, then hung up. A few minutes later, the phone rang again. Looking at the number, it was Eva again. Brett didn't want to answer, He was so tired of the constant scrutiny.

"Pick up, Brett, I know you're there…pick up!" Eva said into the answering machine. 'Very well, we *will* finish this when I get home!"

Click.

Brett just couldn't wait for that, he thought sarcastically. He drank another beer, knowing he'd need the numbing sensations before the evening was done.

The next day Sandy was gone until almost one o'clock p.m. so she didn't know that Brett had been trying to contact her every ten minutes all day long until she checked her caller ID when she returned. Damn it, she wondered, what was that all about? Going to a neighbor's house, she asked to use her phone.

She wished Eva didn't block her number!

Dialing Brett's number, she waited for him to answer.

"Brett? It's me, what's up?"

"Eva saw your e-mail about your key and gave me nothing but shit about it!" Brett was angry as well as drunk. He slurred his words, angry at Sandy, but also at circumstances being what they were.

"How did she see that?" Sandy asked.

"She accessed my e-mails at work. You gotta stop contacting me!"

"From her work? Brett, I didn't write that blatantly, I tried to be so very inconspicuous!"

"I know, but she sees everything now! Thanks a lot!" He hung up the phone.

Sandy was not rebuffed. Quickly she dialed back. "Brett, how are you otherwise? I think about you so much! You didn't say…"

"Somebody's on the other line, I gotta go!" he said in reply and hung up.

Sandy hung up the phone, looking at her neighbor.

"Sorry, I can't call him on my phone, his wife blocked my number…"

Just then the phone rang, Sandy looked at the caller ID. It was Brett.

"Hello?" she asked.

"You have to understand, it's been pure hell for me. She tortures me every chance she gets," Brett said.

"I know, hun and as I said, I try to be careful, to keep it business."

"This hasn't been easy on me. I wish things were what they were. I miss you," Brett said quietly.

"I miss you, too. You know, you don't have to stay and take her torture. Why? I left Harry for that very reason!"

"I am a felon, I have no job prospects, no money. Honey, I worked for thirteen years to have what I have. I can't just walk

221

away from all of that."

"You can come here. Please. I'll help you." Sandy was sincere.

"No, Eva expects me to do that. That'll piss her off. I may as well just finish my time in prison, she can divorce me and I'll start over fresh." Brett always took the drastic steps when he was up against it. Sandy learned to just let him spill his guts and be done with it.

"Sandy, I beg you, please, if she calls you, play dumb. I told her that you were just stirring the pot. She doesn't believe it though."

Sandy hated that he passed the blame onto her, all the time, even with his PO when she asked him about his out of town story. Yet, Sandy forgave him for that weakness, too.

After a few more minutes, Brett felt a bit better. Talking to Sandy always did that for him. Her gentle way eased his mind. He missed her so much, yet was afraid if he let on, she'd be at his door again! Instead, he said he had to go.

Sandy felt bittersweet as she said, "I love you, kiddo. Take care," listening to the click. He was gone. She put the phone back in it's receiver, then listened to her neighbor's tirade. Of how Brett was no good for her and he'd better not be coming around.

"He won't, don't worry," Sandy said. She felt disheartened as she excused herself to go to her next job.

As she drove, her distracted mind was not on the road or what was happening. So she didn't see it when a large SUV crossed into her lane until it was too late. She swerved into the barrier just as she crossed over a bridge, the car going up over the barrier and landing on it's roof on the freeway below, right in the path of an oncoming semi truck. The truck smashed into it, pushing it for several hundred feet before the stunned truck driver was able to stop.

For Sandy, life stopped right there.

The news media had a field day with the story. A local celebrity in a car accident. Details at five.

Brett was watching the TV in between cooking for Eva. Steamed broccoli, grilled chicken and a rice side dish. Just then, the news anchor caught his attention:

"This just in, we have a news crew on the scene of I-94, where a major car accident has traffic stopped for several miles. It seems the victim was pushed off the I-694 freeway by an SUV onto I-94 below, into oncoming traffic. The driver of the car is in critical condition..."

"Sucks bein' her," Brett thought, as he stirred the rice.

..."We have identified the driver of the car to be Sandy Malone, author of several books in the *"Winston the Wayward Spaniel"* series..."

Brett's mind froze. Sandy? Oh my God! Sandy! He raced into the den, turning up the television. Sandy's picture was shown, the words now being lost as the blood rushed to his ears. "Oh, Sandy!" he thought. "What have I done? I've wasted time and now, you're dying in a hospital somewhere..."

Eva walked in from work.

"What's up?" she asked, seeing Brett's horrified expression. Turning to the television, she saw Sandy's picture.

"She was in a car accident," Brett said quietly. "My sweet Sandy," he thought.

"Nothing you can do about it, shit happens. What's for dinner?" Eva asked, heading upstairs to change. Brett could not grasp the hatred that Eva had for Sandy. To show absolutely no emotion at all!

Eva could care less. "If that bitch dies, I'll finally be free of the crap that Brett's been dishing out lately," she thought as she stripped off her nylons, wriggling her toes. "Of course, if she dies, he'll be impossible to live with, too. Horse a piece," Eva thought bitterly.

Brett stayed by the television. Then he called the station to see what hospital she was in, writing down the information. Eva came in just as he tore the paper off the pad, putting it in his pocket.

"Let me guess, you're sending her flowers," she said sarcastically. "Forget dinner, I'm not hungry!" She went back to the bedroom, shutting the door.

Brett watched her go, then went into the kitchen to put dinner away. He wasn't hungry, either.

He paced and fretted, circling the den. Was she alive? Would she die? Damn it, she survived the cancer, she'd fought it so hard and now this! Why did he have to fight what he felt? Because Eva said so. He'd wasted time, and now time was of the essence!

"Eva?" Brett went upstairs, calling out to the closed door.

"What?"

"I need to go. I have to go to the hospital."

The door whipped open. "Why? Why do you feel it's so necessary?" Eva wanted to know.

"Because...she's my friend. I have to go."

"After all she did to you! She lied to you! She humiliated you! She made a mockery of you! Fine! If you leave, don't come back, do you hear me? Just don't come back!" Eva slammed the door once again, the dishes rattling in the cupboards.

Brett retreated to the den. Damn it, Sandy may not have much time left!

At nine p.m. he turned on the news once more, the story now having made it on the Associated Press. Sandy Malone... author... major car accident...critical condition... hospitalized....

"Well, she wanted notoriety, she's got it," Brett thought bitterly. He thought of the CD they made together, *"Stories of Hope."* She needed a Story of Hope right about now. He was not a praying man, having given up on God many years ago. Yet, he found himself praying to a god he wasn't sure even existed.

"I've fucked up my life, yet you sent to me a beautiful girl who made mistakes, but it was in her desire to win me over. I can't waste any more time. I'll do anything, just save her, please. Her time isn't up." He paced some more, lighting up cigarette after cigarette until the room was hazy from smoke.

Sandy lay in critical condition. In her foggy mind, she knew she would never see Brett again and for that, she shed a single tear. Life was over, why bother hanging on? Brett had what he wanted, he had Eva. She'd lost the best thing that had ever happened to her. She allowed herself to slip into an unconscious state where the pain could no longer follow her.

The next morning, after Eva left for work, Brett tried calling a friend of his who could maybe give him a ride. No luck. Damn it. He looked at the keys on the counter. He could take his van, but he had no license. He looked at the keys once more, picking them up. A gold key caught his eye. It was Sandy's house key. He wondered how her kids were handling the situation. Was her ex husband doing the "poor me" thing? Brett couldn't stand it anymore, he was taking a chance, but he had to go see her. Clutching the keys, he drove himself to the hospital.

On the way, he thought about the day when he took Sandy's key off the ring. Yes, he was warming up her car while she checked out of the hotel. He did it on the spur of the moment, because of...why? Deep inside, he hoped she would call him, but instead she had let almost two weeks go by before she even inquired. She had kept her promise. Unfortunately, Eva was aware of it also. He pulled into the parking ramp and entered the hospital, asking at the information desk where Sandy was.

"Are you a relative?" the lady inquired.

"Uh, yes, I'm her fiancé," he lied. Now where did that come from?

"She's on the fifth floor, room 516."

"Thank you, " Brett said.

Going to her room, he peeked in. She was hooked up to tubes and wires, monitors blipping out readings. Her head was bandaged, she was sleeping. At least he hoped so. Standing next to her, he leaned down, kissing her cheek so very gently, stroking her face.

"Sandy? Sandy, I'm here, hun. It's Brett. I'm here. I love

you, kiddo."

From deep in the recesses of her mind, Sandy dreamed she heard Brett's voice. In her mind, he held out his arms, calling to her. She saw his sweet face and, running to him, embraced him in a hug, looking deep into his beautiful eyes. He called her name again, from afar, she answered him.

"I'm here, Brett. I love you, too. I'm so sorry I hurt you. I'll always carry that regret all my life. I'm not perfect, I've made mistakes, just…Please, Brett forgive me."

"I do, hun, I forgive you, I'm here." He gently took her left hand in his, stroking the finger that also had his nickname tattooed on it. Symba. She believed in him so much, so damn much! She committed herself to him, and how did he treat that trust she had? He blew her off!

"Brett? Don't leave me…please…please…" Sandy's eyes blinked once, twice.

Brett watched as she struggled to stay conscious. Tears rolled down his face. He wiped his eyes. His PIA…she was such a pain, but she was also his pleasure. He needed her strength.

The doctor walked in, stethoscope in hand, chart in the other. He went to Sandy, listening to her heart, checking her pulse.

"Are you the lucky husband?" he inquired.

Brett shook his head, "uh, no…fiancé. Brett Pearson. How is she?"

"I can tell you this, it could have been worse. I really don't know why she even survived at all. That semi should have crushed her, actually, going over the bridge alone should have killed her." He straightened out the covers. "You have quite the trooper there, it seems that she is hanging onto life for you." He turned and left the room, in a hurry to finish his rounds.

Brett looked at Sandy, the doctor's words echoing in his head…"she seems to be hanging on for you…for you…for you…"

"Sandy? Sandy, it's me, Brett, wake up, hun."

226

Slowly and with effort, her eyes opened. She looked about the room, aware now of the monitor beeping. Focusing her eyes, she saw the most beautiful sight she could ever hope for. "Brett?" she whispered.

He looked at her, his blue-gray eyes full of love. "You're gonna be alright, hun. I'm here."

"I was so scared..."

"Shhh, don't talk, it's enough to know you're okay," Brett said. "Sandy, I'm not perfect either, but you have given me reason to change. It's not all about me. I just don't know why you love me as much as you do."

"But I *do* love you," Sandy whispered, before closing her eyes once again, the pain medication making her sleepy. "I love your compassionate heart, your gentle soul, your love of life..."

It used to annoy him somewhat that Sandy would tell him that a lot, but now, as precious as each moment was, it warmed his heart to hear it once more. "I love you too, hun."

Pulling up a chair, he allowed himself to live in the memories they had made.

The squirrels that ran around his backyard: Sandy always helped to feed them. When a little white squirrel took up residence there, Sandy was thrilled, naming it Lil Fluffnums and even writing a short story about it. After ten days, it disappeared. For many days thereafter, Sandy worried about it's whereabouts.

Brett took delight in what he called beeper birds. Sandy gently laughed. "What's a beeper bird?" she asked.

"When you come out, I'll point them out to you."

Sure enough, he did. Only Sandy laughed when she heard their melody. "Hun, that's a chickadee. What they are saying is fee-bee! Fee-bee!"

"No, it's bee-per, bee-per!" Brett insisted. Sandy let him believe what he wanted to.

He loved the way they could work side by side, sharing laughter, jokes and stories.

He remembered the wedding show they worked at

together. The night was young as they tore down their equipment. Brett was in no big hurry to go home to Eva, so they sat in the loading dock area, outside the building, watching the nearly full moon do a slow walk across the sky. It was warm and Sandy was in love as Brett kissed her, then ran his hands under her skirt, around her thigh and settled in her groin. He slowly rubbed her, increasing the speed and tempo.

Turned on by the whole idea of doing this right outside the building in front of a major roadway, Sandy began to breathe hard, holding his shoulders as she quietly exploded her release into his ear. Hugging him tight, she whispered, "thank you," kissing him once more.

No woman had ever thanked him before. Sandy always did. She never took their moments for granted, knowing how limited they were.

"Thank you, sweetheart," he said quietly, getting out of his chair. "Thank you for everything."

He turned then and walked out of the hospital room.

When he arrived at home, Eva's car was in the driveway. "Oh great, now what?" he thought, walking up the sidewalk.

"You went to see her, didn't you?" Eva asked him.

Brett looked at her, guilt written all over his features. "Yes," was all he said. He wasn't going to bait her, anything he said nowadays was held under strict scrutiny.

"Brett, it's over. I can't do this anymore. Your involvement with her is killing me."

"Eva, I...please listen..."

"No, I don't want to hear it. I can't fight both of you," Eva said quietly. She had made her mind up earlier that morning.

"Please, give me a minute to explain," Brett begged.

"No, don't you see? She will always be a shadow in my life. I compare myself to her. I wonder what you're thinking when we make love, is it to me or to her? I can't do this anymore."

"Eva, I ...." the words were lost.

So, the moment had arrived. Brett was now homeless.

Eva watched his reaction, as if reading his mind, tears in her eyes but resolve in her heart. It was a relief, actually.

"I'll stay at mom's for a while, until you get your stuff together. Take your DJ equipment, your CD's, anything that's yours. I won't stand in your way. I've already contacted John, I'm filing for divorce."

Brett looked up, aghast. So this was it, then. The suddenness of it gripped him in a panic.

"Where will I go? I have nothing, except everything that I've given to you," Brett pleaded.

"You'll get half the proceeds of the house. I'm selling it. Brett," Eva took his hand. "It's better this way. I can't argue with you anymore. You win. I've already packed my things." Quietly she got up, leaving the room.

Brett felt despair. It was over. Why did it hurt so much? She gave him freedom, she didn't even argue his whereabouts that day. Then again, he always said she wasn't stupid. Fingering his set of keys, he pulled them out. Sandy's gold key stood out. He knew now why he took it. He knew he would have need of it someday. Turning, he looked at the calendar. Someday was here.

It was Friday.

Brett walked to the basement, looking at his stuff. Three mobile units, none of them had been used in quite a while, despite Sandy's best efforts at promoting him. All those car shows, mall shows, church bazaars...and where had he been? Doing exactly what Eva had told him to, that's what! He would call the company he bought them from and see if they would take two units on consignment. A loss for sure, but he had no place to store them. Going upstairs, he went and pulled out a suitcase, slowly packing his clothes. He would move in with Sandy, it was what she had wanted. Her house was small, but it was a house. He would figure out where to go from there.

Laying in the hospital bed, Sandy thought of her successes...few, and of her failures, many. The one big one was in letting Brett down. He was her light, her reason for living. Why she had to blow the best reason she had for living, she didn't know or even understand it herself. The memories assailed her as suddenly, a familiar song played on the radio in the next room. "Hearts." Sandy's felt a crushing pain in her chest as the tears flowed down her cheeks.

"set your hearts along the river…"

She remembered how Brett would take a swig of beer, then share it with her, his mouth on hers as she drank it greedily. His love of Led Zeppelin, playing his music LOUDLY, sharing his stories, his laughter, of which he didn't do nearly enough, the list was endless.

"love me, teach me, know me…" the hypnotic beat of the drum as it pounded into her senses. This was *their* song, why was she hearing it now?

"…how we talk, how we teach our children…"

Brett taught her so much…"Brett, I'm so sorry," Sandy begged him. "I failed you so miserably. You relied on me and I blew it! You trusted me!"

"Two hearts are better than one…" Yes, she found that out. When they split up, Sandy's heart broke into so many pieces.

"…better believe our heart's entwined…" Sandy had thought theirs always would be.

"One heart's for love, one's for giving.." Forgiving, was she really?

"…as we flow down life's river…I see the stars glow one by one…all angels of the magic constellations…" the song sang.

Sandy saw stars also. They were so bright as the room became dark and the pain finally ended for her.

The ringing of the phone jarred Brett back to his senses.

"Hello?" he said, looking at the number, it was Joe's cell phone. Sandy's house. Uh-oh, not good!

"Brett?" He heard crying in the background.

"Yes?" He immediately knew that something had happened.

"Brett, it's Joe. The hospital just called. Mom.....mom... died..."

"What?" Brett asked incredulous. "I was just there awhile ago!" This wasn't real, it couldn't be happening. Just like with his own mother years before! He had visited with her that morning in the nursing home and by afternoon, she was gone, no indication that anything was amiss other than the problems she had which were kept under control.

Everything happened now in slow motion.

"Mom had this number written down, she always said to call you if anything happened to her..." Joe couldn't speak above a whisper. His older brother was there, trying to comfort the siblings who now had to face the realities of life. "We're going to the hospital, they said they'd keep her in her room so that we can say goodbye. Just thought you'd want to know."

"Th-thanks, Joe. Hey, dude, I'm sorry, I loved her, too," Brett's voice was a ragged whisper.

"Yeah, that's why she cried for you every night. She lived for you, man. You left her. She loved you and I thought, THOUGHT, that you loved her, too." Joe spoke out of hurt and anger.

"Hey, man, let it go, we gotta get going," Brett heard an older male voice say.

"Gotta go," Joe said, hanging up.

The silence was deafening. Brett knew what he had to do.

He pushed the accelerator as fast as he dared. Driving without a license, speeding, he had been drinking as soon as he returned home, yup, he was a prison case waiting to happen. He didn't care. He had to see Sandy one last time.

Running through the halls of the hospital, the elevator ride seemed interminable, until finally the doors opened. He strode to Sandy's room. She lay in bed, still hooked up to the heart monitor, a nurse at her side.

"I'm sorry, Mr. Pearson. We don't know why, but her heart suddenly just quit. We tried, but we couldn't get it going again."

"Can I be alone with her?"

"Yes," she said, excusing herself.

Brett went to the bed, taking Sandy's still warm hand in his own.

"Honey, I'm here, but you're not! I was so close, so damned close to having you! Eva left me. I was packing. I was coming to you and now, you're not here. What will I do without you?" He looked about the room, his life a maelstrom of emotions, all of them bad. The light that was his life was gone. He remembered his words, how he'd told Sandy he only knew her for nineteen months, but Eva for thirteen years, he owed Eva the allegiance that Sandy had begged him for.

Time was of the essence...was, and now it was gone. Done. Over.

Was this how Sandy felt when he had dismissed her so abruptly? Lost, forlorn, the grief beyond belief as it sucked him down, threatening to envelope him in it's darkness?

He looked to Sandy again, so gentle. Yes, she made some big mistakes. Why, why couldn't he have just told her right away, yes, I forgive you? Instead, he had carried that hurt even to the end when they last made love. He had to hurt her for the hurt she had caused him.

Sandy. Her legacy would live on, he would see to that. *"Winston the Wayward Spaniel,"* the CD's he narrated, the writing projects he knew she was still working on. That reminded him of something. He picked up the phone, calling the number he knew by heart.

Joe answered it.

"Joe, Brett. Your mom had work on her computer that I need to access. Is that possible?"

"Yeah, man. We were just on our way to the hospital, but

Jake had a flat tire, so he's fixing it, then we'll be there. Are you there now?"

"Yeah, I'm here. I'll stay till you get here. I don't want her to be left alone."

"Thanks, see ya." Joe hung up.

Brett put the phone back. Going over to Sandy, he took her hand. Stroking her hair, kissing her sweet lips for the last time, he looked at her. Even in death, she was beautiful.

"Hun, I will carry on your legacy. I will promote the hell out of your work. This time, I promise, I'll sit at those book stores, the mall shows, everything I wasn't there for, I will be from now on. You will not have died in vain. I'll see to that."

The room was dark now, with only a dim light illuminating the bed. He sat there for a long time, reliving the memories.

It was Friday evening.

It wasn't fair, he thought. The day should have been dreary, dark, dismal, cold. Instead, the sky was blue, with puffy clouds sailing across the sky. Brett held onto the urn that held Sandy's ashes, Winston at his side. He stood in the middle of an old, abandoned railroad bridge that Sandy took him to once, telling him that it was her favorite contemplative place. Now, as he held the urn, he went to the railing, tipping the ashes into the river. Slowly, the ashes mingled with the water, swirling downstream until it disappeared, one with the nature that she loved so much.

"Good-bye, my girl. I love you. I always will." Looking up, he wondered which cloud she was watching him from.

As Brett sat at Sandy's computer, he went into her documents, clicking on the many stories Sandy had there. He was surprised also, she saved every instant message transmission, there they all were, organized by month. Then, the one story that he was looking for caught his eye. *"Because of Friday."* Sandy had started it so long ago. Brett spent the next several hours reading it. My God, she was so honest, he remembered almost he laughed, then after some thought, added the ending:

"Brett looked at Sandy, laying in that hospital bed. He forgave her for everything that she had done and why not? She had forgiven him so long ago, the day she told him that she would never leave him. In reality, she didn't. She always said she would never cut him loose and that promise she kept.

"His plans included taking her home, spending the rest of eternity with her. Eva had left him, she couldn't handle sharing him any longer. The house they shared for so many years, considered the dump of the neighborhood when they moved in, the one he put so much hard work and effort into, sold immediately for a much higher price, giving Brett some much needed cash. He wanted to start over and make a new life for himself. He told Eva he would always be there for her if needed. He owed her that much. She cried, thanking him for that.

"Tomorrow, Sandy. The doctor said that you should be well enough to leave here tomorrow," Brett said with a smile.

"Tomorrow? What day is that?" she asked.

"Um, I think it's the twelfth," he said, opening the curtain to let the sunshine in.

"No, what day?" In the hospital, it was so easy to lose track of time.

Quietly Brett replied, "it's Friday."

From her position on that cloud built for two, Sandy smiled. She loved happy endings, and Brett seemed content with the one he had just completed!

"I'm waiting for you, kiddo. Right here, this is your spot." She smoothed out the seat next to her, settled back and waited.

This is the old railroad bridge that "Sandy" used as her special spot, it is mine as well.

This story is very similar to the life I have lived since I have met Sammy. He has been my inspiration, my reason to continue with the work we have started.

It is my hope that you have that one special person in *your* life, one who makes you laugh, makes you want to live each day to the fullest. Never settle for second best. Your soul mate is out there...go find him or her...never take anything for granted.

Nothing lasts forever...NOTHING!

Printed in the United States
203168BV00001B/211-261/P